# ESTELLA

*and the*

# DREAM TRAVELER

## MERCEDES PARADISO

Published by Mercedes Paradiso, LLC.
www.mercedesparadiso.com

Library of Congress Control Number: 2024927365

ISBN: 979-8-9912170-2-6 (paperback)
ISBN: 979-8-9912170-3-3 (ebook)

**Books by Mercedes Paradiso**

Estella and the Dream Traveler

**Poetry**

thunder and daisy

For Isaiah, Nora, and Izabella

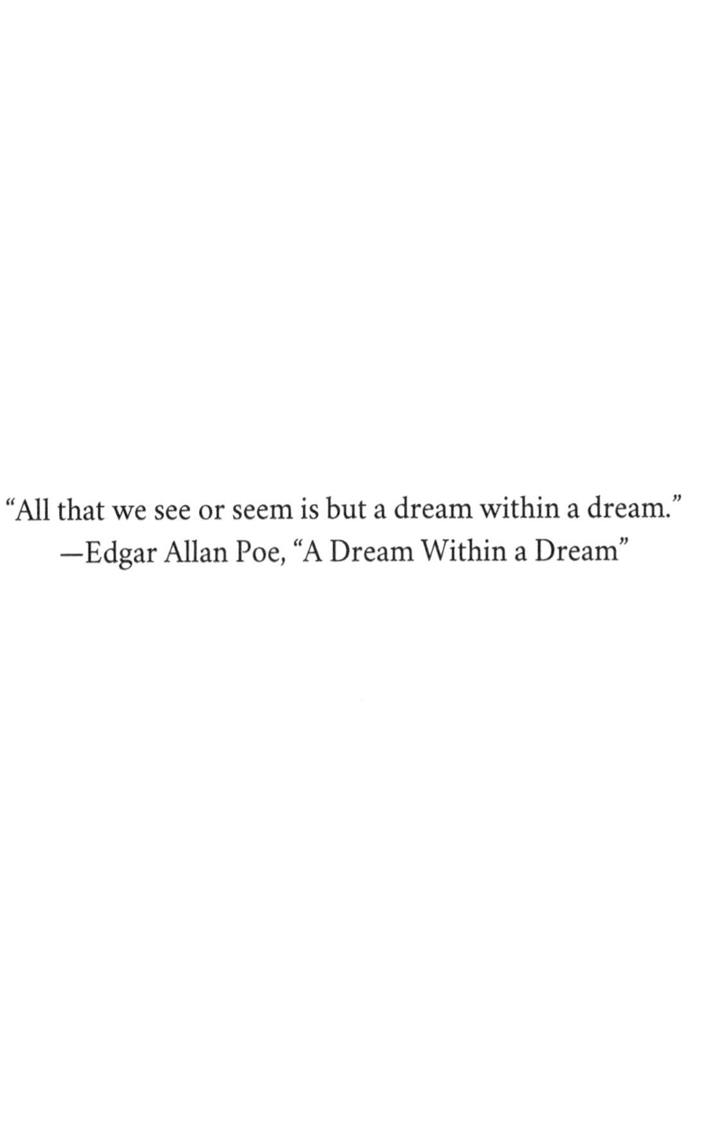

"All that we see or seem is but a dream within a dream."
—Edgar Allan Poe, "A Dream Within a Dream"

# Chapter 1

Estella Larsen tightens her grip on the steering wheel as she turns a corner. Her head buzzes, and the road before her darkens at the edges. *Oh, no, not now...* Her heart pounds. This vision will be a powerful one. She quickly pulls over to the side of the road before her eyes can completely cloud over with blackness. One of these days, she's sure these visions will be the end of her. If it weren't for the telltale moments before a vision begins, the few seconds of warning, she would probably have already met her demise.

It's him—the faceless man. She can make out his silhouette, but shadows always cover his face. She's been having recurring visions of this mysterious man for months now, and each one puts her on edge. What does he want? He never speaks. Is someone coming for her...? After every vision, Estella's imagination runs wild. Sometimes, he's the man of her dreams, and other times, he's her worst nightmare.

It's the same as always: he's dressed in black from head to toe, walking towards her from a distance. The vision soon dissipates, and she sighs in defeat. She has learned nothing new.

Estella's car shakes in the wake of each passing car as she waits for an opening, until she's on her way again. This is her fourth attempt at scattering the ashes of her late husband, Lucas. The last few times, she only managed to get in her car; she couldn't even bring herself to start the engine. Today, however, Estella has set out on the winding drive to the San Andreas Fault Trail in the foothills of the Santa Cruz Mountains. Naturally, Lucas and Estella never discussed their end-of-life preferences; they were too young to consider such things. But she knows that floating on a breeze into the depths of a crack in the earth outside Silicon Valley would have appealed to Lucas.

Just after Palo Alto, Page Mill Road turns into a twisting two-lane road. Estella hugs the switchbacks leading up the mountain and looks over at the passenger seat, where a knapsack containing a bag full of Lucas's ashes rests. Though her eyes land on the knapsack only momentarily, she drifts over the center line in those seconds. A blaring car horn tears her eyes back to the road, her heart thundering in her chest from the sudden surge of adrenaline as she jerks the wheel, frantically getting back in her lane. Visions behind the wheel are one thing, but if she doesn't focus, she'll end up as dust, too. That's the last thing her daughters need.

With a sigh of relief, Estella pulls into an empty gravel parking lot near the trailhead, then gets out of her car with the knapsack, holding what's left of Lucas in hand. It's been a while since the last rain, and the dirt under her feet is dry and dusty. She wears a light jacket, perfect for the mild April weather. She's dressed appropriately not by chance, but because she's done her research; she knew it would be mostly sunny and sixty-eight degrees here today. She consulted with ChatGPT on the weather, reviews, and the trail map. Estella likes to prepare and plan. But she never could have prepared herself for Lucas's death, which shocked the planner in her to the core.

From the wide-open parking lot, Estella can see Silicon Valley in the distance. From this vantage point, it looks so innocuous, not like the future-generating beast that it is. It's not the same in 2028 as when they first moved there. The post-pandemic rise of AI has changed its landscape.

The airiness of the parking lot disappears at the trailhead, where a lush canopy of trees closes in on her. With her knapsack, she feels like Little Red Riding Hood setting out into the forest—though Little Red Riding Hood's basket wasn't full of a loved one's ashes. Estella hates the thought of her once-brawny husband reduced to ash. These ashes can't protect her from any Big Bad Wolf—or any weirdo lurking in the woods surrounding the trail, for that matter.

Though Estella has gone on many a solo hike before, vulnerability and profound loneliness quickly creep in. There's not a soul in sight—no one to hear her screams if she gets into trouble. On instinct, she pulls out her phone, marks her location, and shares it with her mom, Hannah. At least now, her family would know where to find her body. It's no wonder that Estella has held onto Lucas's ashes for over a year. Spreading them is proving to be a nerve-wracking ordeal—and her nerves were frayed to begin with. Over a year ago… That's when, after she quit her job and ended her successful legal career, Lucas was killed.

Along the trail are various stations providing information about earthquakes and the San Andreas Fault. Estella dutifully reads the information at each station as she makes her way along the trail, which zigzags along the fault line. She stops and waits when she arrives at a point close to it. She's not ready to spread Lucas's ashes yet. Her head still aches from the vision. She's been getting visions for as long as she can remember, and most aren't powerful enough to give her a headache. However, her visions of the faceless man have been particularly potent.

Estella waits in the shade until her light jacket fails to keep out the cold. She heaves a sigh. She's made it this far, and the thought of having to make the trip again compels her to move forward. *Rip it off like a Band-Aid,* she thinks. She scans the landscape for a place to rest Lucas's ashes. The fault line lies beyond the trail, but she doesn't see a giant crack in the earth, like she had imagined. The rolling hills and occasional outcroppings of rock tell a quieter story of the fault's movement. She hears a raven's call and follows it to a gnarled old oak tree, where the bird perches on one of its twisting branches. The tree stands out amongst the others. This will be the spot. She won't forget it.

With shaking hands, she retrieves the baggie and works quickly to empty out Lucas's ashes. Naturally, the wind shifts direction and blows some back onto her—like Lucas's death itself, it's another unplanned occurrence. Flustered, she tries again, waiting for the right moment when the wind will carry Lucas beyond the oak tree and towards the San Andreas Fault.

"Until next time," Estella whispers as the last of Lucas's ashes disappear into the wind.

At night, Estella has trouble getting to sleep. Rarely does it come easy. Through no will of her own, bedtime has become the time to examine all her worries, regrets, and longings. As she does so many nights, tonight she burns for something she doesn't have—a gaze heavy with desire, a touch marked with heat, a kiss laced with need. These are some of the things Lucas can no longer give her. These are the things she wishes for quietly late at night. And these are the things she worries she'll never have again.

She tosses and turns for most of the night, until the street noise from the morning rush wakes her. As if someone is turning up the volume knob on an amp, the sounds of cars and motorcycles zipping by become louder. Consciousness trickles in, and reality stings.

Dreams punctuated what little sleep Estella managed to get. A particularly vivid dream about two strangers in a dark forest has left her with residual unease. She clutches her pillow, willing its shape into Lucas's, hoping the comfort of the embrace will wipe the dream from her mind.

The door cracks open, and when she sees her daughters, Mina and Kaitlin, Estella pushes the dream out of her head. Every day, they wake before the alarm goes off because of the impossible-to-ignore symphony of traffic. Their two-bedroom apartment is just steps from one of Silicon Valley's thoroughfares, leading to the many tech giants sprinkled throughout the Valley. Estella groans as she whacks the pillow that serves as a surrogate Lucas a couple of times, smoothing it back into shape.

"Hey, Mama," Mina and Kaitlin say in unison, perched next to Estella like cats about to pounce. Before she can get a word out, they set to pouncing, and the morning starts with a mix of tangled sheets, fluffy pillows, tickles, and laughs.

After Mina and Kaitlin run to their room to get ready for school, Estella gets dressed. She changes into a casual dress and well-worn sneakers. She doesn't mess around with piecing together a professional-looking outfit, like she might have done in the past. These days, she's more likely to be found wearing oversized cardigans and baggy pants. Her hair remains uncombed, free to do what it wants—sort of like her. After many years of juggling her career, marriage, and motherhood, she craves simplicity.

On the agenda today, like every day, is to write a story, a poem—anything. After Lucas died, Estella realized she was a poet. It's like his death flipped a switch in her, and she's spilled a lifetime of emotion into poems. Her plan, however, has been to write a novel. It's her dream, and one of the reasons she quit her job. But the poems just keep coming. It isn't just what she feels in the moment that comes out in her poems; it's every significant moment she can remember, every past heartache. It's like her whole life, she's been tucking a poem into the back of her mind, and she saved them all until it was time for her to release them.

Later in the day, Estella goes to her favorite coffee shop in downtown Los Gatos to get her usual coffee. She peruses the news on her phone, falls into a social media black hole, and then feels guilty about doing all those things instead of writing.

At the coffee shop, with her coffee and toasted everything bagel with cream cheese in hand, she looks for an open table, but doesn't see one. It's a popular place. They roast their coffee in small batches, and their bagels are freshly baked. She navigates towards the back by the roaster. The aroma of freshly roasted coffee becomes so potent that it feels like she's wading through it. Its seductive scent makes her more desperate for a table where she can sit and enjoy her first sip. Nope—no open tables back here.

She's in luck; she spots an open table and takes it before someone else can. It's a corner spot where she has a bird's-eye view of the happenings, and no one can see her screen. She keeps her work safely guarded, especially from curious family and friends. She's not ready to talk about her writing. She self-published the poems she wrote under a pen name because she didn't want anyone who knew her to read them. Her fear of judgment has prevented her from sharing her inner world with others, which has led to profound loneliness.

After Estella finishes her bagel and sips her coffee, she turns her focus to writing, but finds herself distracted and anxious. She can't shake the image of Lucas's ashes disappearing into the wind, or the memory of last night's vivid dream. Because the dream felt so random, yet real, she searches for meaning in it. Give her a dream, a song, or even a random conversation with a stranger, and she'll look for deeper significance. That's just what she does.

Contemplating her dreams, however, isn't Estella's only distraction. Quitting her job and losing Lucas haven't been her only major life changes lately. They've moved around a lot, mainly bouncing from one apartment to another, trying to find an affordable place to live in the Bay Area. Now, in the wake of Lucas's passing, Estella and her daughters must move again. She's trying to find a whole new identity, and a place they can call home once and for all.

Before Estella can even type a sentence out, her phone buzzes. It's Connor Dunn, a former coworker who is also recently widowed. She hesitates before answering because she fears he'll want to make plans. She knows Connor likes her, but she's not ready to date yet. Against her better judgment, she answers.

Connor gets straight to the point. "I've been thinking," he says, "we should go out to dinner."

Estella immediately regrets answering the call. "Like, on a date?" she asks stupidly.

"Yeah. I mean, it doesn't have to be a date," he backpedals, sensing her lack of enthusiasm.

"Uh, sure. That'd be nice," Estella says, only because she feels bad for him. He lost his wife just a few months before Lucas died. Apparently, she was involved in some kind of accident, but Estella doesn't know the details. Though she's curious, she doesn't want to pry. When Estella told her friends that Connor is trying to date her, they encouraged her to give it a try, suggesting that it would be good for her.

"Great! I'll come to your neck of the woods. This cool restaurant in downtown Los Gatos has a live jazz band on Friday nights. Sound good?"

"Yeah," she says, then gives herself an out. "But I'll have to see if the kids' babysitter is available then."

Now, Estella will spend an excessive amount of time deciding whether to cancel, blaming it on the lack of babysitter availability, or to go on the date because "it would be good for her."

# Chapter 2

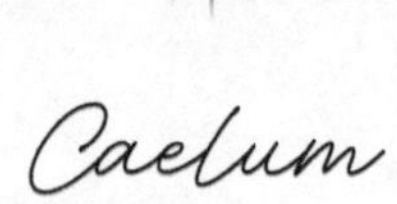

It's getting late in the evening as Caelum pours himself a second glass of whiskey. He drank the first glass like catching up with an old friend; he took his time. As he drank his first drink of the evening slowly, the rocks in his whiskey on the rocks melted. He drops an enormous ice cube into his glass, making one loud clink. While shopping for items to decorate his new home, he purchased an ice cube tray that makes four gigantic ice cubes, each of which fits snugly into a whiskey glass.

Caelum pours the amber liquid on top of the large chunk of ice, which takes up most of the glass. When the room-temperature whiskey hits the frozen cube, it makes cracking sounds, cascades down its sides, and pools at the bottom of the glass. He picks up the glass, swishes it around, the cube clinking against its sides, and takes a long, drawn-out sip. Yet to be diluted by the ice cube, the whiskey goes down strong and warm. On nights like these—which are most nights—whiskey takes the edge off the loneliness.

As he is scarce on connections, it's not unusual for Caelum to drink alone. But it's also not uncommon for a traveler of Caelum's kind to traverse life solo. There are many secrets to keep, and adding people to the mix only complicates things. When a person holds knowledge others don't and can't share that knowledge, being misunderstood comes with the territory. It's why travelers are such a lonely bunch.

Of course, Caelum is not any old traveler, or the kind defined in any earthly dictionary. He's a dream traveler. He travels to all times, places, and dimensions while he sleeps. His power is knowledge of what exists on the "other side" of the veil, including all his pasts, and bits of the future—futures that are only likely; they can change. Other than that, he's as human as it gets. There's no telling that he has access to the secrets of the universe and human existence unless he shares what's in his head. Which he can't. And he won't.

Being a loner in this life makes things easy on Caelum—or so he thinks. He's never been the type to keep to himself, but in all his lives, Caelum has also never felt like he belonged to anyone—anyone but Estella, that is. After they were taken from each other, he thought surely there would be someone like Estella in another life, or he'd come across someone like her on the other side. Nope. She's a strange one, but she's the only one for him. He's explored countless minds, but it's hers he connects with. He's loved in many lives, too, but none of those loves were quite like Estella. Trying to explain their connection is like trying to explain the other side to a non-traveler. It's complex, but also simple. That doesn't make sense ... but does love ever truly make sense?

Caelum takes another swig of whiskey, this one a little smoother, and the silkiness of the intoxicant on his lips is reminiscent of Estella's kisses. He can't get anything like that on the other side. It's one of the many things that make life so precious. He feels her on his whiskey-soaked lips, though they have yet to kiss in this life. He's never felt a kiss quite like hers before—one that's more an intermingling of souls than a meeting of lips, and one he can't shake from his head. He burns for that kiss many nights, but instead, he has his whiskey ... for now.

In each new life a person lives, knowledge of past lives and what's on the other side disappears until they cross back over. So, when a life of Caelum's comes to an end, it's Estella he goes looking for on the other side. But people never know how much time they'll spend on the other side in between lives. Only the Source, a powerful energetic entity, decides that. Estella has gone from one life to another, while Caelum stayed on the other side, waiting for her. Caelum and Estella have been apart for lifetimes.

They'll always have the other side, whenever they both end up there, but he's now been given the gift of another life with Estella—one more chance to feel her in human form. In exchange for rescuing Athena, his friend on the other side, from a wretched half-soul, she gave Caelum her traveling rights. With these gifted traveling rights, Caelum was allowed to enter a life with knowledge of all his past lives and Estella. And he'll be forever indebted to Athena for that reason.

If the kind of information Caelum could access were available to any living person, he wouldn't be such a mystery. Anyone with access to all of time and all dimensions would understand his mission. People would know what lies just beyond the edges of understanding; on the other side, we are eternal, we are deathless. But being here right now is an integral part of the whole. It's a chance to get those kisses, but also to be kind. It's an opportunity to love. The more love a person creates in a lifetime, the more bliss they will carry to the other side. The look and feel of the other side are what a person makes of it. One can create colorful oceans, perfect cities, and a never-setting sun that floats in a sky of orange and pink. If a person has enough love, and they like that kind of thing, the other side could be that for them. For Caelum and Estella, the love they created at the beginning of their journey can build them a glowing neon multi-world paradise on the other side. It doesn't have to be neon, but it damn well could be, if that's what they want.

Caelum walks his only friend, whiskey, from the kitchen to the library, swirling his giant ice cube in his glass, making clinking sounds along the way. Upon entering the library, a chill runs through him—not because it's cold, but because there are no books. It's been said that a room without books is like a body without a soul. The library, mostly empty, is feeling rather soulless. Lounging in a library void of books feels wrong, but Caelum plops himself down in one of the two chairs occupying the room anyway. It's still a library, and there aren't many lives in which Caelum has had the luxury of owning a library. Of course, he was never a traveler in any past life, either. Envisioning his library packed to the brim with soul, he drinks his whiskey, and the room takes on a new shape.

When Caelum and Estella first met, he was someone else. In some ways, he's that person, but he's not that person anymore. Currently, he's Caelum Di Rosa, born in Positano, Italy. But long ago, he made Estella a promise. Now, he's here in the San Francisco Bay Area to make good on it. Having a track record of letting his heart rule his head and being a risk-taker, he doesn't always make the most rational decisions. But one thing is for sure: he's a man of his word. When Estella was taken from him, he promised her he'd always find her, and he has. He's come for her from far away—farther than she could imagine. She just doesn't know it yet. She doesn't know *him* yet. At least, not this him.

Having recently finished the completion of his home and the library he's sitting in, he's just now making his way to Estella. Certain events have kept them apart before Caelum could leave Positano to find her. Now, he has finally settled in the San Francisco Bay Area, looking for a way to get his foot into her world again. For the time being, he gets in her head. As she quietly sleeps, he wanders through her dreams and leaves her wondering, his eyes clouding her thoughts. It's a place he knows he can always go to see her.

Caelum slumps in his chair with only a sip or two of watery whiskey left in his glass and dozes off in his library sans books. Upon slipping into a dream, he heads straight for Estella. He's lucky to find her quickly this time and gets in on one of her dreams.

Jazzy music coming from a phonograph fills all corners of this reality. This dream of hers is quite a trip. The scene is much like a Baz Luhrmann movie, immersive and theatrical. As Estella dreams, Caelum is met by grand gestures and close encounters that quicken his breath. A woman dances around him, swishing her full-length skirt from one side to the other. Her movements are swift and sharp, her look of seduction practiced. His senses buzz, and mellow lights flicker around him when the dancer disappears.

Then the dream morphs into an entirely new dream, which is more Tim Burton than Baz Luhrmann. The jazzy music and dancer have been replaced by a shadowy forest and two dark figures. Snippets of past lives unassumingly weave through Estella's dreams like innocent figments of the imagination. But they're much more than that.

# Chapter 3

Estella takes the Diablo Road freeway exit and follows it to Front Street, which leads her to the Danville Library. *So charming*, she thinks. Shaded by mature trees and sprinkled with park benches, the large grassy area leading up to the entrance looks like an inviting place to read on a nice day. She likes this town already.

Estella made the hour-long trip to Danville to scope out the area. She's been contemplating whether to buy a house in the Bay Area or give up and go back to Seattle to live close to family. But something about growing up in Seattle and feeling like she never fit in has kept her away thus far. Maybe that's why she keeps moving; she never quite fits in. But some place has to stick, she hopes. All that is certain is that it's time to get out of Los Gatos and the apartment Estella and her daughters shared with Lucas. It'll be easier for Estella to move on in an environment that doesn't constantly remind her of him.

Estella continues through downtown. There's something calming about these quiet streets. A coffee shop pops up on her radar, so she pulls over to check it out. This will be the true test; she can't live in a town without a proper coffee shop. A good place to drink lattes and write is essential.

Before she walks into the coffee shop, Estella's phone vibrates. It's her best friend, Emma, who lives in Seattle. Emma is the daughter of Estella's mom's best friend, Kareena. Estella and Emma practically grew up together. They're not sisters by blood, but they are sisters by magic. They have the mark of the moon on the inside of their left forearms to show for it. It's a white crescent-moon-shaped birthmark that all the women in their families have. Not all witches have markings, but the mark of the moon is one of many a witch may have. But Estella doesn't like to use the term *witch*. She doesn't like to call attention to her magic. As her mom, Hannah, likes to say, witches are just exceptional women. That's how Estella likes to think of witches, too. She also downplays her gift of vision, calling it "a strong intuition." But Hannah, on the other hand, lets her witch flag fly.

When Estella turned twenty-eight a couple of years ago, she camouflaged her mark with a tattoo. Delicate, single-needle lines trace the edges of the crescent with a few ornamental accents. Blending her witchy birthmark into a tattoo is another thing she's done to keep her magic on the down-low. But if one looks closely, the space inside the borders of her tattoo is a few shades lighter than the rest of her tan Spanish-Hungarian skin.

Emma got her crescent tattooed at the same time that Estella did. Against her deeper skin tone, Emma's crescent stands out more, so she had hers adorned with more ornamental details. She's like Estella and the younger generation of witches caught up in a recent social media backlash against witches; they decided to keep their magic to themselves.

Estella takes Emma's call and lingers outside the coffee shop's entrance, listening to Emma talk. After raving about some new skincare product she recently purchased, Emma realizes she isn't listening. Estella's strange dream a couple of nights ago is still stuck in her head. But even if she weren't thinking about the dream, she would've tuned out Emma. Fancy skincare products are Emma's thing, not Estella's.

"You there?" Emma asks.

"Kind of. I mean, sorry… I had the weirdest dream the other night, and I can't stop thinking about it."

"I don't know why you overthink things like dreams." Emma never overthinks anything, except perhaps skincare products. Estella envies Emma's lightness.

"It's just that it was so *real*," Estella says. The dream was so lifelike that it didn't seem like a dream. Her surroundings were so vivid that she had wondered whether she was dreaming at all.

"Are you sure it was a dream and not a vision?" Emma asks.

"Yes, I'm positive," Estella says. *Could I have awakened in the night and had a vision?* she wonders. Maybe, but she's not so sure. There's such a fine line between dreams and visions, but it must've been a dream.

"Well, what was it about?" Emma asks.

"I was in some dark and gloomy forest," Estella says.

Her dream began with a question: *What am I doing here?* It's a question Estella asks herself often, usually in a meaning-of-life sense, but in the dream, she had been looking for a physical location. The scent of damp soil filled her nose, and leaves rustling under her feet filled her ears. Wandering around and looking for a way out, she squinted at the few beams of sunshine that made their way through the dense layer of fog and the shelter of the canopy. Beads of dew blanketed the foliage around her, like lightsabers wielded by gods from above. The sunbeams glistened off the dewdrops, illuminating them like tiny lightbulbs. Then fog encroached, extinguishing the lightsabers and flipping off the switch on the tiny lightbulbs. The forest turned dark and gloomy, just like Estella said.

"So? What's so weird about that?" Emma says.

"It felt like I had been there before, even though I've never seen the place. I don't know if that makes sense. But that's not it. There were these people…"

Estella had realized she wasn't alone when two dark figures caught her eye. In the distance were two people, a man and a woman, dressed in black clothes reminiscent of a bygone era. They looked like they had stepped out of a gothic drama. The man was dressed in coattails and a top hat. His pallid complexion contrasted with his earthy brown hair, which flowed from under his hat in jagged wisps. His eyes, a beacon of color, were the kind of green that put the evergreens hiding amidst the forest to shame. The woman wore a long dress and a bonnet. Her skin was a wintry white, and because her pale lips blended into the hue of her skin, Estella was drawn to her eyes—large, chestnut-brown button eyes.

But nothing commanded Estella's attention more than the woman's hair, which was a brilliant copper and danced around her shoulders like fire.

"They kind of freaked me out," Estella adds.

The couple had locked arms and turned to walk towards Estella. As they approached, her heart picked up the pace. She had searched her mind for explanations: she was in an alcohol-laced trance and couldn't remember how she had ended up in the forest; the couple was dressed up because they were characters in a play; the couple was part of some reenactment. Estella greeted them timidly, but was met with silence. Their faces were emotionless, and they were coming in hot—way too hot. Then, before she could move out of their way, the matter of their bodies merged, occupying the same space and time as they walked through her. In disbelief, Estella had scanned her body. She struggled to understand the violation of the laws of physics as she grabbed at herself to ensure she was still solid flesh and bone. That was when the dream had ended.

"They walked through me like I was a ghost, or maybe *they* were ghosts. What do you think it means?" Estella asks.

"It doesn't mean anything. It was just a dream," Emma insists. "Unless it was a vision."

Estella rolls her eyes and says, "I have to get to work."

"Work?" Emma says with a snicker. She fantasizes about quitting her regular job at her family-run bookstore, but can't.

"Shut up. Yes, work. Writing is work," Estella says. With that, she ends the call and enters the coffee shop.

Estella inspects her surroundings after getting a latte and finding a place to sit in the corner of the coffee shop.

It's a cozy indie spot with plenty of tables and stuffed bookshelves, exuding a welcoming vibe. This will be a nice office for her. She pulls her notebook of poems from her bag. Though she plans to write her novel, she keeps dropping poems onto these empty pages.

As she sips her latte and contemplates the opening lines to a new poem, she hears the bells on the door jingle like it's Santa Clause bearing gifts for all.

But it's not Santa. It's much, much better. Inspiration just walked in.

This man strolls into the coffee shop with such bravado that you'd think he owns the place—or rules the world, for that matter. His addition to the room erases everything else in it. What was she writing? He's all there is, his sun-kissed skin and wavy dark brown hair falling right to the corners of his mouth—a place Estella would like to visit.

What is she thinking? These thoughts are so foreign to her. She's not herself.

Lucas was the last person to evoke these feelings, but that was so long ago that feelings of attraction are all but a distant memory. Estella supposes this man is good-looking. His facial features are objectively hand-some, in a proportionally perfect kind of way. He looks to be thirty-something, and over a week's worth of stubble gives him an edgy look. Walking in here with his black jacket over his hoodie, he looks like he's been up to no good. And she likes it.

There are plenty of attractive men wandering around, but it's rare for someone to catch Estella's attention like this. Usually, it takes hours of mind-blowing conversation for her to form an attraction. She dated Lucas for months before she ever even thought of kissing him. Perhaps she's just missing Lucas—or maybe it's something about this guy that makes her feel like he's everything she's ever wished for. Fleetwood Mac's "Gypsy" plays. Estella gets lost in the swirl of her latte, daydreaming about this guy being lightning.

He goes to the register to put in his order, and she feels a pull. Never mind that her cup is still half full; it's time for another latte. She tries to act cool while waiting at the coffee counter, noticing him glancing over at her out of the corner of her eye, because she dares not look directly at him.

She hears faint speech, which turns into "What you got there?" She was so caught up in pretending not to notice him that she didn't realize he was talking to her. She searches herself and finds she's still holding her notebook of poems. Mesmerized by him, she didn't even think to put it down. The notebook is covered in hearts, resembling a little girl's diary, so she hides it behind her back.

"Oh, nothing," she says, laughing nervously. There's an awkward silence, and she feels the need to fill it. "It's my poetry. But don't let the cover fool you. It's a serious book of poems."

Another awkward silence ensues.

"You know, I love poetry," he offers, filling the void.

She says, "Oh?" because it's all she can manage.

He leans closer and says, "I'd love to read your serious poems." His voice takes on a sexy, tender tone with a musical quality.

Is he flirting? Estella doesn't know. She's been out of the game for too long. She looks up and meets his eyes for the first time. They're a luminous green, contrasting brilliantly with his dark hair and tan skin. His gaze strikes her down. Electrified and embarrassed, she can't bear to look him in the eyes again. It's too much feeling. While she's usually somewhat confident, his confidence crushes hers. But she doesn't mind. *Please, please do that again.* Her heart pounds and her cheeks burn. Does he notice?

"I'm still working on them," she says without looking at him. Instead, she searches the counter for her latte, but there's only a matcha waiting for someone. "I'm not sure I'll publish them. I'm working on writing a novel," she says.

"It would be a shame not to publish them," he says, moving closer. His arm brushes against hers, and she feels his touch course through her whole body. "Poetry must be shared," he adds.

Estella lets out another nervous laugh. "Well, actually, I have published a book of poems. I published *thunder and daisy* under a pen name."

She can't believe she's just told this stranger about her book. She hasn't told *anyone* she published a poetry collection. Well, except her mom and dad, of course; there's no hiding anything from them. Oh, and then there's Emma; of course she told Emma about her book. But that's it: three people. Now, four.

The barista calls out, "Estella." She grabs her latte and heads back to her corner table, hoping he doesn't notice the flustered state he's put her in.

"Estella..." he calls after her. She turns back, and seeing him standing at the counter steals her breath. "I'd like a signed copy."

Estella half smiles and turns back around.

At her table, she puts on imaginary horse blinders and avoids accidental eye contact with him. She stares intently at a blank page in her notebook of poems while she works on regaining her composure. Once she can think straight, she'll fill this notebook with pages of poems about him.

When she feels it's safe to scan the room, she notices he's left. She feels a little void inside, like a space once filled with warmth is now drained and cold. But she's also relieved. She can breathe again. She's not sure what it was about that guy, but the intensity of feeling he evoked in her is unsettling, to say the least.

# Chapter 4

✳

*Caelum*

Caelum kills the lights and closes his eyes. He's hoping to fall asleep fast, so he can get to work, but given his encounter with Estella today, thoughts of it prevent him from falling into an easy sleep. He keeps replaying their conversation at the coffee shop. Having known exactly where Estella would be sitting, he spotted her immediately, her small frame hidden under her long, wavy brown hair. Looking for an excuse to talk to her, he asked about her notebook of poems, and it worked. And when she looked at him with her warm amber eyes for the first time in this lifetime, he drank her in as long as she let him, taking in her delicate features—small but full lips and a heart-shaped face. She seemed nervous, but he thought it was a kind of good nervous. It was exactly what he'd hoped for, and now he'll travel in search of their next encounter.

Traveling is an art form. There's a technique to it, which takes many years to develop. At thirty-four,

Caelum is still honing his skills. Knowing he'd find her at the coffee shop today took some trial and error, a few nights of dream travel to the future. He had to direct his energy to different points in space and time, opening a few doors before he found the right one. Given that travelers can travel only when in a dream, he has a limited amount of time to practice.

At last, he finds himself in a dream, looking for a door to open. Gathering intense energy as he envisions Estella and him together in the future, he's led to a door. Doors come in all shapes, sizes, and colors. This one is a heavy oak with intricate carvings and takes some strength to open. He's in luck. He finds Estella in the not-so-distant future behind the first door in this dream.

"Where are you currently living? Are you renting, or do you have a home to sell?" the real estate agent asks Estella.

"Renting," Estella says without elaborating, leaving the agent thirsting for more information.

"So, what do you do?" the agent pries further as she inspects Estella from head to toe, looking for clues.

Estella ignores her question and asks about available homes in Danville.

"We don't have new homes available in Danville. Our new developments are located here in San Ramon," the agent says and crosses her arms over her chest, bringing her expensive watch into Estella's view like some sort of power play. Estella is not impressed.

"Well, this is an amazing home, and San Ramon is nice. And it's right next to Danville," Estella says.

"Inventory is tight, here and in Danville. If you like this home, I urge you to act quickly. Another family is coming in later to put a deposit on it."

Estella doesn't believe her. "First, I'd like to see the other new developments in San Ramon, and resales in Danville," she says.

"I can assure you that you won't find a home in Danville at this price, and our other developments in San Ramon start at a higher price range," the agent says with arms still crossed, now tapping the toe of her pointy shoe on the tile floor. The tapping sound evokes urgency, and Estella views it as another sales ploy.

Estella stares at the agent like she's calculating various unseen factors that weigh on the validity of her statements. "I'm going to get a coffee," she says as she motions towards the coffee maker set up in the corner of the sales office.

Sipping coffee from a paper cup labeled with the home builder's logo, Estella pulls out her phone and clicks the app she uses to search available homes. She does her research and scopes out inventory in Danville and San Ramon to verify the agent's claims.

Estella leaves the sales area and meanders around the model home, moving from one item that catches her attention to the next. She runs her hand along the ivory-colored granite countertops in the kitchen, takes off her shoes to feel the new carpet under her feet, peeks into the walk-in closet in the master bedroom, and messes with the faucets in the bathroom. After touring the house another time and peppering the agent with questions about the development, neighborhood, and local schools, Estella puts down a deposit to reserve the home.

Unsatisfied with what the future shows, Caelum stirs awake. He's a light sleeper to begin with, which does not come in handy when traveling in dreams, but light the candle of Estella in his head, and sleep becomes impossible. Instead of relaxing, having a warm cup of tea, reading, or doing what most people do when they can't sleep, he hauls stacks of books into his library to start setting it up for Estella. Her dream home has a library, so if he's going to wow her with his place, an amazing library is a necessity. Caelum also can't stand leaving things unfinished. Perhaps that's another reason he couldn't let Estella go. In their last life together, they were taken from each other too soon. The library is still an unfinished project, but Caelum will have it complete in no time.

As he breaks a sweat carrying in load after load of books, he grumbles his discontent. A heavy stack of books tumbles from his grasp, landing in an echoing thud. That home in San Ramon is not what Estella wants. It's nice, but it's not at all what she dreams about. It's new, it's spotless, but it's not Estella. He crumples to the floor where the books lay, then cracks open a dusty old hardcover copy of *Great Expectations* by Charles Dickens. "Oh, Estella," he whispers as he turns a page. It doesn't matter what house she lives in for the time being because she won't truly feel at home until she's with him.

# Chapter 5

## Estella

The doorbell rings, and it's the kids' babysitter. After hours of deliberation, Estella did not call off tonight's date with Connor. Her reasons for agreeing to the date are mostly selfish: spending time with Connor will help her get out of her head and save herself from her thoughts.

Upon seeing the babysitter, Mina's face reddens, and she runs into her room. Seeing that Mina is upset, Estella hurries after her, with Kaitlin on her heels.

"We wouldn't need a babysitter if Daddy were here! I don't want a babysitter. I want Daddy!" Mina shrieks.

Shaken by Mina's shrill cry, Kaitlin tears up, her eyes turning into molten amber.

Estella knew this date was a bad idea. She does her best to console her daughters, offering hugs, knowing glances, and shared pain, but it's all inadequate. Nothing she says or does will be enough. She can't give them the one thing they need: their dad.

The doorbell rings again just as the babysitter enters the room holding a container. When she pries the lid off, the aroma of fresh-baked chocolate chip cookies fills the air, and the kids' tears evaporate. With fists full of cookies, Mina and Kaitlin hug Estella, and she slips out of the room to get the door.

Connor has arrived and wears a childlike, wide-eyed look on his face, along with his typically messy but pleasingly plentiful mousy-brown hair. He's such a contrast to Lucas, who had a Viking-esque look. Over six feet tall and built, Lucas took up a lot of space. While Connor is taller than Estella, he's much shorter than Lucas was. Lucas's hair was lighter, an ashy blonde, and he had a lot less of it. He had these deep-set gunmetal blue-gray eyes under strong eyebrows that meant business. But two kids later, with a demanding job, not to mention Estella and her crazy schemes keeping him on his toes, he had looked like a Viking who had been through the wash a few times. Still, he was strikingly handsome until the day he died.

Estella doesn't want Connor to think she put in a lot of effort getting ready for their date, so while she's dressed up, her look is more casual. She stayed away from anything that gives off a sexy vibe.

"Hey! You look amazing!"

Her plan to underwhelm him has failed. Trying to hide her disappointment, she thanks him for the compliment.

If they're calling it a date, it's the first date Estella has been on since Lucas died. Despite it being a year since his passing, it's too soon. She'll end up comparing everything about Connor to Lucas, just like she did the moment Connor walked through the door. Loneliness and the voices of loved ones urging her to move past her grief are the reasons she'll give Connor a try. Tonight, she'll give him her full attention and really try to get to know him. She considers the way a person's mind works to be an essential ingredient of attraction. So, she'll throw a couple of heavy questions at him to see if there's anything interesting behind those big baby blues. He deserves a good try from her.

After a short drive, they arrive at the restaurant in downtown Los Gatos. They're greeted by a lanky woman with thin lips, accentuated by the dark red lipstick she's wearing. She doesn't smile. She just asks them if they have a reservation, and Connor tells her they do. With an air of superiority, she says, "Follow me." Constricted by the tightness of her dress, she takes small steps. They follow her, maneuvering around elegantly dressed patrons and tables covered in white tablecloths. Each table is dimly lit by candlelight, which reflects off the silverware in an inviting golden glow. The candlelight and jazz music make for a romantic atmosphere.

They come to a table for two close to the stage area. Once they're seated, Estella looks over at the band, and the drummer flashes her a smile. She recognizes him and smiles back. It's Gabriel. He works at a coffee shop in town—not the one where she writes, but another she visits occasionally for a change of scenery. The suit he's wearing throws her off, because she's never seen him wear one, but his curly, dark hair and mustache make him easily identifiable. He's probably in his twenties and wears glasses that sit midway down the bridge of his nose. He likes to peer at Estella over the frames while they talk.

Their server introduces herself and goes into her spiel on menu items. Connor doesn't notice the exchange with Gabriel, and he doesn't seem aware that their attractive server is surveying him. He appears to be in his own world. Maybe he's thinking about his dead wife. With that thought, the mood darkens, at least in Estella's head. Attempting to regain a positive state of mind, she focuses on their server, who gives up on trying to engage Connor. She turns her attention to Estella when she gets to the dessert part of the evening specials.

"Tonight's dessert is an almond cake with a honey lavender sorbet and crystallized basil," she says, not taking her eyes off Estella and moving closer. Her magnificent, voluminous, kinky-curly hair floats around her face as she shifts from one foot to the other, reciting her script. Estella asks her a question about one of the menu items, and she smiles before providing details on the braised lamb shank over creamy polenta. Connor stares at his menu all the while. Estella's interactions with Gabriel and their server have been engaging. So far, she's not feeling engaged by Connor, but the date is not over.

A few months before Estella quit her job, Connor had been out of the office for days, and she assumed he was on vacation. But when she finally asked a coworker where he went, she found out his wife died. Word got around that his wife was involved in an accident, but Connor kept the details private. Estella doesn't blame him. Thinking about Lucas without getting a lump in her throat or tears in her eyes is nearly impossible, let alone talking about him.

After Estella left her job, Connor apparently heard about Lucas's death and contacted her, asking if they could get together to chat. She didn't want to get together, and she didn't want to chat. But her friends pushed her to meet with him. They said that they'd understand each other and help each other get through the grief. They are indeed bound by grief, but that's about it thus far. Just because they both lost their spouses doesn't mean they should date. It feels forced.

Connor seems like a nice guy, and he's attractive in a disheveled, boyish kind of way. His hair is always messy, shirt half tucked in, and his baby face makes him look deceptively younger than he is. But Estella doesn't think he's ready to move on. She guesses he knows she's not ready, either. Even if she were, she's not convinced it would be with Connor.

"So, are you going to stay in the apartment?" Connor asks, his eyes still on the menu.

"No. I need to start fresh, somewhere that doesn't remind me of Lucas. We were looking to buy a home when he died, and that's what I want to do—buy a home and stay in it, so the girls can have some stability."

"I totally understand that. After Emily died, I had to move, too. It was too painful to be reminded of her constantly—her favorite chair always empty, her perfume lingering in the air…"

"How do you like your new place?" Estella asks, changing the subject. She knew this would happen—that their lost loves would dominate the conversation.

"It's all right. The commute sucks, but I like the East Bay. My new place is much nicer—more bang for your buck out there."

"Where in the East Bay?"

"San Ramon." He takes a sip of his water, and instead of looking at her, he looks over at the band.

"That's right where I'm headed," Estella says.

"Really?" His gaze finally lands on her.

"I was interested in Danville, but then stopped at one of the new developments in San Ramon. I got sucked in. I have a deposit on a home, but I have a few days to think about it before losing any money."

"You'll love San Ramon," he says. "And we'll be close." He's now more focused on her than he's been all night.

Not sure what to think about being close to Connor, Estella's eyes float away from him to the jazz band.

Connor makes small talk to break the silence. "So, you're staying local. That's cool. I thought you might move back to Seattle. What did you think of Seattle, anyway?"

"I miss it sometimes," Estella says. She thinks of her parents, stepparents, and all her friends. "I miss the people, though, not the weather." As many others have, Lucas and Estella followed tech to the San Francisco Bay Area. Sunshine and the promise of Silicon Valley tech paradise called to them like a siren to a sailor, and the dreary Seattle weather sealed the deal.

Connor and Estella are halfway through their main course, and he hasn't charmed her like Gabriel or their server. Between bites, he's still going on about San Ramon and the housing market. Whatever happened to talking about hopes, fears, and dreams? All this small talk is killing her, and it's doing nothing to ignite the kind of feelings Coffee Shop Guy effortlessly sparked in her.

Changing the subject, she says, "Cheers to date nights, good food, and good music," and raises her glass.

"Cheers," Connor says, and they clink glasses.

Chasing some depth, Estella asks Connor what he likes to read. She tells him about her writing dreams, without divulging any details. She then asks him whether he likes poetry, music, and art.

"I'm not big on artsy stuff," Connor says and shrugs his shoulders. Estella doesn't know what to say, so she says nothing. Then Connor asks, "Are you sad to be leaving Los Gatos? It's such a great place to live."

And they're right back to small talk. Well, she tried.

"I can't stay in Los Gatos. I can't even afford to buy a parking space in this town. And I can't keep paying the crazy rent," Estella says while she watches Gabriel tap a smooth jazz beat on the drums. "It is nice, though," she continues. She is sad to leave. "I just don't really have a choice."

Their server sold Estella on the cake with honey lavender sorbet, so that's what she orders for dessert. But by the time she spoons the last of the sweet yet herbaceous, smooth iciness into her mouth, there has been no discussion of hopes, fears, or dreams. And she's still looking for that elusive spark. Dinner was nice, but she can't say she feels Connor like she felt Coffee Shop Guy, who said even less, but communicated so much more.

# Chapter 6

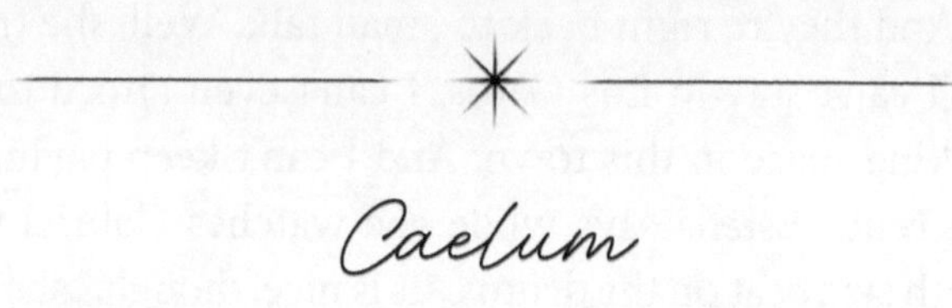

Caelum arrives at a modest home that houses a very rare violin at a very immodest price. He notices paint peeling along the home's trim, clouded windows, and the absence of a welcome mat. Caelum has a thing for rare musical instruments, which led him to this home of a dealer in Los Gatos. What he'll pay to get his hands on the piece is ludicrous, but he must have it.

The dealer, a stout, graying man, flings open the front door upon the first knock. Trust is in short supply, Caelum realizes as he enters the violin aficionado's home. The dealer's hand fidgeting at his side draws attention to a lump at the waist of his pants. He's packing heat—but so is Caelum. Large sums of money make for risky exchanges, but a little danger has never deterred him from getting what he wants.

After exchanging pleasantries, they get straight down to business. The dealer rests the violin case he's been clutching in his other hand on the table in front of them. Perspiration beads up on his forehead in the corners laid bare by a receding hairline as he unlatches the case. Two loud clicks, and it's unlocked. The dealer's fidgeting hand continues to move erratically, revealing a possible muscle tremor rather than nervous energy, or perhaps both. When he opens the case, and Caelum catches his first glimpse of the violin, his breath catches in his throat. There it is, just as he remembers it.

The dealer stretches thin white gloves made of soft material over his hairy hands, taking extra time on the trembling hand before reaching for the instrument. He then presents it for Caelum's viewing. His good hand holds the violin secure, but it moves ever so slightly against the trembling hand. Caelum dares not touch the violin and instead inspects it with a close eye. The dealer points with his chin at another pair of gloves sitting on the table, and Caelum slips them on.

"This is an unusual piece for my collection," the dealer says, delicately handing over the violin. "I had a difficult time tracking it down."

With the violin in Caelum's hands, he's flooded with memories and a mix of emotions. The last time he held it was in another lifetime.

"But at the price you agreed to pay..." The dealer's voice lowers to a whisper, and he eyes the duffel bag of cash in Caelum's possession. "...I was sure to find it."

That, and the clues Caelum planted in his dreams. Caelum could have tracked halfway around the world to get it himself, but he was willing to pay the price to have it delivered to his doorstep. Now is the time to work his way into Estella's world before something else happens to keep them apart, not to get swallowed by his musical obsessions.

Caelum takes the bow from the case and slides it over the strings. His eyes moisten upon hearing the violin speak after all these years, but not one tear escapes. A treasure like this transcends lifetimes. It's priceless, and he does pay dearly for it, handing over his bag of loot to the dealer.

Leaving with the violin securely in its case and his hands tightly wrapped around the handle, Caelum glances back at the dealer's house as he leaves. A portion of the man's new fortune can surely be used on a fresh coat of paint and a welcome mat, Caelum thinks.

On the way to his car, he then crosses paths with the spot where Lucas died. He's quite familiar with the place, having visited it many times over.

Traveling to the future is a funny thing. Caelum will see one version of the future on one trip, but in another dream, it can be completely different. The past is concrete, while the future is fluid, fluctuating like a riverbed at the mercy of its ever-changing waters. He didn't know Lucas was going to die. When he found out it happened, Caelum had to see it for himself. He thought maybe there was something he could've done, but there was nothing he could do to stop it. Because it was already the past, there was no changing it. While Caelum has always wanted to be with Estella, he never wanted her to suffer the loss of Lucas.

On one of Caelum's trips to the past, he had ended up on the corner between the high school and the coffee shop. The oak-and-palm-tree-adorned front lawn of Los Gatos High School was overrun by teenagers on their way to class. The first-period bell rang, and the last of the students shuffled up the stairs through the grand double-door entrance.

As the area cleared of foot traffic, Lucas came out of the coffee shop, holding coffee in a to-go cup and carrying a laptop bag slung over his shoulder. He had worked at Deity Company, which isn't far from the high school, so he must have stopped to get a coffee on his way to work. With the students now in class and no one other than Lucas on the sidewalk, it was eerily quiet—until a black sports car ripped through the scene. It passed in a blur, and Lucas hit the pavement.

A handful of people had come running out of the coffee shop to Lucas's aid, some of them backing away at the sight of his injuries. The first person to reach Lucas was a barista with curly hair, glasses, and a mustache. He dug into his apron and pulled out his cell phone. As he dialed for help, he tried to steady his shaking hands. Moments after the man put away his phone, the unsettling scream of sirens could be heard in the distance, and an ambulance arrived in no time. Unfortunately, it was too late. Life had permanently left Lucas's body.

It also hadn't taken long for Estella to appear on the scene. She had been at another coffee shop nearby and heard the commotion. She was part of a group of curious bystanders who had gathered on the corner. The group stood in relative silence, just a few hushed whispers audible—until a heart-piercing cry emerged from the crowd. It was Estella.

By then, the police had arrived and taped off the area surrounding Lucas. Estella tried with all the strength in her little body to get through, but the police officers held her back. "That's my *husband!*" she cried over and over again, to no avail. She was left sobbing in the arms of the curly-haired barista. She looked meek in his embrace, like a broken bird scooped up by burly hands. They clutched each other as the authorities covered Lucas's still, lifeless form.

In the tragic chaos, Lucas wasn't even given a moment to save himself or see what hit him. To this day, they had never caught the person. Caelum had tried time and time again to travel back to the scene of the crime to find a clue—anything that would lead to Lucas's killer. Perhaps bringing the criminal to justice would provide Estella comfort. That was all he wanted for her. But all his trips were in vain.

There's a certain degree of control, but traveling is not an exact science. Travelers don't always end up in the exact time or place they will themselves into. Sometimes, Caelum appeared at the coffee shop Estella was at when the accident happened, and other times, he found himself on the lawn of the high school. There are some places even travelers aren't meant to be, and some things they're not meant to see. Maybe one day, Caelum will catch a glimpse of the person who killed Lucas, but for now, the only information they have is that the driver was in a black sports car. No make. No model. Just a black sports car.

Cautiously looking both ways before crossing the street, Caelum jets to his car with the violin securely in hand, and in case anyone tries to mess with him, his weapon is easily accessible. The next stop is home. It's time to add this beauty to his collection, where it belongs.

# Chapter 7

The day after Estella's date with Connor, she's in no mood to write, so instead of going to her regular coffee shop, she walks over to the other coffee shop where Gabriel, the drummer, works. She's been avoiding Gabriel's coffee shop for some time because it's close to where Lucas's accident happened.

There are some moments in life that are too painful to recall. They get buried deep into our memories and stay there, lost. Her memory of the day Lucas died is hidden in a dusty corner of her mind behind a door she keeps shut. But she can't leave Los Gatos without saying goodbye to Gabriel. He's at the counter, swirling steaming milk on top of espresso as he glances over his wire-frame glasses at his latte art.

"Hey. I didn't know you were a drummer. You're really good," Estella says.

Still looking into his latte, Gabriel smiles and says, "I've been playing gigs around here for years."

"I don't get out much these days, so I have no idea what goes on around here," Estella admits and looks down at her shoes. Choosing the sanctuary of her mind over the excitement of the world too many times stirs up regret.

"Trying to stay afloat here, and hoping I don't get replaced by a coffee-pouring robot, I've been working jobs, like playing music at that restaurant." He shrugs his shoulders. "We're there every Friday and Saturday night. You should come see us again."

"I'd like to," Estella says. She really would, but she probably won't. She'll think about going, but then end up watching a rom-com or reading a book instead. "I play a bit of drums myself. My mom plays, and, well, my grand-pa is a drummer. He taught her, and he taught me some basics, too. I'm thinking of getting back into it. Maybe taking some lessons."

"Hey, if you need help or lessons, I'm your guy." Gabriel's eyebrows hover higher above the top rim of his glasses like doors opening, an invitation awaiting. "Teaching drums is one of my side gigs."

"That would be great, but I'm moving soon," Estella says.

Gabriel's eyebrows disappear behind his glasses. "Oh. Really?" He looks down at the latte he placed on the counter for a customer, and they both stare at the heart made of foam that floats atop it.

"Yeah. You know… I have to get out of here."

They exchange a look you might see on the faces of those who have experienced the same profound trauma. It's a sad understanding they'll share with only each other.

They'll be forever connected in that way. It's the same kinship Estella feels with her law school friends: they made it through hell, but they did it together.

"I get it. Where are you moving?" Gabriel asks.

"San Ramon."

"Ah, the East Bay. Yeah, I guess lessons wouldn't work, then. That's too bad, but I hope you'll stop by sometime. Los Gatos will miss you."

They smile at each other, but their mouths are twisted into shapes more closely resembling melancholy frowns.

"I'll miss it, too," she says and waves goodbye to her almost-friend.

Soon, it'll be time to part with Los Gatos, but Estella finds it difficult to leave. Her daughters—Mina, her first-born, and Kaitlin, her little one—also seem to love the neighborhood and their school. The thought of having to yank them out of yet another school at the end of the semester when it comes time to move is dreadful. They've already made a bunch of BFFs. They need friends they don't have to always leave behind, and they need stability. Estella wants to give them that, especially now that they don't have Lucas.

Mina, her mini-me, is eight years old. Like Estella, she has warm chocolate-brown hair. Her eyes, the blue-gray of storm clouds, are like Lucas's. Her personality is much like Estella's, a blend of competing opposites: a fun-loving, free-spirited, optimistic dreamer, and also an observant, introspective, neurotic realist. Estella knew Mina was hers when, one night, she was tucking her into bed. Mina said, "Hold on one second," jumped out of bed, adjusted her slumped-over teddy bear to sit neatly upright, and jumped back into bed. With a mischievous smile and a few blinks of her doe eyes, she said, "Good night, Mama."

Kaitlin, on the other hand, is all cuddles and love. Her funny, light-hearted personality is as bouncy as her curly, gingersnap-colored hair, and her spirit as warm as her big amber-brown eyes. With her freckles and dimples, you couldn't pack more cuteness into one kid. But don't let the sweetness fool you; she's smart as a whip, and her charm has a snakelike magic. Kaitlin has charmed Estella into giving up her fluffy blanket when she's cold, her side of the bed when she's sleepy, and her share of dessert on more than one occasion. Kaitlin may be only seven years old, but she knows what she wants, and she knows how to get it.

Like all the women in the family, Mina and Kaitlin also bear the mark of the moon. They haven't come into their magic yet, so they don't know that their crescents are more than just a birthmark. Estella was very young when she started getting visions. Her magic was strong, and she understood it before Hannah even mentioned the word "magic." On the other end of the spectrum, there are some witches who go most of their life without opening their gifts. In any case, there's usually some triggering event, like a life change, heartbreak, loss, or that kind of thing that releases the magic. Estella had thought Mina and Kaitlin would get their gifts when Lucas died. It didn't happen, but they could come into their powers any day now. Estella has been meaning to have the magic talk with them, so that they're not blindsided when it happens. She's just been waiting for the right time to tell them.

After saying goodbye to Gabriel, Estella sips her coffee on a slow walk back to her apartment. Like Alice in Wonderland, she slides down into a rabbit hole of daydreams on her walk home. After months of spinning her wheels and not making much progress toward her life goals, she needs to accomplish something—anything. So, when the girls get out of school, they drive to the new community in San Ramon. Estella wants Mina and Kaitlin to see the house. The next step towards their new life is the girls' approval of the new home in San Ramon. Maybe, if they finally find a home to buy in a place where they can plant roots, everything else in Estella's life will fall into place.

Later that day, when they pull into the housing community, Mina says, "Mommy, all the houses look the same." Kaitlin pipes up and adds, "Yeah." They point out exactly what Estella dislikes about the community: it lacks the old-town charm of Los Gatos or Danville.

"That's because these houses are *newww,*" Estella says, like it's chocolate cake for breakfast.

"Oh," they say, like it all makes sense now.

While the home is small, it's also shiny and new. It's upgraded to the T and staged to the max. How can a person resist? Estella and her daughters simply don't stand a chance. The girls are dazzled by the ballerina-themed room, and Estella can't get over the enormity of the walk-in closet. Even though she has her heart set on Danville, she's also hypnotized by the new, fancy model home. She hears the girls yelling from upstairs, already claiming their rooms.

"This is my room!" Mina shouts.

"No, I like that room! Why do *you* get that room?!" Kaitlin shouts in return.

"Because I'm the oldest!" Mina justifies.

"Not fair! Mom! Mom!" Kaitlin shouts as she barrels down the stairs, her curls moving vigorously with each step and her freckles fading into the deepening red of her cheeks.

With the kids bickering and time to decide on the house running out, Estella's blood pressure elevates, and her heart pounds in her temples. They have two days to back out without losing the deposit. If they buy this home, it'll be ready for them when they return from summer vacation. The kids' school year is ending, and a few weeks later, they'll be off to Budapest for some summer fun. While Estella's dreams of Danville are slipping away, they'll be starting fresh in a new home and town after vacation.

"Let's stop in Danville for dinner," Estella suggests, and Mina and Kaitlin agree.

Danville has one of those cute, walkable downtown areas, dripping with old-town charm and filled with shops and restaurants. She doesn't know what it is about Danville, but something else, extra special, draws her to it. She thinks of Coffee Shop Guy and smiles. So, to Danville for dinner they go.

Estella parks the car by the old train station depot, which only adds to the old-town charm and gives Danville a historic feel. What was this town like when the train was running? Who lived here? What happened here? Movie scenes from old Westerns flash through Estella's mind, and she imagines the possibilities.

The air is warm. It's perfect for walking outside in the early evening, a reminder that summer is around the corner. People are out walking their dogs, on their way to restaurants, grabbing drinks with friends, or lining up for ice cream at the new ice cream shop adorned with a GRAND OPENING banner.

"Ooh, can we get ice cream after dinner?" Mina asks with an extra bounce in her step, a side effect of joy from the prospect. Kaitlin chimes in, "Yeah, can we?"

So predictable. Estella knew the question would escape their mouths the second she saw the ice cream shop. "Maybe," she says, feeling like the mighty ice cream gatekeeper, and adds, "if you behave yourselves at dinner." She smiles, and now both the girls are bouncing on their feet.

The town is buzzing with energy and has come to life this evening. As they stroll down the main street, they approach the cutest lively little restaurant, and Estella steers her daughters in its direction.

Mina is on her best behavior at dinner and spends an excessive amount of time talking about the pros and cons of each ice cream flavor she's considering. Kaitlin, on the other hand, talks a bit too loud and goofs off throughout dinner. Kaitlin doesn't pay much attention to Mina's analysis of ice cream flavors, but mentions that strawberry is the best flavor there is. Later in the evening, a scoop of strawberry ice cream is precisely what Kaitlin gets. Mina has difficulty settling on one flavor, so she chooses Neapolitan. Three flavors in one—problem solved.

# Chapter 8

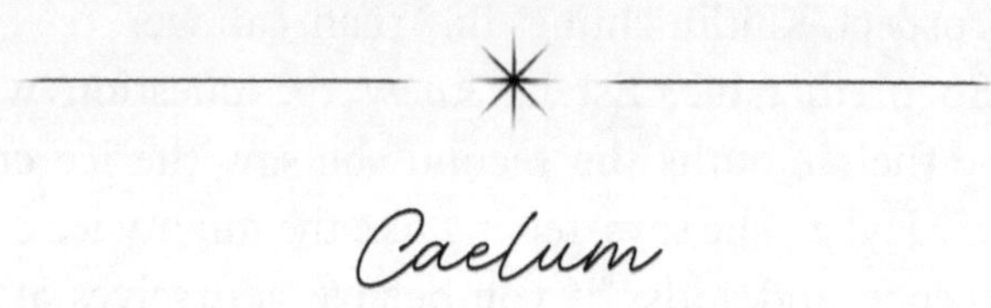

Caelum is up to his elbows in the dirt, but he doesn't mind. Estella likes gardens, so he's planting one for her. Currently a monotone green, it will be full of color soon. The citrus fruits and peppers will add red, orange, and yellow to the garden's color palette. He's only just planted fruits and vegetables to her liking, but they'll be ripe in time for her arrival.

He's working in his garden at his home in Danville—a bit of a drive from Los Gatos, but that's okay. He knows Estella is coming his way soon. His home will also be Estella's home—at least, that's his hope. Based on designs found in her dreams, he's constructed it for her. She's always searching for her perfect place, her forever home, but never seems to find it. Once he has her here, there will be an end to all of that. Estella will grow roots here, and she won't want to leave.

A private, winding driveway lined with lush greenery leads to Caelum's home. It's not a sprawling mansion, but it's a charming home with character, just big enough to fill every corner with love and warmth. The backyard features the garden Caelum is planting and an attention-grabbing view of Mount Diablo.

While Caelum's home is modest, it does include some extras, like the music studio and library. Caelum and Estella share a passion for music and books. Caelum was playing all kinds of musical instruments before he fished Mediterranean waters, and fishing was his livelihood as a young man. Also, his mother taught literature, so music and literature are in his blood. That's just in this lifetime, though; his relationship with music and literature goes back much further. It's amazing how quickly a child takes to playing musical instruments when that child is a traveler who's played in other lifetimes. When he was a boy, Caelum had all of Positano thinking he was going to be the next Mozart. That was when he dialed things back a notch. He learned to manage perceptions and be careful of what he let people see.

Estella has always had a thing for books and music, too—and she's always had a thing for guys like Caelum. It's the same in every lifetime. Estella is drawn to intelligent, deep, kind, confident, and creative people who are also a bit rough around the edges. It may take her some time to realize it, but Caelum will show her that he's what she wants. When they're together again, he'll show her the kind of love that is almost too much to bear. Caelum knows she still loves Lucas, but when they're together again, Estella will realize that she and Caelum are meant for each other and always will be. After all, it was Caelum and Estella long before Lucas came into the picture.

Caelum wanted to get to Estella sooner, but things happened, and he couldn't make it. Born a poor fisherman on the other side of the world from Estella, he had to wait until he was old enough to leave his family. He wanted to do things the right way. While he worked on making his way to her, tragedy struck his family, prolonging his separation from Estella. She then met Lucas before Caelum could step into her life. Caelum knew very well that he might have to spend this lifetime hiding in Lucas's shadow after the unexpected occurrences derailed his plans. But fate brought them together in the beginning, and that's what opens the door yet again.

Using his foot for leverage, Caelum drives a shovel into the dirt, digging homes for blackberry plants. Though he's laboring in his yard, the sunshine warming the skin of his back lulls him into the kind of relaxed state one feels on vacation. The California sun is deceptive like that—a warm, sparkling glow that makes it easy to forget one's problems, at least for a moment.

As he is soothed by the sun's embrace, visions of the past weave their way through Caelum's thoughts. Estella would often steal away into their garden in Esztergom, Hungary, to pick the blackberries. He remembers her purplish-blue-stained fingers clearly. Esztergom, a town on the outskirts of Budapest, is where they first met. It was a beautiful and influential citadel during the late Middle Ages, when Estella and Caelum shared that past life together. Their town was filled with magic, love, and joy. It was surrounded by raging rivers full of life, and a bountiful forest. This is where their story began during medieval times. This is when he found her.

When he saw her for the first time, she was strolling down the main street of their town with her group of girlfriends on a sunny weekend morning. In that instant, he knew that she was his purpose, that she was the reason for existence itself. Her long brown hair fell in thick twists around her shoulders, exposed by the cut of her blood-red dress. How he had wanted to touch those smooth, delicate shoulders… Her eyes, a melt of mahogany and gold, are marked like a seal on his soul forever.

Drawn to her by an irresistible force, he had followed her through the streets, watching her every move, undetected, blended into the crowd with his hat pulled down low. He watched her mouth as she used it to speak with her friends. He watched her hands as she caressed the petals of the flowers decorating the produce vendor's display. He watched her until he could keep his distance no longer.

"May I?" he had asked as he placed a coin in the vendor's hand and pulled a single red rose from the bouquet. "For the lovely lady," he said as she looked into his eyes for the first time. The moment their eyes met, a feeling of warmth made its way through him. This feeling must have also coursed through her, as a rush of blood to her cheeks tinged them red.

She whispered, "Thank you, sir," and turned to see the stunned faces of her girlfriends. They chuckled as they turned away and continued their stroll through town. She had slipped through his fingers with that first encounter as she disappeared down the cobblestone street.

At first, she didn't see him the way he saw her, but Caelum had persisted. He has never been the type to give up easily and always loves a challenge. After their first meeting, in the hope of seeing her again, Caelum spent more time in town than usual. And it was at their second meeting that her love for him began to grow.

On that day, heavy cloud cover had darkened the streets of the town. It was midday when the vendors' stations were at peak bustle. The atmosphere was filled with townspeople chattering, vendors advertising their goods with bellowing voices, and the clopping of horses pulling carts over the cobblestone streets. A group of musicians had assembled on a busy corner to play songs for passersby. Perhaps music would draw her to him.

When the musicians stopped for a break, Caelum had engaged one of the violinists in conversation, asking to play his violin for a song or two. The violinist was a dark-haired, heavyset man with a thick mustache that curled upwards at the corners. With meaty fingers, he held his violin bow tight and refused to let Caelum play his instrument. But when Caelum offered up a couple of coins, the corners of the violinist's mustache curled up higher. With the money in his pocket, the violinist happily handed over his violin and bow.

As the other musicians and Caelum played a lively melody, some of the townspeople gathered. The men clapped their hands and slapped their boots while the women twirled, hopped, and kicked with hands on hips. Others quietly listened to the music and watched the dancers get rowdier as the band played louder.

While Caelum played, his eyes made their way over each face in the crowd—until they got stuck on Estella's. She had been lured by the commotion and stopped to watch the dancers. He didn't take his eyes off her for a second as the band went from playing the dance tune to a soft lullaby, one that would become her favorite song—*their* song. This time, her shoulders were covered with a scarf, and she was dressed in dark tones that blended with the dreariness of the weather. Her eyes, however, were as bright as the first time they ever met his.

When the music turned soft, she took her eyes off the dancers as they dispersed and watched the musicians play. Over the gliding of the violin bow, she eventually noticed Caelum watching her intently, and she dropped a bushel of something wrapped in paper and twine. Mid-song, he pushed the instrument back into the hands of its owner and rushed to her. The violinist didn't miss a beat, picking up where Caelum had left off. At her feet, Caelum bent down to retrieve her parcel from the ground, and she smiled at him when he handed it to her.

He would have liked to think he had impressed her with his music, that maybe she caught a glimpse of his soul when he played for her. Whatever it was, Estella let Caelum spend time with her that day. They had walked through town, talking for hours. They didn't tire of treading up and down the same streets over and over again. The town was an entirely new place with each passing moment they spent together. Once she let him in, she truly saw him for who he was. She knew him like no other—and she never let go.

Caelum had been András Rózsa then, born into the noble House of Rózsa. Estella was Mária Terézia, a commoner when they met. He made her a noble when she became his bride: Mária Terézia Rózsa of the House of Rózsa. They wed with much fanfare in Rózsa Castle and spent their happiest moments there.

In 1526, the Ottoman Empire continued its advances in Hungary. The Battle of Mohács ensued, and the Ottomans prevailed. The Ottoman Empire's victory marked the end of the Middle Ages in Hungary, and the decline of Esztergom, their beautiful home, which became one of four Ottoman fortresses in Hungary.

The entrance to Rózsa Castle was adorned with the family coat of arms, featuring a raven, symbolizing knowledge, transformation, and the arcane. Along with the raven was a rose, representing the Rózsa family name, which means "rose" in Hungarian. Above the raven and rose were three symbols: a sun for the masculine, a moon for the feminine, and stars symbolizing love for humanity. The Ottomans unceremoniously shot an arrow into the Rózsa coat of arms and stormed the castle. As András and Mária attempted to flee their home, they got trapped. He held her in his arms as the fire closed in on them. They burned alive that night. Their castle had been heaven on earth, until the fires of hell consumed it and burned it to nothing but ash.

This is their past.

Caelum drops his shovel on the ground and leaves it there. He's had enough of gardening for one day. Estella will have her blackberries. While Caelum has seen a beautiful future awaiting Estella and him, it's not guaranteed. He must do what he can to make sure intervening factors do not prevail. He can't let what happened in the past happen again. He must make sure nothing gets in the way of the future he has with Estella. No piercing arrows. No raging fires. Nothing.

# Chapter 9



Sleep continues to be an elusive, slippery thing. Should Estella buy the San Ramon house, or back out while she still can? Something about it just doesn't feel right. Sleepless hours pass as she mulls over the question. When she finally does fall asleep, it's a restless night filled with bad dreams.

In a sweat, she awakens from a nightmare. Reality presses down on her. She doesn't know if it's your standard buyer's remorse, but she's feeling like a bird with clipped wings. The two sides of her—the one that craves stability and peace, and the other that craves freedom and adventure—are at odds. When one side gains too much power, the other side protests. Right now, the wrong house is taking up too much of the equation.

Trying not to wake the kids as she slips out of bed, Estella goes into the kitchen to make coffee and calls her mom, Hannah, to vent. This is something Estella does on a daily basis: venting to her mom. And if there's nothing to vent about, she calls to talk about nothing.

Estella often calls her dad, Julian, too. But Julian and Estella's stepmom travel a lot. They split their time between Seattle and Spain, where Julian's side of the family is from. Also, Julian doesn't get the witchy stuff. He doesn't have magic. Hannah is Estella's go-to person because she's always there for her, and she gets her witchy problems.

"I'm second-guessing the San Ramon house. I'm thinking of backing out and getting my deposit refunded. I don't know if it's the right house. I mean, I just don't know!" Estella tells Hannah.

"What do you mean?" Hannah asks. Before Estella can answer, she continues, "The girls need some stability. They need a home. Let me help you."

Estella hates it when her mom or stepdad offers to help her with money. She never had to worry about money growing up, but now that she's an adult, Estella wants to know that she can make it on her own. She doesn't want anyone to help her. She's going to be an indie author, and she's going to sell books. She just has to get past the fear of people judging her so she can actually sell the books.

"I don't need help or money or anything. You know we have money saved up, and I plan on selling my books. We'll be fine," Estella says.

"How about just a down payment? At least let me help with that," Hannah says.

"You know what? Never mind. I'll figure it out," Estella says. When is Hannah going to learn that she doesn't need help? "I have to go," she says and hangs up.

Estella pushes the conversation with her mom out of her thoughts, and her dreams from last night drift back in. She had two dreams. The first one was pleasant enough: it was a brief encounter with Coffee Shop Guy. The second was the nightmare she awoke from in a panic this morning. It's still fresh in her mind. In the dream, Estella and her daughters were in a house when an earthquake hit, and the house started to crumble. They made it out just in time. She's certain this dream was a message telling her to get out of the deal. There's still time! They have one more day to cancel before they lose their deposit.

Feeling the urgent need to have a word with her daughters, she scoops up Kaitlin from her bed, and they tiptoe over to Mina's bed. She is fast asleep, covered in a fluffy white goose down comforter up to her chin, a floating head in a puffy cloud.

Wide awake now, Kaitlin belts out, "Wake up!", destroying the serenity.

"Huh?" Mina whispers.

"I said, wake up, will you?" Kaitlin then plants her hand on Mina, trying to shake her into reality. The weight of Mina's body dampens little Kaitlin's efforts, and Mina rocks ever so slightly.

"What is it? What's wrong?" Mina says in a manner as peaceful as she looks in her cloud of covers.

"Girls, I don't think we should buy that house," Estella says.

With her head still buried in her fluffy white pillow and her voice still drenched in sleep, Mina asks, "What house?"

"The house with the ballerina room."

Mina's eyes peel open, and she pops up to a sitting position, comforter falling to her waist. She's no longer a peaceful, floating head; she's the rational bust of Pallas and Estella, the maddening raven in Edgar Allan Poe's "The Raven."

"What?" Mina says, and her eyebrows move into Angry Birds formation. "I like that house! Daddy would've liked that house." Mina's eyes fill to the brim with tears. "I miss Daddy!" she cries, and Kaitlin's eyes spring fresh tears, too.

Estella gathers Mina and Kaitlin close, wrapping her arms around them. "I miss him, too," she says. The conversation is becoming more complicated than she'd hoped, and she is unsure of how to proceed. All she can do is hold her daughters in her embrace until they calm down. Once their eyes are dry, she continues carefully, "I had a nightmare. I know it's because of the house. I got the feeling that it's not meant to be our home," Estella says. Though she tries to hide it, her voice is laced with emotion.

"But Mommy, you said nightmares aren't real," Kaitlin says, her big toffee-colored eyes searching Estella's.

She puts her hand on Kaitlin's shoulder in a calming gesture, and though it is so difficult for her to do, she reins in her emotions. As calmly as she can manage, she says, "I know. But this is different. Buying a house is too big of a decision to make so quickly. I want to make sure we get the right house, so we can stay there and not have to move again."

"I don't like moving!" Kaitlin declares.

"Me, neither!" Mina adds, her eyebrows still scrunched together. A carbon copy of Estella, Mina's expression crinkles in the same way as hers when she's upset, duplicate mouths pressed into tight lines and duplicate eyebrows arranged into the same shape.

"I know. Remember where we went for dinner and ice cream after we saw the house with the ballerina room? We'll find a house in that town, Danville, and we'll stay there. Did you like Danville?"

"They have yummy strawberry ice cream," Kaitlin offers.

"Well, that's a good start, isn't it?" Estella says, then turns to Mina, and asks, "What do you think?"

Mina's eyebrows soften, and she lets out a sigh. "I guess so. But you promise we'll find a house, and that we'll stop moving all the time?"

"I promise."

# Chapter 10

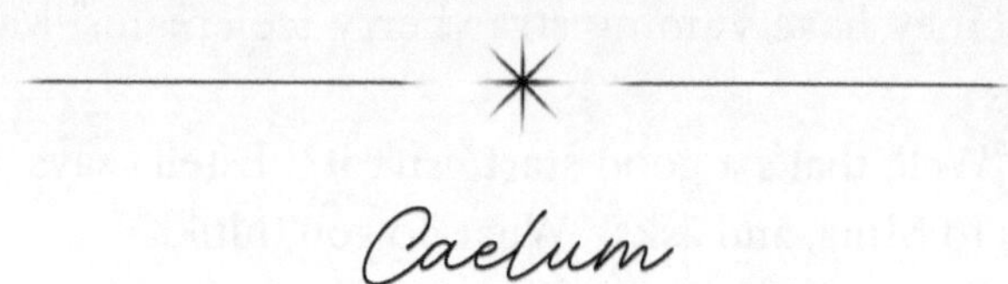

Filtering through the library blinds in dusty beams, the sun puts a spotlight on the empty chair next to Caelum. It's a chair without Estella in it, a reminder that he's alone. He's taken a moment to rest and sip his beer as he works on stocking the bookshelves. It's too early for whiskey, so his companion for the moment is an IPA. Living a dream traveler's life is proving to be more difficult than Caelum had anticipated. Secrets are harder to keep than he thought. So, he's been drinking more in this life. He sleeps a lot to escape the isolation, because friends and family are always only a dream away. But this makes him weak. Life is to be lived, not a precious moment wasted or diluted. If only those moments could be shared… He's never been good at being alone.

Caelum continues to work hard to get his place ready for Estella and her daughters—stocking the bookshelves with books, hanging artwork on the walls, and gathering equipment for the music studio. The library is no longer an empty, soulless room; the bookshelves are almost completely full. He sets his empty beer glass down and goes for the last load of books.

As he carries the last stack into the library, Caelum picks apart Estella's recent dreams. Her dreams are steering her to Danville—to him—and she listens to her dreams. She knows her dreams are much like her visions; they have meaning, with messages hidden within. She's an active dreamer, tuned into the other side on an exceptional level, even for a witch—at least one that's not a traveler. If only she could travel with Caelum, she would understand it all; he could show her everything, and she would love him again.

But it's not that easy. She's not a traveler, and Caelum can't tell or show her anything that has to do with the other side. He has no authorization to do so, and if he breaks the rules, he could find himself in some deep trouble. He'll have to get her to fall in love with him naturally, knowing nothing more than what they experience together, here and now, in this lifetime. She'll know about their past and all there is to know only when she crosses back over.

Alexandre Dumas's *The Count of Monte Cristo* sits on top of the last stack of books Caelum is filing onto the shelf. It's one of his favorites, and one that his mother gave him. He thinks of her as he dusts off its burgundy cover etched with gold. He cracks it open, and the scent that escapes its pages kicks up memories from childhood. Here in his empty home without Estella, he's Edmond Dantes imprisoned in the Chateau d'If.

As Caelum squeezes the last book in the stack to fit tightly on the library shelf, he recalls Estella's latest dream—one that caught him by surprise. She dreamed of him. Stepping out of the darkness of her dreams, Caelum approached Estella. Their movements, each one a short story, were a conversation before any word was given a voice.

"Touch me," she then said, sliding her hand down his forearm. She took his hand in hers and placed it on the area of her waist exposed by her shirt. The touch of her skin created movement throughout his body, a rush of blood, a quickening of breath. Taking full advantage of the invitation, he pulled her closer and slid his hands under her shirt and up her back. The movement gained velocity. He pressed his body close to hers and went in for a kiss.

"Wait… I can't. I'm married. At least, I was," she said as she pushed him away. Then she disappeared along with the dream.

Estella has seen Caelum only once, at the coffee shop in Danville. He must have made an impression to have shown up in her dreams. He was a mere thought in the darkness, and he couldn't resist taking it to the next level. How could he not take the opportunity to be close to her when she dreamed him up?

But Caelum is not so sure she's thinking about last night's dream encounter. Estella's recent dreams have also been filled with worries. The changes going on in her life weigh heavy on her mind. She has decisions to make, daughters to raise, a house to buy, and books to write. She got lost down a path paved with promises of recognition, respect, and other attainments of misplaced value.

Caelum is not so lost, only because he's a traveler with knowledge of the other side. Having a general idea of the path carved out for him, he sticks to it, and rarely ever does he veer off course. On the other side, we all have a clearer understanding of ourselves. Sometimes, Estella takes detours, but then her dreams and visions lead her back to her path. That's what she's in the process of doing right now: returning to her highest purpose.

With the library complete, Caelum has one less distraction, so he goes looking for another one. He picks up his empty beer glass and goes to the kitchen for a refill. When the bitter, ice-cold foam reaches the point of spilling over, he sucks it down in a breath and carries his beer to the music room. He reaches for the best companion of all: music. He doesn't feel like playing; he just wants to listen. So, he puts on some blues and cranks up the volume to drown out the quiet of his own company.

Now that Estella doesn't have Lucas, she's lonely, too. Her loneliness doesn't reach the depths of Caelum's, but she still feels its sting terribly. Estella has her daughters, and even though her family and friends aren't nearby, she can confide in them. Caelum, on the other hand, has no one to confess his secrets to. He has some family left in Positano, but a traveler's problems can't be shared.

Situated in Silicon Valley, the epicenter of this tech-driven world, Caelum and Estella are starving for some humanity, and their own humanity is leaking out at the seams. It's been hidden behind the screens of their smartphones, stifled by the rat race, and choked out by the increasing number of distractions that take away from the most basic and powerful contact: looking someone dead in the eyes and truly seeing them for the human being they are. The utility that technology brings to the masses, connecting people to others and to ideas that they may have never connected with otherwise, is indisputable. But there's nothing that can replace an embrace from a loved one, the feeling of live music, or a lover's kiss. They desire a connection that can be felt only in the presence of another person. Caelum and Estella want to feel human. They *need* to feel human. And they need each other to feel human.

Blues and beer fill in for flesh and bone, breath and body.

# Chapter 11

*Estella*

"Ouch!" Estella's thumb has a heartbeat. She pounded it with a hammer, trying to nail up *Green Face*, the Roy Lichtenstein lithograph her mom gave Lucas and her as a wedding gift. The American pop art is an abstract face created by broad brushstrokes and comic-book-inspired dots. At times like these, she really misses having Lucas around. Moving is never easy, but they had moved around so much that Lucas had become a pro. He would've had their artwork up on the walls in no time.

"Mina! Can you get me a Band-Aid?" Estella calls.

Mina comes running, and Kaitlin follows.

"What happened? Mina asks. Lecturing Estella, she puts her hands on her hips and says, "You weren't being careful, were you?" Mina has taken to mimicking her, mothering Kaitlin and Estella herself.

"Are you okay?" Kaitlin asks.

"I think so. But I could use some help hanging the pictures on the wall. Hand me that picture, please," Estella says as she motions to the print of Van Gogh's *Wheat Field with Cypresses*. It reminds her of New York and spontaneity. She bought it at The Met gift shop on a spur-of-the-moment trip. But for Estella, spontaneity is a thing of the past. These days, she takes comfort in planning.

It all happened so fast. They're just about settled into their new place in Danville. After Estella backed out of the San Ramon deal, her realtor quickly found the perfect place for them and managed to arrange a pre-market deal. The seller was moving because she could no longer afford to live there. She has something in common with Estella; her husband has recently died. Because they have suffered the same fate, the seller empathized with Estella. She felt Estella and her girls should be the new owners and agreed to sell Estella the house before putting it on the market.

They closed escrow around the time the girls finished their school year, and they were able to move in before leaving on their summer trip to Hungary, which is just a few weeks away now. While the girls have been to Hungary a couple of times, they were too young to remember the details. This summer, Estella hopes to create memories that will last them a lifetime.

Their new place isn't the house Estella envisioned, but it's a good townhome in a great location. Even with the money Lucas left them, it turns out a house in Danville is out of their reach. They may not have the space or yard of a true house, but it's just big enough for Estella and her daughters. The best part is that it backs up to the Iron Horse Trail, which runs right through downtown Danville. The coffee shop and library are just a bike ride away.

Now that they're getting situated in Danville, Estella is on the hunt for a local music shop offering drum lessons, and a gym. Recently, Estella rode her bike past the library and noticed an adorable cottage painted yellow with white trim. She didn't realize it was a music shop until a brass bell hung above its front door chimed, calling her attention to a young girl carrying a violin case exiting the store. A wooden sign on a shingle next to the door read *Diablo's Music* in gold script. The shop is not far from the library, where Front Street meets Diablo Road. It's another spot in town that's just a bike ride away.

Estella has been interested in developing her drumming skills for a long time and had planned to take lessons after she quit her job. But then Lucas died, and her plans were put on hold. So, after she hangs up this last picture, she's leaving the kids with the babysitter and going to check out Diablo's Music. After that, she's signing up at the local health club, the Diablo Valley Club, or the DVC, as the locals call it.

Estella walks into Diablo's Music, and right away, she likes the authentic feel of it. It's small, but cozy. On the plush couches, people sit with instruments in hand, chatting, playing music. The customers trying out guitars for sale play an incohesive mix of different riffs. There's warmth in this place, a realness you can't get just anywhere.

When Estella asks about music lessons, the man at the counter asks for the student's age. His assumption that she's buying lessons for someone else tells her they don't get many students like her. She says, "Thirty," like it's a dirty word, then adds, "The lessons are for me."

Embarrassed, he quickly redirects her attention to a list of drum teachers. She picks the first person on the list.

Next, she moves on to the DVC, where she's greeted by very fit people wearing skintight clothing and taken on a tour of the club. Some women at the café bar, wine in hand, huddle together and whisper, their attention fixed on Estella as their eyes travel up and down her body. Their eyes then dart over her shoulder and fixate on something behind her. By the looks on their faces, they're captivated. Curious, Estella turns around and follows their line of vision. Standing with his back turned to Estella and talking to the host at the front counter is the figure of a good-looking man.

He turns around, his eyes meeting Estella's—and a swift burning destroys the quiet within her. It's Coffee Shop Guy, and the impact of his gaze pushes her off her footing. She stumbles slightly to catch her balance. His thick brown hair is messy, and under his gym clothes, muscles in all the right places make themselves known. His eyebrows float up into arches, and a smile crosses his lips. He must recognize her. She responds with a quick, shy half smile and turns away out of nervousness. Envy marks the faces of the women at the bar; they must have noticed their exchange.

"Right this way, Mr. Di Rosa," the host says.

So, that's his name. Where has she heard "Di Rosa" before? Estella doesn't need to finish the rest of this tour; she's seen enough. *Charge my card!* She turns back to look at the women, all of them laser-focused on Mr. Di Rosa's amazingness. Then, she steals another look at him.

He glances at the women at the bar, then turns his gaze back to Estella. When their eyes meet, he smiles again. Looking at Estella now, the women's faces crumple, and their eyes narrow. Estella gets the feeling the women at the bar don't like her already. As she's never been one to fit in with most crowds, the feeling isn't alien.

# Chapter 12

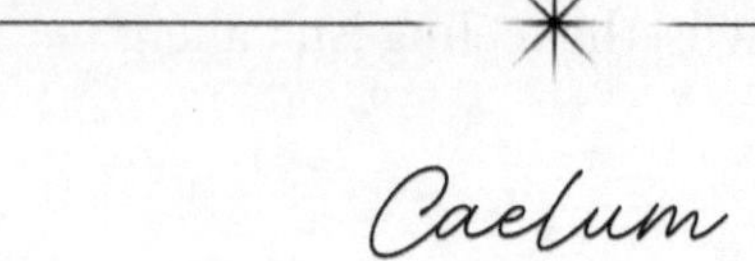

Behind a worn wooden door pockmarked with knots, an elderly woman sweeps dust from the broken tiled entrance to the courtyard of an old apartment building. This is the third door Caelum has opened in his dream, and there's still no sign of Estella. Being that Caelum is in Dreambuktu, he's off his game tonight. He's not thinking clearly, because he's letting his emotions get the best of him again. Estella has seen him in Danville twice now, and he's anxious for their next encounter.

There's a force connecting them, drawing them together, but buried deep in Caelum is fear. Though he firmly believes they're meant to be, lovers in one life aren't guaranteed to be lovers in the next. He gets easily swept up in the immensity of his feelings and forgets that there are boundaries. He's not practicing wu wei, the ancient art of simply letting things happen. Caelum must take his time to let things unfold. He knows that trying too hard will only work against him. But he's grown impatient. He's tired of waiting.

Caelum arrives at another completely different door. This door is nothing fancy, but that doesn't mean it's not worth opening. It's the kind of door you'd find in a modern office building. This is likely the last door for tonight.

Not surprisingly, Caelum finds himself amongst a row of cubicles. He hears a constant pinging sound and searches his surroundings to see where it's coming from. Next to him, a finely dressed woman huddled over her desk scrolls through social media on her phone. Someone—perhaps her manager—keeps messaging her. Apparently, some things, like aesthetically pleasing posts, are more pressing.

Estella is nowhere to be seen. Caelum looks around to make sure he's not missing anything, and what he sees dampens his mood. Everything is some hue of gray. The carpets are dark gray with some lighter gray print. The paint on the walls matches the lighter gray print on the carpet, and the cubicles are some kind of in-between gray.

"Caelum," someone says in a low whisper.

"Who said that?" Caelum swings around to look behind him, but other than the woman absorbed in social media, there's no one around.

"Caelum."

"Where is that coming from?" He pokes his head into the rest of the cubicles in the row, all empty.

"Over here." An adjacent conference room door opens halfway.

Not sure what to expect, he pushes the door open, and amidst the drab office backdrop stands a vision with a head of copper locks. She peers at him through a mess of bright red hair, which takes up an abundance of room around her. He'd recognize those eyes anywhere—brown, so big that they give her a look of perpetual mild surprise. His own eyes widen just looking at hers. She raises the left corner of her mouth into the crooked smile she wears so often. When she rests the corner of her mouth, the smile crease next to it, visible only on that side, remains etched into her face like a lone parenthesis.

"Athena!" he shouts and wraps his arms around her. "What are you doing here? Where have you been?"

"I died in a recent life and returned home to the other side. Without traveling rights, I've been off the grid." There's an edge to Athena's tone.

"When I used my traveling ability for the first time and couldn't find you on the other side, I figured you were given a new life. You must have jumped into that life right after I was given mine," Caelum says.

"It wasn't my time for another life, but I made a bargain with the Source," Athena says. "Although I wasn't granted the gift of travel this time around."

Only the Source grants traveling rights. After Athena gifted Caelum her traveling rights with the Source's approval, her rights were gone.

Caelum picks up on the urgency in Athena's voice. Confused, he asks, "What was the rush? I mean, why bargain for a life and not just take one as it may come?"

"Because I couldn't wait for a life to come. I had to follow you to warn you." The drama in her eyes kicks up.

Caelum's confusion turns to concern. "About what? Couldn't you have waited until I visited the other side?"

"I would have been useless waiting around on the other side. You know, finding a soul, or half-soul, that doesn't want to be found is tricky, even from the other side. I had to jump into this current lifetime so I could help find him, uncover his identity, track him, and stop him."

Caelum starts to pace as his confusion and concern grow. "Who? And without the ability to travel, how did you know your mission?" Without traveling rights, her previous collective knowledge would've been erased. "How would you even know there's someone to track?"

"There's much to explain. Part of the bargain with the Source was that I'd be activated when the time was right, when the Source had the information we needed. Unfortunately, it took longer than expected, and shortly after getting to Alexander, I died."

"Alexander! He exists in this life?" Caelum's mind spirals at the thought of Alexander being alive. He could be anyone. They could've already crossed paths without Caelum even knowing it. "But I threw that half-soul back into the in-between!"

"And I can never repay you." Emotion sweeps Athena's face, and she covers her quivering mouth with a hand.

Caelum feels the walls of his dream closing in on him, and his pacing gains speed. He wouldn't even be here if it weren't for getting rid of Alexander. And now he's out? What if he wants revenge? "How on Earth did he escape the in-between?"

"With help, of course," Athena says.

"Help? Who, other than Cassius, would have the power to help him?" Cassius is the worst of the half-souls who dwell in the in-between.

Athena needs not respond.

"No. Don't tell me…" Caelum says.

"It's true. They're working together to destroy humanity, so that they can create more half souls to worship them in the in-between. They want to rule the dark place and in order to do that they need power. They need followers. Look, I don't have long. You know dreams fade." The urgency in Athena's voice reaches a fever pitch. "You need to visit the other side to be enlightened," she pleads. "Why haven't you come to the other side? Why haven't you come to visit your family?"

"I didn't know you had returned." As he gets a rein on his emotions, Caelum's tone mellows. "I would've visited the other side had I known that. I've been busy. I've been working on getting Estella back. It hasn't been easy, but now that Lucas has crossed over…"

"I know what happened to Lucas. Given I've been back on the other side for about a year now, I've had time to catch up."

"A *year*?!" His mellow tone goes out the window. "And you couldn't find me sooner?" It isn't always easy to track a person down in their dreams, but a *year*? Realizing how long it's been since he's visited loved ones on the other side, he feels guilt creep its way in.

"I feel you fading. We need to talk about Alexander! His new identity. His name…"

"Who is he? Athena? … *Athena?*"

Damn. She's gone. All too often, dreams dissolved by the light of day end at the most inopportune times.

# Chapter 13



With a pair of drumsticks that her grandpa, Laszlo, gave her, Estella nears Diablo's Music. She's ready to embark on a new musical journey. Laszlo gave her the sticks when she left Seattle for the Bay Area. She's always wanted to play like Laszlo, or even her mom. She knows that probably won't happen, because Laszlo is pretty darn good. But she likes to try, and it's in her nature to dream.

Laszlo taught Estella a few things about the drums when she was a kid, and she spent a little time playing with a garage band when she was a teenager. But then she put her drumsticks down. She got it in her head that people wouldn't take her seriously unless she was a lawyer or something like that, so she pushed aside her true loves: writing and music. She became an attorney out of fear—and she quit that career out of love. Estella found herself when she started to love herself for who she is and always will be: an artist. Her mother, Hannah, had made similar choices with her career and had done her best to make sure Estella didn't make the same mistakes. But despite her efforts, history repeated itself.

Once inside the music shop, Estella checks in with the guy working the front desk. He looks to be around her age, and he's giving off Hawaiian vibes. A few streaks of gray hair catch her eye as they stand out in obvious contrast to his long, dark brown hair. He's wearing a Fender T-shirt, ripped jeans, and flip-flops. Not to mention, he's pretty ripped.

"The lesson rooms are in the back. You're in room eight," he says.

Estella turns to head to the back when she hears the guy at the counter ask, "So, is this your first lesson here?"

She turns back around, and they chitchat for a little bit. She finds out that he started working at the music shop not long ago. He plays guitar and ukulele, and his name is Kaleo Kalani, but she can call him Kal for short if she wants to. It turns out he is Hawaiian—well, half Hawaiian and half Norwegian. Within the short conversation, Estella lets him know she's new in town, recently quit her attorney job, money's not everything, and she wants to really live life and do things she enjoys, like playing the drums.

Why is she such an open book? She's afraid to share her writing with anyone, but she'll spill her guts to a handsome stranger. It's liberating and far less risky. Estella wishes she could play it cool, keep a tight lip, and maintain an air of mystery. There's that saying, "loose lips sink ships," that always comes to mind after she's said too much. She wishes she had the presence of mind to heed that warning, or at least remember it before, not after, she's spilled the tea.

"Hey, since you're new in town, maybe you can use a friend or two? Some of us from the music shop are going out on Thursday night to listen to some live music at Jack's. Want to come?"

"Yeah, maybe," she says casually and adds, "I'm busy getting ready for a trip, but I guess I could stop by for a little while." She could use some friends around here. *Please be cool and not a creep,* she thinks. "Is Jack's the place on Main Street with the blue neon sign?" she asks.

"Yeah, that's Jack's. The music is good, and the people are friendly. Here, let me get your number," he says as he fishes out his phone from his back pocket. Estella gives him her cell number and he sends her a text: *It's Kal. Hope to see you at Jack's on Thursday at 9.*

"There you go. Now you have my number. But feel free to call me whenever you want," he says, smiling and continuing to smile.

Estella looks down at the floor. "Uh… I have to get to my lesson now."

She makes her way to the lesson rooms again, but takes a quick glance back at Kal before reaching the hallway. He can't seem to wipe the smile off his face. She blushes as she disappears down the dimly lit hallway, every square inch plastered with posters of rock bands, to the door marked eight, and she knocks.

"Come in," says a muffled voice on the other side.

Upon entering the room, she's blown away by the owner of the voice. There sits Mr. Di Rosa, drumsticks in hand. Did she dream him up?

"What are you doing here?" she asks, shock bypassing her filter. Quickly correcting herself, she says, "Sorry, I didn't expect to see you here... I mean, I didn't know that you're my drum teacher." She could swear she's heard his name before.

"Please, sit. Funny that we keep running into each other," he says. He looks amused. *He's got such a great smile, it should be criminal,* she thinks. "Well, Danville is a small town."

"Yeah, I guess it is," she says with a hint of unease. How will Estella function, sitting so close to him, just the two of them in this small room? She won't be able to hide her nerves at this most intimate proximity. He looks amazing, too. All he's wearing is a pair of jeans and a plain white T-shirt, but he makes the understated attire look achingly exceptional. She's done for.

He examines what looks like a student sign-up sheet. "Estella," he says slowly. "Doesn't Estella mean 'star'?"

"It does," she says with a little smile.

"Well, that's an interesting coincidence, because I was named after a constellation of stars. Growing up in Italy, I was called by my nickname, Celio, but my parents gave me the name Caelum, which is the constellation that brought them together."

"Brought them together?" she echoes, her voice catching on "together" because her throat has gone dry.

"They had attended the same school and worked on the same astronomy project. The Caelum constellation was the subject of their project." They share a quick glance and smile. "So, we already have something in common. We're named after stars."

Estella can't think of a single word to say.

"So, you want to play drums?" Caelum asks with a grin.

So, Estella launches into the same spiel she gave Kal. And here we go again... "Loose lips sink ships" is completely lost on her. They talk about Estella's history with drums, and as a warmup, Caelum shows her a paradiddle, which she then plays.

"Very nice," Caelum says and scooches closer. "But your hand placement on the sticks isn't optimal. Can I help? Is it okay if I touch you?" he asks.

Her first thought is, *Hell, yes!*

"Umm, okay," she says instead.

He places his hands on hers and moves them to the optimal point on the drumsticks. The whole time he is touching her, she doesn't breathe, and when he pulls his hands away, she drops her sticks.

Caelum then gives Estella her first lesson, a basic drum pattern. He shows her the beat and then shows off a little, embellishing and layering other patterns on top of it. His playing is giving her so much feeling that she doesn't know what to do with herself.

When he's done playing, he asks, "Cool?"

Almost inaudibly, she whispers, "Mm-hmm," in the most nonchalant way she can manage, trying her best to hide how much he's made her feel. Even this smallest of utterances is dripping with so much emotion that he must pick up on the fact that he has moved her. Her feelings could be written all over her face, for all she knows. She's not the best at hiding these things.

When their lesson time is up, Caelum walks Estella to the front of the shop, where Kal is hanging out. As she's leaving, she can feel both their eyes on her. It's that almost sixth sense when she can't see the person, but she can feel their gaze. As she's walking out, they say, "Bye, Estella," and she can't help but feel a little special.

# Chapter 14



As Estella walks out of the music shop, Caelum pays close attention to her every move. Her hair and hips sway in an effortless, dance-like rhythm. But he's not the only one watching her. Next to him, Kal looks her up and down like a hungry animal. Caelum doesn't know who this Kal guy is, but he doesn't like how he's watching Estella walk out the door. He also doesn't like how Kal calls Estella by her name as if they've been acquainted. He must have engaged her in conversation when she came in.

Sizing him up, Caelum scans Kal from head to toe. He doesn't like the way Kal looks him up and down in return, as if he knows what he's thinking. This guy better not be a problem. What if he's Alexander? After Caelum's conversation with Athena, everyone is a suspect. He'll have to meet with Athena on the other side soon and keep his eye on Kal in the meantime.

Darin Densmore, a lanky dude with long, stringy hair, enters Diablo's after Estella leaves. Caelum has jammed with him a couple of times and thinks of Darin as a damn good musician and a decent guy. Darin isn't working today, but has come in to pick up his guitar, which sits behind the counter in a case buried under a thick layer of stickers.

Just out of earshot from Caelum, Darin and Kal chat for a bit before Darin reaches for his guitar. "See you Thursday night," Darin says to Kal as he bolts out the door, carrying his sticker-covered guitar case.

After Darin leaves, Caelum is left with Kal, who talks up the features of a particular Fender Telecaster as he helps a customer interested in buying an electric guitar.

"This guitar plays like butter," Kal says to the customer. He tosses his long hair around and contorts his mouth every which way as he busts out an over-the-top solo.

Caelum rolls his eyes. Waiting for his next student to show up, and to question Kal after he wraps things up with the customer, he thumbs through a guitar promo catalog as he reclines on the couch.

After the customer leaves, Caelum corners Kal. "You new here?" His voice comes out harder than he wants it to.

"Kind of." He must've picked up on Caelum's less-than-warm tone, given that Kal's tone matches it.

Trying to make small talk, but really probing for information, Caelum questions him. "So, what's your story? You from around here?" This time, he overcompensates on tone, and his voice cracks on "here," making the honey-coated words sound forced.

The shop phone rings.

"Uh, I need to get that," Kal says. And with that, he's off the hook.

Caelum's next student arrives, and throughout the lesson, he can't keep Estella off his mind. He keeps thinking about their lesson and that dream she had of him. He thinks back to how it felt to touch her in the dream and wonders what would've happened if she hadn't pushed him away. Then his student tears into the crash cymbal, and the thoughts of Estella are beaten out of Caelum's head. Abruptly, he's back in the room and focuses on his work.

Once the student leaves, he traps Kal in the back by the water cooler. "So, before we got interrupted, where did we leave off?" he asks.

"I don't know," Kal says and shrugs.

"So, you just started working here..." Caelum says, hoping Kal will elaborate. What Caelum really wants to ask is, *"Who the hell are you, and what do you want with Estella?"*

"What did you say?" Kal asks through the cacophony. Multiple music lessons are going on, and the walls are thin. Drumbeats, violin screeches, and bass thuds surround them. As they both head towards the front of the shop, away from the mélange of sound, Caelum does the talking, and Kal doesn't offer much.

"So, what's going on Thursday? Is Darin's band playing?" Caelum asks.

"No. But you know The Black Door?" Kal offers. "His friend's band is playing there."

"Right. I remember Darin mentioning that," Caelum lies. He'll invite himself whether Kal likes it or not. A bar setting may be a better place to get some information out of Kal.

On Thursday, before things start to heat up there, Caelum arrives at The Black Door. He doesn't want to miss Kal and Darin, so he makes sure to arrive early. Some barflies have already settled into their seats at the counter, and the band is setting up. For a bird's eye view of the room, Caelum takes a stool in the back corner. Time passes as he slowly sips his whiskey, and the room fills up with one person after another. None of these people are Kal or Darin. By the time Caelum's glass is filled with nothing but a lonely, half-melted ice cube, the band is already halfway through their set with no Kal in sight. Patiently, but with anger building by the minute, Caelum watches the band until they finish their last song to confirm that Kal is a no-show. That asshole.

# Chapter 15

Estella shifts restlessly in the back seat of an Uber, her fingers tapping against her knee. Peering out the window, she sees the blue neon sign reading JACK's appear in the distance. The sign includes an arrow pointing at the bar's front door, beckoning those in search of something, anything, to enter its doors. As Estella exits the Uber, the music spilling out from Jack's gets louder, and her heart pounds with the rhythm.

As soon as Estella enters, she scans the room and other people trickling in. There's Kal. He's on the other side of the bar, close to the band. He's smiling at her big, not only with his mouth, but with his eyes, too. He's got his hair up in a bun, and his massive shoulders frame his smiley face. He looks so darn cute that Estella has visions of Hawaiian gods, Norwegian gods, and Hawaiian-Norwegian gods. The music gets louder as she nears Kal, and the sound starts living in every cell of her body. She scans the faces in the room, but not a single one belongs to Caelum. Maybe he's running late.

"Hey! I was hoping you'd show up!" Kal yells over the music. "This is Darin," he says and motions to the guy standing next to him. "I don't think you guys have met, but Darin also works at Diablo's Music a couple of days a week."

Darin has long, stringy blond hair that he keeps tossing behind his shoulders, and turquoise-blue eyes. His slim body is drowning in baggy jeans and a V-neck T-shirt.

Estella introduces herself and asks, "So, what do you do with the rest of your time when you're not working at Diablo's?"

"Music," Darin says simply. And with that word, Estella likes him already. Moving with fluidity, Darin gets up close to her and asks if she'd like a drink. It looks like he's already had one himself. "I like those shoes," he says, looking down at Estella's brick-red, lace-up suede booties. Estella is pleased that he notices the shoes she spent a little too much time picking out.

Before Estella even gets a chance to talk with Kal, Darin monopolizes her, and she enjoys the attention. Kal sips his drink and throws glances her way, accompanied by subtle smiles as she talks with Darin. As they chat, Darin makes big gestures when he's trying to make a point and gets close enough to invade her personal space. He's one of those close talkers. But Estella doesn't mind. They talk about music and his band. Darin talks passionately, and Estella loves talking about music, so she lets him go on and on. Though she's known him for only twenty minutes, it feels as if Darin is an old friend.

Kal gets up from his chair and inserts himself between Darin and Estella. Kal smells like a popular beach at the peak of summer, or a pina colada, one of the two.

"What do you guys think of the band?" Kal asks. "They're losing their guitarist to another band, and they asked me if I want to play for them. Maybe, next time you're in here, you'll see me up there with the rest of them."

Estella looks up at the stage as the band starts the intro to the next song. She recognizes it immediately: "Beast of Burden" by the Rolling Stones, a song she's always loved. The raw mix of defiance and vulnerability in the lyrics resonates deeply. It speaks to her desire for love and connection without feeling weighed down or taken advantage of. She watches the singer belt out the lyrics, then glances over at Kal to find him inspecting her. When their eyes meet, his eyes dart back to the band.

"They're pretty good," Estella says, as Kal nods his head, wearing that bright smile of his and looking pleased.

Estella watches the scene at Jack's unfold before her as the place quickly fills with people. At first, there's only one woman dancing alone, teetering on high heels. She gets so into her dancing that she almost topples over. In no time, a random guy approaches her, and they start dancing together. Suddenly, they're kissing. That was fast! After they start making out, they disappear from the dance floor, leaving it empty. But then, as if a clock has struck to signal that it's now okay to dance, the floor becomes packed with people.

Darin calls out, "That's my boyfriend," as he points to the sea of people on the dance floor. He makes his way over there and disappears among the dancers while Estella stays at the bar with Kal. She plans to probe him for information on Caelum's whereabouts, but not right away. She doesn't want to seem too interested in Caelum.

Estella's eyes tick towards the entrance to Jack's every time she sees someone walk in, and she gets a little disappointed every time it's not Caelum. But after the letdowns pile up, she finally asks Kal if Caelum is coming tonight.

"Oh, I don't know. I don't really know the dude," Kal says.

And that lets the air out of Estella's balloon. It's probably for the best. Caelum wouldn't be good for that stability she's trying to regain, and even though she's fascinated by him, she doesn't know if she's ready to date yet.

Estella stays at Jack's for a while longer, chatting nonstop with Kal. She learns a lot about him and even gets comfortable enough to tell him she's writing. But she doesn't go into what she's writing about just yet. Kal likes to read epic science fiction, which isn't Estella's cup of tea. But when he mentions his love for classic literature with a hint of darkness—authors like Edgar Allan Poe, Mary Shelley, Bram Stoker, and Oscar Wilde—she almost throws her arms around him.

She learns that Kal worked for a Silicon Valley venture capital firm many years ago, until he realized how miserable it made him. He quit on a whim and moved into his uncle's place in Hawaii. After spending a little time there, the mainland began calling him back. He never considered returning to the venture capital game; instead, he took the money he made at the firm and invested it in a local health and fitness club.

"Not the DVC?" Estella asks, stunned.

"Yep. You been?" Kal asks, like owning a premier club is no biggie.

"No way! I mean, yeah. I just signed up." Estella stumbles through her words. "But I would've never thought… I mean, how do you find the time to run the DVC *and* work at Diablo's?" is what makes it out of her mouth.

"I have a lot of associates working for me. That allows me time to focus on things I enjoy, like helping out at the music shop a few hours a week, playing in a band, and making my way down to Santa Cruz to do some surfing once in a while."

"Cool," Estella says. The word comes out wrapped in awe, and it hangs between them before she says, "Want to meet up at the coffee shop on Railroad Avenue sometime?" Making friends with two interesting people in one night is like spotting a snow leopard in the wild, at least for Estella.

"That'd be rad," Kal says.

Estella isn't sure if it's because he smells like suntan lotion or because he told her he surfs, but now Kal is giving her major surfer vibes. As her mind fills with surfer boy images, Darin grabs Estella's shoulder, bringing her back to the current situation at Jack's. After all that time spent on the dance floor, Darin has sweated through his shirt. He tosses his damp hair from one side to the other.

They decide to call it a night, but agree to make Thursday nights at Jack's a regular thing. Even though Estella didn't get a chance to see Caelum, she had fun and made a couple of friends. Maybe that's what happens when someone steps out into the real world. She leaves Jack's high on happy feelings and new friendships as rare as snow leopards.

# Chapter 16

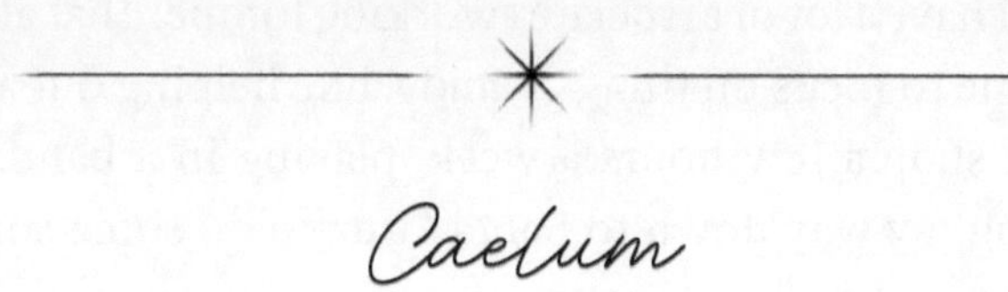

Caelum taps away at his computer. While Estella will be on summer vacation, Caelum has some of his own traveling to do. He's going on a trip—a real trip. It's been a while since he's been to Positano, so it's about time he pays his aunt and uncle a visit. And since he'll be in Europe, he plans to make another stop or two along the way. Though Caelum is not big on fancy things, he splurges by booking a couple of nights at a nice hotel. He finds happiness in little comforts—a chocolate on his pillow, and the gentle massage of a rainfall showerhead.

Because of his ability, being able to travel through time and get inside people's dreams, he's found ways to make money. Any traveler you meet will be a person of means. You wouldn't know it, but some of the most powerful people in the world are travelers. Caelum knows how to get his hands on money and enjoys having it, but he's careful not to seek more than a comfortable amount.

Too much money isn't always a blessing. The last thing he wants is to draw unnecessary attention to himself.

But creating a reality that would please Estella isn't exactly cheap. A custom-built home, books to fill a library, and a music studio are things that require funds. If Estella ever wonders how a poor fisherman from Positano made his money, he'll owe it to some hard work and well-placed investments.

After booking a last-minute flight, Caelum throws some necessary items into his trusted suitcase. Sure, he could buy a sleek, new suitcase at any time, but he's had this thing for decades. It looks like it's been run over a few times, and the wheels squeak on occasion, but it does its job.

When his Uber arrives, Caelum drops his suitcase into the trunk and jumps into the back seat. Going back home is always bittersweet. While he looks forward to seeing his aunt and uncle, Caelum misses seeing his parents and brother in human form. His parents and only sibling died in a car crash when he was just sixteen. Caelum can still see them by visiting the other side, but as Athena pointed out, it's been a while since his last visit. Ever since Lucas passed, Caelum has been so consumed with getting Estella back that he hasn't kept up with his family visits. A trip to the other side is long overdue.

Caelum's family is always there for him, and he finds comfort in that. They'll each be hanging out on the other side until they're offered another opportunity at life. We never know when that time will come, and the amount of time we spend on the other side between lives is different for everyone. But visiting loved ones who've crossed back over is another perk of being a traveler.

After the accident, Caelum frequently traveled to the other side to visit his family, often spending most of his time sleeping or locked in his room. His aunt and uncle believed he was lost in his grief and urged him to seek help. If only he could've enlightened them and eased their worries, but whispering a word of his travels to those who don't share his abilities is against the rules.

At the airport, the Uber driver jumps out and heads to the rear of the car. By the time Caelum reaches the curb, the driver has already popped the trunk and is fishing out his suitcase. He drops it to the pavement with a clunk, then fixes his eyes on it, puzzling over it for a moment.

Before handing it to Caelum, he asks, "Is this thing vintage?"

Yes. But so is Caelum.

# Chapter 17

In the days leading up to the trip to Budapest, Estella has been a bundle of nerves, and today is showtime. She loves to travel, but hates to fly. Actually, she enjoys flying, as long as she doesn't dwell on the possibility of the plane going down in a fireball of death. If she can snag a window seat, she finds comfort in the pinnacles of the clouds. For her, there's a polarity to flying, a yin and yang formed by the chaos of being at the mercy of forces beyond her control, and the serenity of gazing into the heavens.

"Are you guys sure you want to travel halfway across the world for vacation? How about we take a road trip to visit Grandma instead?" Estella asks Mina and Kaitlin.

Knowing how Estella gets before flying, Mina says, "Relax, Mom. It'll be okay. Think of how much fun we'll have."

Estella can always count on Mina to be the voice of reason. "Yes. But getting there will not be fun," she laments.

"You can hold my hand at takeoff," Kaitlin says and displays her hand inches from Estella's face. Estella chuckles at the sight of Kaitlin's adorable little hand, and her shoulders descend a few inches from her ears.

"You're right. I'm being ridiculous. But I will take you up on that offer to hold your hand at takeoff," Estella says.

Suddenly, Estella feels a buzzing in her head. *Oh, here we go...* she thinks. "Let's make sure we pack everything we need to bring with us," Estella tells the girls, then bolts to her room. She keeps her visions to herself for now.

When Estella closes the door behind her, her bedroom slowly fades and is replaced by a different scene. She's surprised to see a book and not the faceless man, given that he's been dominating her visions for months. With its worn pages, the book looks ancient. It lies open on a table and comes closer into view. Estella hears strange whispers as her vision closes in on the open pages of the book. Words begin to sharpen into focus just as the book slams shut. Estella jumps, and her vision vanishes, leaving her even more anxious than before.

What a day to fly halfway across the world.

When they arrive in Budapest, Estella feels like she used to in college after an all-nighter of drinking and no sleep, except she didn't have a drop of alcohol on the flight. As they make their way through the gate, Estella sees three familiar faces: her uncle, Matthias; her aunt, Monika; and her mom, Hannah. Estella's stepdad usually comes on their trips to Budapest, but he couldn't make it this time.

Matthias waves his arms above his head to get Estella's attention. In his early twenties, his hair took on Elvis Presley's signature 'do. He went gray prematurely, and his hair turned completely white by the time he reached his thirties. With his frosty, flowy hair, jolly disposition, and belly inflated by Dreher, a staple beer consumed in copious amounts by the Hungarian masses, he is Santa Claus in the flesh.

Monika grips Estella in a powerful hug, and she's pulled out of her head and into a Budapest mood. Monika is a small woman with a big personality. She's had the same pixie cut for as long as Estella has known her, dying it to maintain its original coffee-brown color. Frozen in time, her hair looks like it hasn't changed over the many decades, though the rest of her has.

Monika is the glue that holds the family together, always reaching out to others and hosting family gatherings. It gives Monika an opportunity to gossip as she prepares elaborate feasts, which often include *gulyás* (Hungarian goulash), *nokedli* (spätzle), *rántott hús* (schnitzel), *töltött káposzta* (stuffed cabbage), and *szilvás gombóc* (plum dumplings). And there's always *pálinka*, Hungarian fruit brandy. Turning down this moonshine offered by persistent hosts won't be easy.

Mina and Kaitlin's faces light up when they see Hannah. "Grandma!" they cry.

Hannah crouches down and scoops Mina and Kaitlin into a hug. They then run over to greet Matthias and Monika.

"And how's my little witch?" Hannah says to Estella, whose eyes dart in every direction, checking to see if there were any passersby within earshot. Mina and

Kaitlin hear Hannah call Estella "her little witch" all the time, but they don't quite understand that it's not just a term of endearment.

"Will you keep it down?" Estella snaps. She can't stand it when Hannah uses the word "witch" so recklessly in public. At times like these, she wishes she could trade her gift of vision for invisibility.

"Don't be silly," Hannah says and wraps Estella in a hug. When she lets go, Estella sees that Hannah's sleeves are rolled up, and her crescent is on full display. Estella crinkles her brow. Hannah must pick up on Estella's disapproval, because she then rolls down her sleeves.

"You might want to consider a tattoo like mine," Estella says.

"Don't you think a tattoo may call even more attention to it?"

"No," Estella huffs and crosses her arms. "People can assume it's just a tattoo, not that I'm covering a mark. But there's no question that yours is a witches' mark."

"And so what if it is?" Hannah says defiantly.

*One of these days, her desire to put her witchy heritage on display is going to bite her in her witchy butt*, Estella thinks.

"Can we go now?" Estella says. She's eager to get out of the airport and into all the things she wants to do in Budapest, like visiting her favorite spots and eating all her favorite Hungarian foods.

Many of Estella's best childhood memories are of times spent in Hungary. There's a soft spot in her heart, however, for one place in particular: Monika and Matthias's vacation home in the Hungarian countryside. She'd like her daughters to have their own cherished memories, so while they're in Hungary, a drive to the countryside is a must.

Estella's time at the vacation home is always filled with joy, music, laughter, and in typical Hungarian fashion, overindulgence in delicious food and drink. Her favorite times have been spent under the dark night sky illuminated by only the stars and fire, under which is usually perched a cauldron of bubbling-hot goulash. They often gather around the fire, drinking *pálinka* strong enough to make one's eyes water upon the first whiff.

One such time, in the middle of a hot, humid summer, a thunderstorm had broken out as Estella and her family sat by the fire at night. At first, they felt only a few drops of rain. But they weren't the kind of raindrops one could ignore. Estella could feel the weight of each drop, and where they landed soaked her clothes straight through. Suddenly, the sky tore open, and in a flash, rain extinguished the fire they sat around. They ran for cover, seeking shelter under the porch overhang, which must have been made of tin, because the sound of the rain hitting it rang in her ears like bullets. In the absence of the campfire, the moonless night was as dark as they come, except when bursts of lightning ripped across the sky, seemingly right in front of their noses. Each time lightning struck, it illuminated the sky, making it appear as bright as day for moments at a time—night, then day; night, then day.

Estella gasped. During a flash of lightning, she had seen what appeared to be the figure of a man. Monika assured Estella that they were safe, despite the proximity of the lightning strikes. Estella described to Monika what she had seen, and Monika said, "It must be one of our neighbors caught in the storm."

The storm had continued—night, then day, night, then day—replete with thunderous booms and the roaring of the enormous raindrops hitting the tin roof overhang. It was a moment Estella will never forget. Having grown up in Seattle's mild drizzle, she is not accustomed to that kind of intense weather. To Estella, it was novel, exhilarating, and unforgettable, much like most of the time she spends in Hungary, a world so unlike the one she grew up in, a thousand worlds away from the suburbs of Seattle.

# Chapter 18

*Caelum*

The city of Positano is sprinkled along cliffsides jutting out of the Mediterranean Sea. Steep roads and staircases are a part of living in Positano, but so are the insane views of the Amalfi Coast. It is exactly 258 steps from the road to Caelum's front door. No longer in Positano shape, he feels the comforts of California life in the burning in his legs. He's less fond of his trusty old suitcase when he has to lug it up these stairs. After he takes a moment to catch his breath, he knocks on the door.

"*Ciao*, Celio!" his aunt and uncle shout.

Tommaso, Caelum's uncle from his mom's side, looks like a male version of his mom, Aurora. They both have lighter hair and dark brown eyes, just like Caelum's brother, Giovanni, inherited as well. Caelum, on the other hand, got his father Dante's looks, an opposite contrast of dark hair and light eyes.

Tommaso looks just the same as he did when Caelum saw him years ago, except his tan is a shade darker at this time of year. His aunt, Vittoria, is a couple of years older than Tommaso, her brown, shoulder-length hair highlighted with more gray than Caelum remembers. But she has twice Tommaso's energy and is quite trim. Climbing the stairs to the house is enough to keep a person fit.

The Positano villa is very old and has been in the family for generations. It needed a lot of work to get it into the condition it's in today. Thanks to some of Caelum's investment money, the villa now boasts a clean layer of paint on replastered walls, sleek modern appliances, and tiles free of cracks. The new decorative indoor tiles are a cheerful teal and soft yellow. But the place to be is on the terra-cotta-tiled balcony, shaded by white arches, with views of the Mediterranean that astound.

Espresso is set out on the coffee table in the living room. *"Prego,"* Tommaso says, motioning towards the table. Caelum is taken back to his childhood when he sees the display of espresso cups and saucers made of sturdy white porcelain with blue flowers adorning the edges. The set belonged to his mom, handed down to her by his grandparents. They take a seat around the table, and as they've done countless times, they chat over espresso. Caelum has missed the local espresso! He marvels at the richness and savors every drop as they catch up on life.

Sitting comfortably in his lounge chair, Tommaso has his legs in a cross with his ankle over his knee. He likes to take up a lot of space and make big movements. In one such animated movement, he runs his fingers through his hair, pushing his dirty blond locks, streaked with gray and longer on top, neatly to the side. He uncrosses his legs and leans in close, looking at Caelum with intensity, his eyes the color of the espresso they're drinking.

"When are you going to get married and bring home some *bambinos*?" he asks pointedly.

Caelum fidgets in his chair as he sucks the last drop of espresso out of the tiny cup. As he's been waiting for an opportunity to be with Estella, he's never brought a serious girlfriend home—and his aunt and uncle give him shit about it every time they see him.

"I'm working on it, I assure you. I have my sights set on someone. I just have to get her to fall in love with me. And she already has *bambinos*—two daughters."

*"Bravo!"* they cheer, and Tommaso brings his heavy hands together in one loud clap. "Of course, she will fall in love with you. Who wouldn't?" he adds with excitement.

"You bring her next time," Vittoria adds gently.

Changing the subject, Tommaso slaps the tops of his thighs with those hefty hands of his and asks, "What's the plan? What would you like to do while you're here?"

"Tonight, nothing. I'm already feeling the jetlag." Caelum needs a good, long dream so he can go looking for Athena on the other side, and finally pay his family a visit. "But tomorrow, let's go to Fornillo." This time of year, the main beach, Spiaggia Grande, is overrun by tourists. Yes, the views are beautiful. Yes, it's where everybody takes post-worthy pictures. But during the peak of summer, Caelum avoids it at all costs. Fornillo is another picturesque beach, but smaller and less crowded.

"And what would *caro mio* like for dinner tonight?" asks Vittoria in her soft voice. "Let me guess," she says playfully, *"spaghetti aglio e olio?"*

"*Si, Zia* Vittoria." She knows Caelum. It's easy-to-make pasta with garlic, olive oil, red pepper flakes, and parsley—simple, but it's Caelum's favorite. Sometimes, simple is best.

After dinner, Caelum settles into his bedroom for the night. By his bedside sits a vintage Venetian hand-blown glass lamp, another relic from his childhood. He turns it on, and the room glows with its warm, dim light. A cooler light cast by the moon, almost full, comes in through the sheer, ivory-colored curtains. Pushing them aside, he cracks open the rustic, wood-framed balcony door, and the curtains dance as a gentle wind fills the room. The air outside is warm and fresh with the scent of the sea. With the soft breeze caressing Caelum and jetlag taking hold, he falls asleep quickly.

Now, where's his key? When traveling through dreams, there are only two places where keys are needed: the other side, and the in-between. Finding his key is easy; he always keeps it in the same spot, a familiar corner of the dream world where he knows it'll be safe, a trusted place from his past. He opens the door to where his key rests, in the very room he sleeps in. However, if he opens the top drawer of his nightstand while awake, it won't be there. Objects don't carry from the real world into dreams and vice versa; this key exists only in his dreams.

Finding his key to the other side takes no time at all, but getting a key to the in-between—that's a different story. No one really wants a key to the in-between. After Caelum forced Alexander back into its depths, he tossed that key away in a place no one will ever find it. He pulls his key to the other side from the drawer. It's delicate and made of gold, with the bow in the shape of a four-leaf clover. With this key, the other side is just one often-visited door away.

As soon as he crosses over, Athena appears, fists resting on her hips.

"It's about time," she says.

"I'm here, aren't I?" When Caelum cracks a smile, Athena flashes her crooked grin in return.

"We need to get down to business. But before we talk about Alexander, I should tell you about the other travelers sent to protect Estella and ensure she fulfills her purpose. She must write her book, and the Source said we must see to it."

"Other trav—"

Caelum is interrupted by visions of his mother, Aurora, and his father, Dante.

"*Caro mio*, where have you been? Did you forget about us?" his mother asks and then turns to greet Athena.

"Aurora, Dante," Athena says obligingly, but she's clearly miffed by the interruption.

"Where's Giovanni?" Caelum asks. Typically, his brother appears alongside his parents, but he's nowhere in sight.

"Gio's in a new life. Perhaps if you'd visit once in a while, you'd have known he crossed six months ago," Dante says.

"Good for him," Caelum says. He'll miss Gio until they're reunited again, but time is a different concept when you have eternity.

*Crash!* The door to the balcony slams shut, and Caelum's loved ones vanish into thin air. Thunder rumbles outside as he turns in his bed to face the sound, the sudden noise ending his dream travels for the evening.

He gets out of bed to inspect the door and balcony. Upon him opening the door, a much stronger wind blasts into the room, and the curtains' dance is now more paso doble than waltz. The moonlight is dimmed by passing clouds, and the balcony is dark, empty, and quiet, the only sound made by the summer storm brewing in the distance. That must have been one strong gust of wind to shut this heavy door. Caelum will have to finish his conversation with Athena another night.

# Chapter 19

After spending a couple of weeks in Budapest, Estella and her family pile into Uncle Matthias's old car and make the hour's drive out of the city to the vacation home in the countryside. For most of the ride, Estella quietly stares out the back seat window at the ever-changing scenery. Typically, Lucas would've squeezed his large frame into the car with them. He's been on every trip the girls have taken to Hungary. Family vacation won't ever be the same without Lucas.

As they near the vacation home and the cityscape gives way to cornfields, sunflower fields, and then a forest, Estella's mood takes a slow slide south. The surrounding trees of the Hungarian countryside look like the trees in that dream she had—the one with the two strangers in a forest. Reflecting on the past breeds tears that stream down Estella's face, and one family member after another notices.

"Why are you crying, Mama?" Mina asks, her face crinkled with concern.

Kaitlin, who's sitting next to Estella, reaches over and wraps her little arms around her. Mina and Kaitlin are unsettled by Estella's crying. They aren't used to seeing their mother cry, as Estella rarely sheds a tear in their presence. She has tried her best to be the picture of strength for her daughters, especially after Lucas's death. But Lucas's absence, changing careers, moving, and being a single mom come together into a whirlpool, taking Estella's emotional strength down with it.

"I'm feeling nostalgic," Estella says. It's a half-truth. "Don't worry about me."

"This place reminds you of your childhood, doesn't it?" Monika asks and reaches over to put her hand on top of Estella's. "We've spent so many good times here together," she adds.

Estella nods in agreement, wiping away her tears.

They pull up to the rusty gate at the entrance of the vacation home, and Matthias gets out of the car to open the gate. His Santa hair is shockingly white and stands out against the surroundings. The place looks exactly as Estella remembers it, frozen in time, just like Monika's pixie cut. The *megy* trees are brimming with little balls of bright red fruit. The sour cherries are a more vibrant red than sweet cherries, and while still sweet, they're also tangy.

When Estella was a kid, she picked a handful of sweet cherries from the trees. While gorging on them, she peeked at a cherry after a bite and saw a small, squirming worm inside, or *kukac*. Wailing in disgust, she spit out the mouthful immediately and nearly retched. Monika, who had witnessed the scene, casually chuckled and said, "The worms love the sweet cherries." This is how Estella learned to eat only the sour cherries from the trees.

The grape vines draped over the porch are also full of fruit. The grapes sparkle a bright yellow in the sun, as if they themselves are drops of sunlight. Standing on the porch under its tin roof, Estella recalls the spectacular thunderstorm she witnessed here those many years ago. The place is as magical as Estella remembers it, an abundant paradise. Before she can unpack their bags, Mina and Kaitlin find their way into their bathing suits and are already splashing in the sprinklers.

After a few days in the countryside, they squeeze back into Matthias's jalopy and make the drive to Lake Balaton. No summertime trip to Hungary would be complete without some time spent at the lake. With tourist season in full swing, the lake is speckled with many boats. The break in thunderstorms and the arrival of a cloudless, sunny day drew out the boaters, sparking a festive atmosphere.

The sounds of music blasting and laughter echo from surrounding boats as they glide through the marina, making their way out onto the open water of the massive lake, the largest in Central Europe. Matthias steers the boat, as Lucas isn't there to take over as captain. Sailing the boat would always give Lucas something to occupy himself with. Because he didn't speak Hungarian, he often blended into the background like drab curtains in the presence of Estella's Hungarian family. But on occasions when Lucas had a couple of beers or shots of *pálinka*, he'd tap the few Hungarian words he'd learned. Estella's family loved this. They enjoyed hearing the American speak Hungarian; it sounded so wrong that it was funny, but it was the effort that counted.

The kids squeal with delight, thrilled by the excitement of being on a boat. The main sail clatters against the mast in wild fury until they catch a strong wind. Against the wind's force, the sail makes one loud snap and shapes into a tight, smooth curve. The boat picks up speed as the wind relentlessly whips Estella's hair against her face. She feels the cutting sting of the sharp strands against her cheeks, but it doesn't bother her. She's caught up in the rush of the experience. It's nice to feel something—to feel alive.

As the afternoon fades into early evening, they find themselves in the company of only a few other boaters. Much of the excitement from earlier in the day has disappeared, along with the good weather. Clouds have rolled in, and the waters of Lake Balaton now resemble black glass.

They turn into a small cove to change direction and make their way back to the marina. The cove is lined with charming villas, and geraniums pouring from the balconies bring the scene to life with their eye-catching red hues. As Estella admires an immaculately maintained rustic cottage with a thatched roof—the kind you find in old paintings of the Hungarian countryside—she sees another sailboat approaching. As the boat nears, she makes out its name painted in black letters on the hull. It declares itself Sors, or in Hungarian, "Fate." Estella says the boat's name aloud: *"Sors."*

And then she sees him. There's a familiarity to him.

He's too far in the distance for her to make out the details of his features, but she's immediately reminded of Caelum. But it couldn't possibly be him. Caelum takes up more space in her head than he needs to, and now she sees him where he's not.

The sailboat slowly creeps by, and their eyes fix on each other across the distance for what feels like an eternity packaged into a few seconds. In the stillness, it seems time slows to a trickle. The only sound comes from the creaking of the ship's ropes. The man's eyes are partially hidden under the brim of his hat, so she can't quite make out their color or read his expression. But the muscles in his jaw look clenched. He's angry, perhaps. Maybe they've intruded into his private cove. *Could he be the faceless man?* Estella wonders, stomach lurching.

Fantasy man takes control of his boat to steer it away from the cove. Whoever he is, Estella can imagine by the way he moves that he's self-assured and assertive. He strikes her as a man who takes charge and knows what he wants. He seems like the kind of guy who would make life interesting and exciting.

And there she goes, letting her imagination run away with her yet again. Who is she these days?

Estella doesn't know what it is about Hungary that ignites passion within her. It's a magical place that stirs up romantic feelings. She can't help but wonder, will she ever fall in love again? The fire that burns within her— the one that makes her feel like a balloon about to float away into oblivion—was tethered by Lucas's sanity, his coolness, and his calmness. But when Caelum looked into her eyes, it was as if their souls spoke the same language, like she could see the same fire in his eyes. Caelum makes

Estella a balloon again, like the ones that escape from parties and float higher and higher, disappearing into the clouds. What will become of Estella without Lucas to keep her grounded?

# Chapter 20

*Caelum*

The perfect boat rental, *Sors*, stands out among the many others bobbing around in the marina. Disguising himself enough so that Estella doesn't recognize him, Caelum wears his hat low and maintains a distance. On the lake, he lets her see him. It's risky for him to show up on her trip, but he's a sucker for making irrational decisions when it comes to Estella. If she recognizes him, he risks scaring her away, but he wants her to wonder about him in this place that is so special to her.

That magical connection she feels to Hungary—the connection that can be felt in her dreams—is very real. Estella's aunt and uncle's vacation home is located in a small village nestled in the forest surrounding Esztergom. Caelum and Estella once roamed this land together. She's close to their home of long ago—close to the place where they first met and fell in love. Estella gets caught up in a whirlwind of emotion when she's in Esztergom for deeper reasons than she knows; she feels their past in these shadowy forests.

After visiting Positano, Caelum took a flight to Budapest and then made his way to Lake Balaton. Because he was so close, he had to see her. Because she's traveled to where they first met, he had to be with her, even if it's from a distance. All Caelum can hope for is that she sees him in a stranger's face and feels him across the divide. He's grown tired of keeping his distance, and now that he's found his way into her life, being apart from her is painful.

Caelum's boat drifts closer to Estella's as her eyes remain glued on him. He hides under his hat and reaches for the mainsheet. The clicking sounds made by the rope moving through the pulley shorten in interval the harder Caelum pulls on the rope. The approaching storm sends a cool breeze in his direction, the mainsail puffs, and he glides away.

That was close, and a great deal of effort for only a moment shared. But Caelum thinks it was worth it.

A dark yellow full moon hangs in the sky outside Caelum's plane window on the flight back to the Bay Area. While he has been moving around Europe, he suspects that someone is tracking him in his dreams, and he senses they know his mission. A few nights ago, before Caelum met with Athena and his parents, an obscured face appeared in his dream—a face he could have sworn he had seen before. It wasn't Kal, so it's another face to keep track of. While another meeting with Athena should be first on the agenda, Caelum's suspicion about Kal takes over.

The cabin lights dim for overnight service, voices drop to a whisper, and the buzzing vibration of the plane's engines eventually lulls Caelum to sleep.

He awakens in a dream, and with a concentrated drive to find Kal, he takes a door he is sure Kal is hiding behind. Upon entering, Caelum gets soaked, and thunderclaps ring through his ears. His clothes hang on him, drenched and heavy. He tries to keep the rain flowing through his hair and over his face from getting into his mouth. It's the darkest of nights, the night of the new moon, and he can't see a damn thing. Where is this dude?

Lightning tears through the sky, illuminating his surroundings for flashes at a time, giving him small clues. He must be in the countryside somewhere. Then, he sees a modest abode in the distance and carefully moves in closer. There are people sitting on the porch, taking shelter from the storm.

Undetected, Caelum creeps closer and tries to make out their faces, which are hiding in the shadows and lit by the glow of only one small lantern. Right in front of the porch, lightning rips the sky in half. In that moment of illumination, he sees Estella's startled face, her eyes fixed on something in the distance. Caelum follows her gaze.

There he is, that son of a bitch! What is Kal doing here in her dream?

Caelum knows this place well. They're at Estella's aunt and uncle's vacation home. They're in the past. This event occurred when Estella was a teenager. Then Caelum sees another version of Kal—and that version turns to look at Caelum.

Two Kals! He's a traveler!

The only time two versions of the same person can be seen in a dream is when one of them is a traveler visiting another moment of their own existence. He's dreaming about an event that happened to him in the past, which means Kal had been there at that time and place all those years ago, following Estella, lurking in the shadows around her. What does he want? Who the hell is he?

Caelum gives chase. He's running through the wet grass in the pitch black and feels nothing other than his blood raging through his veins—not the cold, not the wet, not the tree branches hanging in his path that scratch up his arms. He's out for blood.

Lightning strikes again, and Caelum sees Kal running in front of him. Kal glances back at Caelum, who is inches from grabbing him.

"Stay away, Caelum!" he yells over the sound of heavy rain and thunder.

"You're a traveler! What do you want with Estella?" Caelum yells into the dark.

Caelum closes the gap and tackles Kal to the ground. Their bodies collide, rather than pass through each other like a swirl of dust. Travelers can't move through other travelers in dreams, but they can pass through anyone or anything else if they choose.

Caelum pins him down, his knee in Kal's back. With one hand, Caelum secures Kal's arm behind his back, and with his other hand, he shoves his face into the soggy ground.

"Who are you?!" Caelum demands.

"None of your business! Get the hell off me!" Kal yells.

Caelum presses his face deeper into the drenched, mushy dirt. "Who are you, I said?!"

"Okay, okay, I'll tell you—but you have to let me up."

"Not a chance."

"Come on, I can't talk to you like this! I'm eating dirt here," Kal says as he spits out mud.

On high alert and ready to strike again, Caelum slowly and carefully loosens his grip. He doesn't trust Kal one bit. Kal gets up and wipes off his face and mouth, his drenched white T-shirt streaked with mud. As he breathes heavily, chest heaving, Caelum can see in his eyes that he hasn't surrendered yet.

"Keep out of my dreams, Caelum," he warns. "This has nothing to do with you. Don't you see, I had to keep her safe from the storm."

Then, Kal's fist heads for Caelum's face. It doesn't connect; it fragments. They have awakened.

Caelum is back in his plane seat, sweating, anger coursing through every square inch of him.

He's going to kill Kal.

# Chapter 21

✳

## Estella

A warm wind blows through Estella's hair as she rides her bike down the Iron Horse Trail into town. It's a short and pleasant bike ride to the coffee shop. The trail is bordered by yellow and orange wildflowers that look like polka dots of color on an otherwise unremarkable background of dry grass and dirt. Old, gnarled trees provide a little extra color and a welcome canopy of shade on a hot day. After spending most of the summer in Hungary, Estella and her daughters returned to Danville with just a couple of weeks of summer vacation left. They have spent those weeks adjusting back to California time and getting ready for school. The girls have now started the fall semester at their new school, and Estella has turned her attention back to writing.

Exceptionally motivated, Estella finds a seat in the coffee shop and begins typing feverishly, draining words from her mind through her fingers. They're living in a new town—another new start. The air is thick with change, just the way Estella likes it. She's never been one to avoid change; to her, it's exciting. Sure, it's a bit scary, but at least it's never boring. Every so often, she prods at the walls of her reality, checking for weak spots and areas for improvement. And that's exactly what she's doing now, typing away, not only crafting a story, but also a new life.

Estella is interrupted by a conversation at the next table over. Two women in their twenties gossip so loudly that Estella can't help but overhear.

"Can you believe he's dating her?" one of them says. "I mean, she's thirty—that's, like, *old*."

The young woman catches her watching and looks away, embarrassed, as she flashes a fake smile. Amused, Estella chuckles to herself. They'll be thirty in no time. At thirty, she is reinventing herself. There's no age limit on that. She's just getting started.

Shortly, a new voice from their table says, "I like your shirt."

Estella tilts her head down to look at her Oktoberfest shirt, then turns toward the source of the compliment. Connor has replaced the women at the table.

"Oh, hey! What are you doing here?" she asks.

"Just getting a coffee. I live one town over, remember? Mind if I sit?" he asks as he makes his way to her table. "So, you've been to Oktoberfest in Munich?" he continues, pulling up a seat before she has offered him one.

"Yes," she replies blandly, wondering how long this interaction will last—especially given she's finally making some progress on her writing.

Connor's gaze falls to her notebook of poems—the one covered in hearts. "Cool, me, too!" he says, not asking about the notebook, and Estella is relieved. He wouldn't be interested in her poems anyway; he pretty much said so himself on their dinner date. His hair has that messy thing going on again, but it looks good on him. His big blue eyes peer at Estella over his coffee mug as he takes a sip. *"Sprechen Sie Deutsch?"* he asks and flashes a goofy smile, which gets a laugh out of her. Yeah, he can be cute, she supposes.

*"Ich spreche ein bisschen Deutsch,"* she replies. A while before she quit her job, Estella decided to study the basics of the German language. This was mainly to help her navigate Oktoberfest, but also to explore new ways to connect with others. She's since switched her focus to the universal language of music by getting back into playing drums. Nothing makes her feel more connected than music, like a bona fide citizen of the world.

"What are you working on there?" Connor asks.

She quickly shuts her laptop. "Oh, nothing. You know, just researching random things," she lies. But Estella does often research random things on the internet, especially when she's writing, so it's a little white lie.

"Like what?" he presses.

Estella doesn't feel like discussing her writing ambitions with not-into-artsy-stuff Connor, so she searches her mind for a not-so-white lie.

"I'm looking for a job." This is definitely a lie, but it's the first thing to come to mind. It's also about the last thing Estella really wants. She just wants to write the damn book she's dreamed of since third grade. The content has changed over the years, of course. She's been collecting life experiences, saving them up for the right time.

"Another attorney gig?" Connor asks.

"Nah. Like I said, I'm researching. I'm not sure what I want to do."

Without her fully realizing it, the thought of quitting her job had been in Estella's mind long before she actually did it. It was a process, a subconscious desire—or rather, a necessity—that had been percolating for months, maybe even years, without surfacing in her consciousness. That is, until her entire being blinked red and sounded the alarm. While her time as an attorney was an important part of her journey and formed her into the person she needed to be to move on to the next step in her life, she learned that she won't feel complete unless she creates something of her own—a piece of her soul to share with others, not something packaged under some organization's seal, containing some profit-making vision she doesn't care a thing about.

"I was thinking about our dinner the other night," Connor says, changing the subject. "It was nice. I'd like to do it again. Hang out, I mean. Dinner, a hike, coffee, whatever."

"We're having coffee now," Estella points out, fully aware that it's not the response Connor is looking for. He lowers his eyes to gaze at the bottom of his empty coffee mug. Feeling guilty for hurting his feelings, she says, "Sure. That sounds nice."

"Great! Have you hiked Mount Diablo yet?" Connor asks. He looks even more boyish when he's excited. "The views are amazing. You can see into eternity from up there."

# Chapter 22

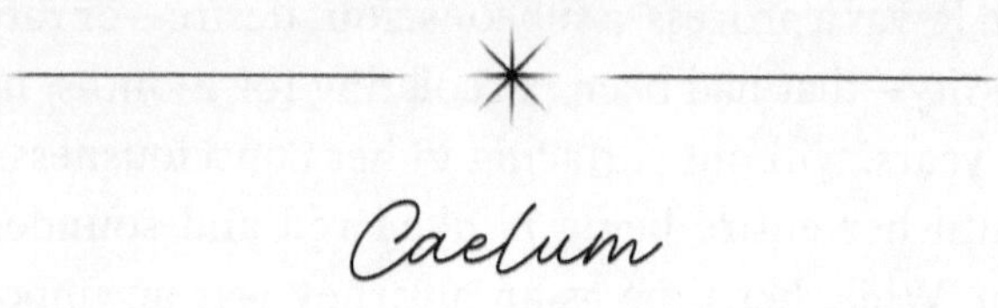

On the treadmill at the DVC, Caelum cranks up the speed as he replays the dream encounter with Kal. The steady thump of his feet hitting the treadmill drowns out dance hits meant to motivate gym-goers. He keeps coming back to the same conclusion: it's highly likely that Kal is Alexander. Athena can confirm this, so it's imperative that Caelum meets with her tonight. As he works up a sweat, pounding out his frustrations on the treadmill, he feels a pair of eyes on him. A thin, dark-haired woman then trails in front of him, arches an eyebrow, and scans the length of him with her vacant eyes before moving past him.

When Caelum finishes his run, he's covered in a layer of sweat. His heart rate and breathing gradually slow as he dabs his face with a hand towel. He then goes to the water fountain, and as he leans over to take a sip, he feels someone push into his backside. Startled, he turns to see who bumped him.

"Excuse me," she says, looking him up and down with her pale blue eyes as she curls her lips into a smile.

It's the woman who just eyeballed him on the treadmill. He recognizes her as one of the women who was sitting at the bar the first time Estella saw him here. Did she just grab his ass? They sure get bold in this place. As he tries to step around her, she shifts her statuesque body to block him, her dark, razor-straight hair swinging at her jawline.

"Hi, I'm Valentina," she says, standing so close that he can feel her breath as she talks.

"And I'm late," Caelum says as he slithers around her and hightails it to the locker room for a shower.

Before he goes looking for Athena tonight, he has some important business at Diablo's—and that business involves Kal.

When Caelum arrives at the music shop, Darin is in the spot Kal typically occupies on Estella's lesson day.

"Hey, man. Where's Kal?" Caelum asks.

"Oh, he quit. Said he doesn't have the extra time for Diablo's anymore, so you're stuck with me," Darin says.

*Yeah, he'd better run and hide...* Caelum will have to deal with Kal later.

Darin looks like he got run over by a truck. His long blond hair, usually in constant motion with him, hangs lifeless in front of his face as he sits slumped over on the chair by the register.

"You okay, man?" Caelum asks.

"Yeah, I'm okay, I guess," Darin says and lets out a long sigh. "I got dumped. Again. The thing is, I really liked him, but it's like I'm destined to be alone."

"Don't say that." Caelum moves over to Darin and grips his shoulder. "You're not destined to be alone. No one is ever really alone." If only Darin knew how true that is. "If you ever need anyone to talk to, I'm here for you, man."

As Darin laments that his last three relationships didn't even last a year, Estella arrives. When she enters the shop, Caelum and Darin both perk up. Caelum smiles big. Darin, still feeling the sting of lost love, doesn't smile, but he straightens his back.

During their lesson, Estella's eyes stay on Caelum, watching him as he plays drum exercises. He takes the opportunity to look back into her eyes. He tries a couple of times, making her visibly uncomfortable, but something about today makes it hard to hide what's on his mind. Through his gaze, he shows her how he feels.

She meets his gaze with equal intensity, telling him everything he needs to know. She takes him to a place he never knew existed. He didn't think it was possible for his desire for her to deepen, but she has taken him there, overwhelming him with the power of it. She gives him so much, just doing nothing but holding his gaze. In their eyes, they're one. Without a word, without a touch, they're closer than ever. Though she's on the other side of the room, there's no distance between them.

Later in the evening, Caelum lays in bed, burning over the story in Estella's eyes. How the hell will he get to sleep tonight? While meeting with Athena is urgent, he doesn't think a wink of sleep is in the forecast. The harder he tries to get Estella off his mind and get into a dream, the more he psychs himself out.

A nightcap will surely lend a helping hand. After Caelum pours himself a whiskey, he settles into a seat in the music room. After a few sips, he unlocks the cabinet where he keeps his cherished violin. With his violin from another life, he plays a song from that same period, a sixteenth-century folk song from Transylvania, back when it was part of Hungary. It's a slow, low melody, one Estella used to know. Nothing undoes Caelum like the haunting sound of a violin. He plays and sips, and as the hours pass, the tone of his songs grows darker and darker. Images from long ago carry him to a ship of dreams, and he sets sail to the past.

After dozing off, Caelum wakes in a dream, retrieves his key to the other side, and goes searching for Athena. But something feels off; he can't sense her presence in the vastness of the other side.

"Caelum," says Aurora.

Caelum's parents have come to greet him. He can tell something is wrong by the way Aurora says his name and the worry etched on their faces.

"Have you seen Athena? I need to speak with her," Caelum says urgently.

"She's gone," Dante replies. "We haven't felt her presence for days. She must have started a new life."

# Chapter 23

Estella always gets nervous before her lessons with Caelum. Today, she doesn't have the time to even think about getting nervous. When she stops at home, she grabs her drumsticks and runs back out the door. She's on her way to see him, heart thrumming, blood flowing, butterflies in her stomach fluttering.

Instead of Kal at the counter, she finds Darin and Caelum. It looks like they were talking about something heavy, because Darin isn't bouncing around with energy like usual. She's about to ask Darin what's wrong when Caelum shows up at her side and leads her toward the lesson rooms. She glances back at Darin to wave and tell him she'll see him later, but he's looking down at his hands resting in his lap.

Caelum plays a drum pattern, and Estella watches him. She looks up and sees him staring intently into her eyes—not a word, only his music and his eyes. She quickly looks away. It leaves her uncomfortable as she wonders, *What is he looking at? Is this what drummers do—zone out while they're playing music?* She peeks up at him again to check the situation. He's still looking at her! *WTF?* Unnerved, she quickly looks away again. His eyes—they're beautiful … and they're all over her. Nothing else, just her. It makes her feel so … *real.*

Estella tries to brush it off as just a random accident, chalking it up to Caelum being lost in his music and staring into space. To distract herself from his eyes, she focuses on his hands instead. But those hands, so incredibly sexy… Soon she's imagining them all over her. *Okay, forget the hands,* she tells herself. Drums, music—that's why she's here. *Concentrate on the music you need to learn,* she coaches herself.

She looks up—and his eyes are burning fire into her eyes again. This time, she can't help but hold his gaze. Now, he has her curious—and totally turned on. This is no random, accidental locking of eyes. It's too much feeling, so she diverts her eyes again.

A few seconds later, she musters up the courage and looks right into his electric green eyes, already hooked, already addicted. For what feels like a lifetime packaged into a single minute, their souls are speaking—sexy, raw, transcendent. They're no longer in this world. Their gaze has become a key, unlocking a door to another realm—one they've instantly stepped into together. Not a single cheap word could capture what's being said in the silence, and no amount of conversation could ever reveal as much about him as his eyes are revealing to her now. He knows exactly what his gaze is doing to her: making her mad with desire.

As Caelum taps a mellow beat on the drums, a slow smile spreads across his face without him breaking his gaze. The intensity is overwhelming. She blushes, looks away, and lets out a nervous laugh, releasing just a bit of the tension building inside her. Estella can't recall anything in her life that has ever turned her on this much—not a touch, not a whisper, not even a kiss. His eyes are her complete undoing. Who would've thought a look could hold so much power? And in this moment, all she wants is to be his—*completely* his.

Caelum breaks the silence. "You know, I'm thinking you should come to Jack's and play a song with my band. I think you're ready," he says.

"What? No way! I'm not that good." As if the day hasn't been intense enough, Caelum keeps pushing her out of her comfort zone. It's quickly becoming too much for a sensitive person like Estella.

"Sure you are," he insists. "You already had the basics down before our first lesson. Trust me, you'll kill it. You'll be on drums; I'll play guitar. We play on Friday—not this Friday, but the next. That'll give you some time to practice. And if it makes you feel better, we can start with an easy song."

"Hmm..." Estella says hesitantly, as a dust devil of thoughts kicks up in her mind. Her, on stage, playing drums with a band. With Caelum. In front of people. Her whole body tingles at the thought of performing with a real band in front of a live crowd, but the idea of spending more time with Caelum is simply irresistible.

"Well?" Caelum interrupts, pulling her out of her thoughts.

"Oh, okay," she says, surprising herself. "Why not?"

"Heck, yeah!" Caelum looks like he just won a prize. "I have your number in your registration info, so I'll text you. We can talk about what song to play, and I'll see you at our next lesson before the show."

After her lesson, Estella rushes to the front of the store to tell Darin about the gig. She finds him at the drum set display, looking more like himself as he grooves and moves. When she shares the news that she's going to play her first show, Darin raises his drumsticks overhead and belts out an enthusiastic, "Yeah!"

As soon as Estella tells Darin about the show, it starts to feel real.

# Chapter 24

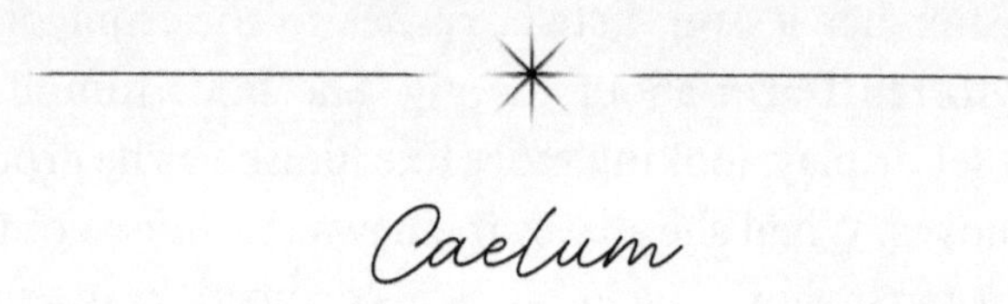

Caelum pulls the handle of the drawer on his nightstand, and a gleam of gold flashes. His key to the other side is exactly where he left it. The murmured voices of Tommaso and Vittoria drift in from the other room. His aunt and uncle might walk in at any moment, but they wouldn't see him. He's in a dream, on his way to the past.

The dream world and reality rarely ever overlap, but that's not to say they never intersect. Some people—typically witches—can see the dream world while awake. Such experiences are called visions, and Caelum knows Estella has them. He may be a traveler, but he's no witch, and he doesn't have visions. However, in very rare occurrences, people who aren't witches may experience a vision if that person is chosen to see something. These visions are important messages sent from the other side. Messages in dreams can feel insignificant and are often forgotten, but no one forgets seeing wild things when they're wide awake and sober.

Caelum is traveling to the other side tonight to look for information on Athena's whereabouts and this new life she's started. Maybe she left behind some clues or a message for him. Her departure from the other side creates a major problem: she can no longer confirm whether Kal is Alexander's new identity. This vital information, along with her knowledge about other travelers, is lost now that Athena is in another life.

Connecting with and having the support of other travelers is crucial. Then Caelum would have more than just his whiskey to turn to. It's hard to quantify how many travelers are out there, but it can't be more than a handful. So, when travelers find each other, they stick together and adhere to the rules: absolute secrecy. You don't share what you know with non-travelers. Break the rules, and your time in this life is over—and don't expect to be trusted with traveling rights ever again.

Caelum steps into the foreverness of the other side, feeling a sense of home not felt anywhere else. Aurora, Dante, and other familiar energies from past lives greet him. They revel in one another's light, but he learns nothing new about Athena. She hasn't passed along any information regarding Alexander's identity.

They leave Caelum to his mission as he roams to the past, closer to the last time he saw Athena in Positano, dreaming in his room. It takes him three tries before he decides to take a closer look from a different angle.

Like watching a movie, he observes his past self checking the balcony after the door slams, then returning to bed. Double-checking to ensure that his past self didn't miss anything, he peers out at the balcony again—and sees a shadow where there had been none. It moves.

Out of the shadows peeks a long, slim leg clad in sheer black pantyhose and a pointed high heel. Trying his best to remain unseen behind the balcony curtains, Caelum uses one eye to peek just beyond the curtain's edge. Is this another traveler following him in his dream, or a person who was present at that moment in the past? Maybe it's Athena, or perhaps it's another traveler, one of Alexander and Cassius's half-soul cronies. He can't take any chances.

The pale moonlight travels up the leg to reveal the rest of the woman as she steps out of the dark corner of the balcony. It's not Athena. Caelum isn't sure who this woman is, but her shape is familiar. She moves to the edge of the balcony, and his eyes are glued to her. That hair—he recognizes that sleek, shiny hair.

The woman turns to look back at his balcony door, and Caelum holds his breath. With her face now in view and the moonlight reflecting in her icy blue eyes, he slowly lets out the breath he's been holding. He knows her. It's the woman who hit on him at the DVC. What did she say her name was? Val…? Valerie? No… Valentina—that's it. She moves toward the staircase at the side of the balcony to make her exit.

"Valentina!" Caelum calls out. If she's a traveler, she should be able to see him, but she doesn't even flinch. "Valentina," he repeats as he moves closer.

The tapping of her shoes quickens as she descends the staircase. She doesn't look back; she hasn't acknowledged his existence. He can't be sure if she's a traveler, or just some crazy stalker, or if she's working with Alexander.

# Chapter 25

Estella

Estella rifles through her closet, searching for a top—most of which are black—as she and her best friend, Emma, get ready to go out. It's Emma's first time visiting Estella at her new place in Danville. Knowing she wouldn't have much time to practice drums during Emma's visit, Estella spent hours earlier practicing on the drum kit she set up in her garage. She's not only preparing for the show at Jack's, but also hoping to impress Emma with her improving skills.

Tonight, however, Estella is taking Emma to Jack's to meet Darin and Kal. Her plan is to show Emma around town and spill the tea—the tea being Caelum, Connor, and Kal. Estella needs advice from her best friend and fellow witch. Since she doesn't advertise her magic to the world, she doesn't know any witches in the Bay Area. In fact, since marrying Lucas and having kids, Estella hasn't made any new friends besides Darin and Kal. She left all her friends in Seattle when they moved.

Deciding what to wear to Jack's, Estella keeps it casual with a simple black tank top that cuts low in the back and features little crisscross straps. She slips on a pair of relaxed boyfriend jeans and black ankle booties. For her hair and makeup, she doesn't do much—just two flicks of eyeliner for a subtle cat eye. Her friend, on the other hand, goes all out in a tight dress. Typical Emma.

"So, who did you say we're meeting tonight?" Emma asks. She hops on one foot as she slips on one of her heels.

"We're meeting some new friends of mine, Darin and Kal, at the neighborhood bar, Jack's. It's chill. You'll like it."

"Are they cute?" Emma asks. Of course, this is her top concern. She looks at herself in the mirror and smears red lipstick over her top lip, from one corner to the other, then continues down to her bottom lip, completing the circle. She's all poofy dark brown hair, big brown eyes, and some red-ass lips. *Aww, she's trying a bit hard, but she sure looks cute.* Estella chuckles to herself.

"What?" Emma says defensively.

"Nothing."

Emma raises a fluffy eyebrow at Estella.

"Yeah, they're cute," Estella says. "But Darin has a boyfriend—and I think Kal is into me."

When they arrive at Jack's, Estella scans the room as the music thumps through her body. Next to her, Emma's shoulders move to the beat. The scene hasn't changed much. Estella spots Darin and Kal in the same spot by the bar. There's a comforting familiarity in seeing them there, exactly where they were last time, as if that's how it will always be. Their faces light up when they see Estella, and they look at Emma with curiosity.

"You brought a friend," Darin says. "Love your hair!" he says to Emma, flipping his own hair from one side to the other. Emma thanks him for the compliment, running her fingers through her hair to add fluff. "And matching tattoos." He points out Emma's crescent moon tattoo on her inner left forearm. She instinctively hides her arm behind her back.

"We're besties," Estella justifies. She trusts Darin and Kal, but doesn't plan on telling them any time soon that she and Emma are witches. These days, whenever someone finds out she has visions, they expect her to do things for them—or worse, they judge her, or think she's a freak.

"I have a moon, too," Darin says. He pulls up the sleeve of his T-shirt to reveal a tattoo of a wolf and a full moon on his shoulder. Estella and Emma share a glance, and Estella knows what Emma's thinking. Could he be a witch, too? He might be covering a witch's mark, or it could just be a tattoo.

"Nice," Emma says and smiles. Darin makes easy friends. He's good like that.

Darin and Emma make their way to the dance floor, and Estella stays at the bar with Kal.

"What are you drinking?" Kal asks.

Estella thinks about it for a moment, remembering that they're at a dive bar; no muddled or freshly squeezed mocktails here. "I'll have a vodka soda, but hold the vodka," she replies after Kal flags down the bartender to place their order. "I've been trying to reach you. You didn't show up at Diablo's, and you haven't been picking up your calls. Is everything okay?" She's been dying to tell Kal about her first gig.

"Everything is fine. I lost a key associate at the DVC. He moved back east, so I just don't have time for Diablo's anymore," Kal says.

"That's a bummer." Diablo's won't be the same without Kal.

"Come see me at the DVC," Kal says, handing Estella a soda water with a lime wedge perched on the rim.

"I'll look for you next time I'm in," Estella says, squeezing the lime into her drink. "So, guess what? I'm playing my first gig at Jack's next Friday!" she blurts out before Kal can even take a guess. "I'm playing with Caelum's band, and I'm so nervous! Please say you'll be there." She looks at Kal with puppy dog eyes, hoping for his support.

"Don't be nervous. You'll be great," Kal replies, sucking the foam off his beer. "And of course I'll be there."

Estella takes a deep breath and sips her tasteless but excitingly bubbly soda water, feeling a bit of ease knowing Kal will be there.

"So, tell me about your book," Kal says, catching Estella off guard.

She chokes on her bubbly water. Damn, she doesn't want to get into it. She almost forgot she had briefly mentioned her writing to him. She's surprised he remembers. "It's a work in progress."

"Come on, give me something. A genre, anything."

"Okay, okay. There's a little bit of magic, and … well, I'm a romantic, so there has to be romance."

"Anything else?" he prompts.

What more can she tell him? She looks into Kal's trustworthy eyes—at least, they seem trustworthy.

"There's a battle between a dark force and all of humanity," she offers. "Cliché, right?" she adds. "I know you've heard the theme before, but I want to put my own spin on it. A message about solidarity and love to help save humanity."

"You want to know what I think?" he asks. She gives Kal a quick nod and widens her eyes in anticipation. "Humanity needs a book like that right about now. It seems we're headed for dark times. Things haven't been the same since the pandemic and the rise of AI. Maybe your book can help spread the message. We must keep our spirit alive; it's our connection to being human. We can't lose that. Your voice will join the chorus of voices carrying the same message, growing louder and louder until it cuts through the noise," Kal says.

Estella changes the subject, but Kal's words about humanity's spirit linger in the back of her mind. It's the core of what she's been writing about: how we're all connected, despite our differences, even when modern-day spirits are low. Fragility, weaknesses, and imperfections are swiftly stamped out. There's always something just one click away to ease the pain and make us forget. But we need to remember. She knows we must feel the pain to move past it; otherwise, the darkness lingers and accumulates. Over time, it creates cracks, allowing more darkness to seep in. Maybe Estella's book will help; maybe it will keep the dark from seeping in.

Estella's mind wanders back to Caelum as if he's a default setting, and she thinks about how she feels when she's in his presence. She scans the room again, looking for him. Every person coming through the door isn't Caelum. He's nowhere to be found. She must forget about him and finish her book; she can't take it anymore.

"Want to dance?" she asks Kal.

"Heck, yeah!" Kal replies, as if it's the question he's been waiting for all night.

Estella surrenders, completely and absolutely, to the music. She dances it all out, pouring out everything she has until there's nothing left in her. She dances away her grief over losing Lucas, her lust for Caelum, and her feelings of fear and inadequacy.

Kal moves in closer, swooping one arm around Estella's waist, pulling her into reality. She looks up at him and sees what he wants written on his face. He closes the little space left between them, their bodies pressed together, moving to the music.

Just then, Darin and Emma burst onto the scene.

"Hey, guys!" Darin yells, and Estella guesses he's about four drinks deep. He squeezes between her and Kal, and soon they're all dancing, the four of them moving together until they close the place down.

Whenever Estella is with Emma, she forgets that she's a grown-ass adult who has grown-ass responsibilities. They spent so much time having fun growing up that when they're together, Estella slips back into her teenage self.

Today, while Estella and Emma wander through Danville, Estella wonders if they'll run into Caelum. She does her best to push him out of her mind for most of the day, but memories keep slipping back in—the way he looked into her eyes at the coffee shop, the intensity of his gaze in his lesson room. Estella doesn't see him at the DVC as she gives Emma the tour, but she remembers the moment she first spotted him here. She isn't the only one with her sights set on Caelum. She's only seen him here twice—once that first time, and then another time briefly after that. He didn't see her that second time, because a tall, pretty woman with a neat bob cornered him at the water fountain.

Caelum might as well come with a warning sign: Caution: Look, But Don't Touch. Estella and her daughters are just beginning to find a sense of normalcy after their move to Danville, and getting involved with someone would upend that. The last thing her daughters need after losing their father is a strange new man breezing in and out of their lives.

"I need your opinion on something," Estella says to Emma as they sit down at the DVC café after ordering smoothies. "Do you think it's too soon for me to date?"

"Not at all. But you have to feel ready," Emma replies, taking a sip of her smoothie. "This is good." She pulls back and admires her pink strawberry-banana smoothie.

"That's the thing. I don't know if I am. Part of me feels like I'd be letting go of Lucas, but another part feels like a plant that's dying. I don't know how else to say it. I need love. I'm also worried about how the girls would feel, seeing me with someone who's not their dad." Estella takes a sip of her smoothie. "This is a good smoothie. Very banana." She crinkles her brow and raises a hand up to her forehead.

"Brain freeze?" Emma asks.

"No," Estella says through gritted teeth. "Vision."

The guy sitting at the table next to them glances over, watching them a little too intently. Emma twirls a finger, and an empty chair tips over. The guy quickly stands up and leaves. Emma doesn't have visions herself, but just like her mom, Kareena, she can move things with her mind.

"You promised not to use your power in public. Can't you control yourself?" Estella groans, scanning the room to see if anyone else noticed.

"What did you see?" Emma asks, dodging the question.

"This time, it was the faceless man and this old book. First, I kept getting visions of this faceless man, then the book, and now I see them together in one vision."

"Do you think these visions have anything to do with the book you're writing?" Emma asks.

"I don't know… Maybe," Estella says, taking a sip of her smoothie.

"How's the book writing going, anyway?" Emma asks.

"I've made some progress," Estella replies, then catches Emma glaring at her. "What?" she asks defensively.

"Are you going to tell people about your book, so they can actually read it? You need to get over your fear of what other people think," she scolds. "Look at your poetry book—you published it and didn't even tell anyone."

"I'm working on that," Estella says, setting her empty plastic cup on the table. "Now, can we get back to our discussion about dating? I wasn't done talking about that."

"Okay, but if you don't start promoting your books, I will," Emma says. The notion makes Estella uncomfortable, and she fidgets in her seat. "About dating: don't worry so much. If it's meant to be, everything will work itself out. So, who's the guy? The drum teacher you told me you have a crush on?"

"Actually, there are three."

Emma chokes on her smoothie. *"Three?"*

"Yeah, well, there's the drum teacher. His name is Caelum. And you met Kal. And then there's Connor, the other guy I told you about. We used to work together. He's widowed."

"Oh, right, Connor. But which one do you like? I mean, *really* like?"

"Caelum. I don't know what it is about him, but I can't stop thinking about him. I've even had dreams about him."

"So, go for it!" Emma says, making slurping sounds with her straw as she sucks up the last of her smoothie.

"I don't know. I need to get to know him better. My feelings for him kind of scare me. He's intense, sexy, and smart. He seems too good to be true. Then there's Kal… He's handsome and sweet, but it's Caelum I keep thinking about. Connor seems nice, too… But again, Caelum."

"Something's telling me you like Caelum," Emma says jokingly. "Stop trying to figure things out with your head and go with your heart."

Easier said than done. "I don't trust my heart to make good decisions."

# Chapter 26



It's Saturday, and the DVC is crowded with weekend warriors. Every table in the café is occupied with people drinking post-workout power smoothies. Caelum snagged a table early, and he has conducted a stakeout for the past couple of hours. With his laptop open for research, he takes sips of his own smoothie—a green one. The taste is earthy—not in a good way—but it's supposed to be healthy, so he takes another sip.

Caelum came looking for Valentina at the only place he's seen her in the waking world. If she doesn't show up, he'll go looking for her in a dream tonight. If she's a traveler, they can meet and chat in the world that exists while they sleep. If not, he'll find out everything he needs to know about her during his dream hunt.

Caelum types *Valentina Danville* into the search bar on his laptop. A few Valentinas pop up, and he clicks on the links, but none match this Valentina. One has wavy blonde hair, while the Valentina he seeks sports dark, sharply cut hair. Each lead turns out to be a dead end. A last name would be helpful, but it's no surprise that the host at the front desk wouldn't share it when he asked about Valentina this morning.

A loud thud startles Caelum, and as he turns to see what happened, he accidentally knocks over his smoothie. The green drink splatters on the floor beside his table. A guy picks up the book he dropped, wipes some smoothie off it with a napkin, and mumbles something as he takes off. The clerk behind the café counter witnesses the chaos and approaches with a dish towel to clean up the mess.

As Caelum helps her wipe up the green sludge with a handful of napkins, he asks, "Hey, have you happened to see a tall, thin woman with dark chin-length hair come in here?"

"No. Sorry."

"Her name is Valentina," Caelum adds.

"Oh, you mean Ms. Black."

Bingo. "Yeah, Valentina Black," Caelum replies.

"I see her come in here all the time. She always gets this smoothie," she says, holding up the dish towel now tinged green. "Are you waiting for her?"

"You could say that. I'll grab another smoothie while I wait, but this time, let's make it strawberry banana," he says as they walk to the cash register.

After Caelum pays for the sweeter-but-better-tasting smoothie, he settles back into his seat and types *Valentina Black Danville* into the search bar. The page loads, and her icy blue eyes stare back at him. *Now we're talking.* One step closer to finding her, Caelum feels his mood lighten, and he takes an extra big sip of his new smoothie. Crushing strawberry seeds and bits of ice between his teeth, he clicks on her picture.

Strange. According to this website, she lives in New York, and she's a literary agent. The website lists successful authors she's worked with, her favorite novels, and fun facts about her. Apparently, she likes traveling. *No shit.* Caelum knows exactly what kind of "traveling" she likes to do.

But the fact that she works with books is interesting. It can't be a mere coincidence that Valentina represents authors, and Estella is currently writing a book—one that the Source wants her to write. There must be some connection. Maybe Valentina is one of the travelers Athena mentioned. She had said there are other travelers here to help Estella, so perhaps Valentina isn't one of the shady half-souls after all. Maybe she's here to assist Estella with her book.

After finishing his second smoothie, Caelum packs up his laptop, concluding his stakeout of the DVC.

Later in the evening, Caelum slips into bed and pulls up Valentina's website to study it further. He pores over every detail, but nothing seems helpful for his dream hunt. Frustrated, he searches her name again and clicks through the search results. He discovers that she has a speaking engagement at the upcoming International Antiquarian Book Fair in New York, at the Park Avenue Armory. She's set to present an ancient philosophical text, which will be auctioned off for a staggering sum. Bidding starts at two hundred fifty thousand dollars. It must contain the answers to all of life's mysteries for that kind of cash. This is too intriguing to pass up. There's no reason Caelum can't take a detour to the future.

While Caelum often uses his dreams to take trips to the other side or explore dreams, travelers can also use their dreams to time travel to any point in time. They can choose whether to feel the scene, but there's no interaction like there is in real life, and they remain unseen by those in the waking world. Instead, they pass through the scenes and the people in them like holograms. Unless, of course, there's another traveler present. Travelers can always interact with other travelers.

People have tried to interact with the past since the beginning of time, but there's no messing with the past to change the future. What's done is done. Even if the past could be changed, future outcomes always change, too. The future holds no guarantees.

In tonight's dream, Caelum will make a quick pit stop at Valentina's future speaking engagement before traveling back to the past to intercept her on his Positano balcony. There was only one version of Valentina there, so she was either physically lurking around his bedroom in Positano, or she was a traveler tracking him in his dream. If Valentina is indeed a traveler, Caelum is sure to find out.

There are a couple of surefire ways to identify fellow travelers in dreams. One method is seeing two versions of a person, like when Caelum saw two Kals—his past self and his traveler self. Another sign is if they're solid; a traveler can't pass through another traveler. They interact in dreams as if they're made of flesh and bone. When Caelum finds Valentina, will she be solid, or thin as air? He just has to get close enough to find out.

Before dozing off, Caelum envisions the time and location of the book fair.

The words ENDURANCE, FIDELITY, INTELLIGENCE quickly appear before his eyes—and he realizes he's reading the inscription on a bronze statue of a dog. He's standing at the Balto statue in Central Park, New York City. Damn, he's getting good at this. His dream lands him just a short walk from the book fair. With this kind of accuracy, next time, he might end up right in the enemy's lap.

Upon arriving at the book fair, he's met with spectacled faces, neckties, scarves, and people carrying books like they're holding onto treasure. The bookish vibe is strong. In the expansive open space, a sea of booths showcases rare books, first editions, and other valuable items. A symphony of conversation mixed with antiquity fills the air.

Finding Valentina amongst the myriad of booths will take an eternity. But as Caelum makes his way up and down the aisles, he catches a glimpse of her face. Only it's not her physical face; it's her picture on a cardboard display advertising the time and location of her presentation.

Next to Caelum stands a man who looks like he stepped out of *The Great Gatsby*. As the man scrolls through his phone, Caelum leans in to check the time. Gatsby doesn't mind; Caelum's a ghost to him. Valentina presents in five minutes, so Caelum floats through the crowd to get in position. Her presentation is in the Colonel's Room, away from the bustling open space filled with booths.

The Colonel's Room is an elegant space adorned with high ceilings, grand pillars, and deep mahogany wainscotting. Large portraits hang on the walls, and an opulent chandelier casts a warm yellow light throughout the room. This warmth and grandeur contrast sharply with the industrial open space filled with booths.

Valentina soon enters the room, and her commanding presence immediately draws attention. Her striking looks capture the gaze of everyone present. She steps up to the platform in front of the microphone and glances around the audience. Voices hush, and all eyes are on her as she prepares to speak. Her gaze drifts to someone in the back of the room, and their eyes lock—his a deeper shade of blue than hers.

"Ladies and gentlemen, I present to you *The Book of Origin and Fate*," Valentina announces. She holds up a book that looks like it has been buried for centuries. It's bound in tarnished metal, stamped with intricate designs, and secured with a latch. From where Caelum hovers, he can almost smell the passage of time in its pages.

"What are you doing here?" someone demands from behind him.

He turns to see another Valentina.

"Fancy seeing you here, fellow traveler," Caelum responds. "So, you're following me in my dreams, are you?"

"I tried talking to you at the gym, but you blew me off. Remember?" Valentina mutters.

"If you had started with the bit about being a traveler, I would've listened. You know, I caught you in a dream on my balcony in Positano. That's why I've come here looking for you."

"Oh?" she replies, her eyes darting back and forth.

"Don't you remember? After all, you were the one tracking me. I called after you, and you ran. Why didn't you reveal yourself then?"

"Oh, right... I did try to get in touch with you, but I had to get to the other side, so I left. I didn't hear you calling after me."

"So, who are you? Are you one of the travelers sent to help Estella? The ones Athena told me about?"

"Athena?" she echoes, surprised.

"So, you don't know Athena?" Caelum asks, suspicion marking every word as his voice rises. "Then who are you, and what is your business with me?"

"No, no," Valentina stutters. "Of course I know Athena. I'm here to help Estella with her book," she adds. "For the Source. I'm with the Source."

"Aren't we all?" Caelum replies, eyeing her skeptically. "So, where is Athena?"

Valentina bites her lip before responding. "She started a new life, so we won't be seeing her for a while."

"Damn. She has information I need. Did she tell you anything about Alexander? He's entered this life, and Athena knows his current identity. I need to know who he is."

"I know nothing of Alexander," she says briskly.

"Is that so? It sounds like you know something."

"No. I don't even know who that is. I'm here to help Estella," Valentina says, her tone softening.

"A million dollars!" the man with the blue eyes in the back shouts.

*What the...?*

"Who is that? I saw you look at him earlier."

"I don't know him." Valentina raises her palms in innocence. "I may have glanced at him for a moment. What can I say? He's good-looking."

"Sold!" screams the auctioneer.

"He's the winning bidder," Valentina says, and then the dream begins to fade.

# Chapter 27

"Play music," Estella says to her virtual assistant. *Music will help,* she thinks. It always does. She tells it to crank up the volume loud enough to drown out the thoughts of everything that could go wrong at her first gig. Singing along just as loudly, she feels her nerves settle. Music takes her to a place where there are no mistakes.

Showtime at Jack's arrives sooner than Estella wants. Despite practicing all day, she feels unprepared, and nothing unnerves her more than that. She and Caelum decided on "Space Oddity" by David Bowie, a song that almost feels too fitting for the moment. She knows every beat, every pause, and could play the song in her sleep, but performing it live is something else entirely. Like a lonely figure venturing into space, she feels isolated and uncertain, an imposter floating in a world she's not sure she belongs in, faking it until she makes it—whatever "it" is, because that goal always seems to shift just out of reach.

As she gets ready for the show, she fishes out a black velvet top that has gathered dust in the back of her closet, pairing it with tight black jeans. If she's going to play drums in a band, she wants to look the part, even if she isn't quite sure what that looks like. Dressing up is just one part of her preparation, a ritual that helps ease her nerves. She doesn't have to do it, but she wants to. For a touch of color, she swipes on cherry-red lipstick. To complete the look, she lets her hair air-dry into its wild, untamed state, textured waves falling around her face.

She's ready … kind of.

Estella steps into Jack's and spots Kal leaning against the bar, his face half buried in a glass of beer and his long hair dusting the bar countertop. Just seeing him there puts her at ease, though Caelum is nowhere in sight—not yet, at least. They're up soon, so he must be around here somewhere.

"Kal!" she calls out, a little louder than intended. Heads turn, and she hides an embarrassed smile.

Kal straightens, setting his beer on the bar with a clink. "I'm about to get up there with the band. You're looking at their new rhythm guitarist," he says. He spreads his arms to give Estella a hug, and when he does, he squeezes her tightly. He smells like the tropics again. Estella wouldn't mind burying her face in his coconut-scented hair, but it's Caelum's arms she truly wants wrapped around her.

They both turn toward the stage, where band members are busy adjusting pedals and amplifiers, tuning instruments in a mix of chaotic sounds. The drummer catches sight of Kal and Estella, lifts a drumstick, and points it in Kal's direction, signaling, *"Get your ass on stage."*

Darin appears as Kal answers the call of the drumstick. He slides into Kal's place at the bar and helps himself to the half-empty glass of beer Kal left behind.

"Don't you need a certain amount of experience or skill to play a gig?" Estella asks, her voice full of doubt.

Darin tips back the rest of Kal's beer, and Estella can't help but think that she needs that drink more than he does, though she doesn't drink anymore.

"Listen to me," Darin says, turning his whole body to face Estella. "You. Are. Going. To. *Rock.*" She looks at him like his words aren't registering. "Okay?" he adds, but Estella remains unconvinced. He bombards her with compliments, propping her up as good friends do, grabbing her by the shoulders and repeating even louder, "You are going to rock!" And he nearly convinces her that she will, in fact, "rock."

The band starts to play, and the beat resonates through Estella. She sips her drink and watches Kal on guitar, noticing how his eyes frequently travel to meet hers, checking to see if she's paying attention. When their eyes meet, he smiles and blushes. *How cute,* she thinks. He can't hide the fact that he likes her, even from halfway across the room while playing with his band.

"There you are," a voice cuts through the music.

Estella follows the sound to find Caelum's face. Caught off guard, she says hi a bit too loudly. He moves in for a hug, triggering palpitations in her chest as if he has a literal grip on her heart. When Caelum hugs Estella, they fit together like skillfully played Tetris pieces, and letting go feels especially difficult. Maybe Estella holds onto that hug for longer than she should, but not as long as she wishes she could.

"What's up, man?" Caelum says to Darin, and they greet each other with a firm handshake.

Caelum moves in close to drown out the music, leaning in to talk in Estella's ear. "We're up next. Are you ready?"

He's close enough for her to feel the warmth radiating from him and catch the scent of laundry detergent mixed with that heat. She takes a deep breath of him, and as she lets it out, she says, "Ready as I'll ever be."

Estella looks at Caelum, and the rest of the room fades into a blurry watercolor painting. *What gig?*

As Kal's song comes to an end, Estella glances up at the stage. This time, he isn't looking at her, and the expression on his face has changed. He looks rough and hard, his gaze fixed on Caelum, whose face has also hardened. Estella doesn't understand what this exchange between them is about, but she gets the feeling that they don't have the warm fuzzies for each other.

As Kal leaves the stage, Estella and Caelum make their way up there.

"You were amazing!" Estella says to Kal as she grabs his arm.

He tilts his chin up and smiles proudly. "Now, it's your turn to rock this place," he says.

As Estella gets up on stage, she sees Caelum whisper something into Kal's ear when they pass each other. What's going on between these two?

Jack's feels much different from the stage than it does from the audience, and Estella realizes that nothing she's done has prepared her for this moment. She's spent hours practicing on her own, but shouldn't practicing with the band be a prerequisite for playing a gig in front of a live audience? If it isn't, the unease in the pit of her stomach insists that it should be. Yet, as she looks out into the crowd and at the band around her, a surge of power flows through her. People's eyes are on her—and it feels good.

Caelum introduces Estella to the rest of the band. They exchange quick greetings, but she's too preoccupied with sensory overload to remember names. She can't see the bassist's eyes, which are tucked under the brim of his newsboy cap, but she catches a glimpse of his exceptionally white teeth when he flashes her a smile. The rest of him appears slouchy, with shoulders that slope and pants that sag. He taps out a bass riff that sounds rich and toasty.

The singer, a young guy with a deceptively wholesome look, gives off an impression that he's no angel. He has a close fade, a clean-shaven face, smooth skin, and rosy lips and cheeks. There's heartbreak written all over him.

As the band tunes up and makes adjustments, Caelum straps a guitar on and guides Estella to the drum kit. He hands her drumsticks, and when she sits on her throne, it feels like she's just taken a seat on a roller coaster.

It reminds her of a trip to Las Vegas with her parents when she was a kid. She remembers wanting to ride a free-fall ride, but she was nervous about getting on because, well, it's a big drop. After Estella worked up the courage to get on the ride, the operator checked her straps to make sure she was secure along with the other riders. That gave her some feeling of safety, which quickly vanished once the ride began. It was a big drop indeed—like free-falling into oblivion—and she'll never forget the rush she felt. As the ride neared its end, she couldn't stop screaming. Unable to handle the overload of euphoria, it escaped from her in uncontrollable shrieks. The operator came over while she was still strapped into the ride, dangling right above him, and he grabbed her foot, grounding her like a lightning rod discharges electricity. It worked. He jerked her back to reality, and maybe, by grabbing her foot, he got a jolt, too. She'll never know for sure, but she likes to think he felt some of that rush before it dissipated.

Despite the feeling of power that comes from being on stage, Estella is still a wreck. She's not a real musician. What if she's not good enough? What if she sucks?

Caelum gives Estella a nod, and as the band starts playing, the magic of David Bowie's "Space Oddity" begins to flow. *Gods of rock and roll, please carry me through.* She stops thinking, and her worries melt away. She just plays. It's like more Tetris pieces falling into place. She becomes a part of the group, a part of the music, a part of something good.

The song ends, and Estella feels that roller coaster rush as the crowd cheers. She doesn't scream her head off like she did on that free-fall ride years ago, but a similar euphoria courses through her veins. Her gaze locks onto Caelum, and for far too long, they stare at each other in amazement. When they snap out of it, Caelum sets down his guitar and approaches Estella, who stands next to the drums with sticks in one hand. Just as the free-fall ride conductor grabbed Estella's shoe to diffuse her rush, she grabs Caelum's arm with her other hand, testing the conductor's method. The look on Caelum's face when Estella touches him tells her he felt a jolt of something.

# Chapter 28

Caelum scans the crowded scene at Jack's until his gaze locks on Estella. She's standing at the bar with Darin, and on stage, he sees that creep, Kal, the man he needs to question, now encroaching on his evening with Estella. Caelum will have to find a way to get at Kal without making a scene. He'll deal with him later.

As Estella turns her head to talk with Darin, Caelum takes in the soft outline of her profile—pillowy lips and wild hair he imagines burying his hands in. Desire stirs unexpectedly, pulling him towards Estella. When he reaches the bar, he greets her and Darin, his voice calm, but he's anything but.

Estella's energetic greeting gives away an edge of nervousness. Her lips are bright red, vivid against her skin. He's never seen her wear lipstick, and it has an effect on him, immediate and intense. Like a bull drawn to a scarlet matador's cape, he can't look away. As she talks, his mind drifts to the thought of a lipstick-smearing kiss between them.

They turn to watch the band play, and the moment Kal notices Caelum standing next to Estella, his face drops. Caelum smirks, puffing out his chest as if to remind Kal that he's standing guard.

The song Kal is playing comes to an end, and now it's Caelum and Estella's turn. As they switch places, Caelum steps close, leaning into Kal's space so he can hear him say, "Meet me in the back after this set. We need to talk."

Caelum puts Kal out of his mind once he's on stage and becomes completely immersed in the moment with Estella. There's nothing more powerful than the connection the music creates. And from the look on Estella's face, she's loving every moment of it.

She kills it, like Caelum knew she would. As the crowd cheers, Estella grabs his arm. Her touch is electric, stopping him in his tracks, and all he can do is stare at her in amazement. It's one of those moments when time stands still, like a worn snapshot revisited years later, but as vivid as the day it's taken.

Once they clear the stage, Darin catches Estella's attention, giving Caelum an opportunity to look for Kal, who's nowhere to be seen. Caelum slips out the back door, weaving through puffs of smoke exhaled into the night air by those who've stepped outside for a cigarette. But there are only the smokers—no Kal.

Then, Kal steps out of the shadows. "Before you say or try anything, let me speak. Just as you're here for Estella, so am I. Just as you're a traveler with a purpose, so am I."

"What do you want with her?" Caelum demands, his teeth clenched as he steps closer, getting right into Kal's face.

"My mission has been to watch over Estella throughout her life, to ensure her safety, so that certain events can unfold that will lead her to her highest purpose. She's here to initiate a shift in the zeitgeist—one that humanity needs. She's a key—one of many—to unlocking doors that lead to truth. She has a message to deliver—and I'm here to make sure she delivers it." Kal holds his ground, staring Caelum down without backing off an inch.

"You think I don't know everything there is to know about her?" Caelum snaps. "She doesn't need your protection. *I*—" He jabs a thumb at his chest. "—can protect her." He's still not convinced that Kal isn't Alexander or some other half-soul.

"You don't understand. It's my duty, and I must fulfill it, or die trying. Those are my orders, directly from the Source."

*The Source,* Caelum repeats in his head. If Kal has orders from the Source, there's no way he'll back down. That is, if he's telling the truth.

"Half-souls are working to bring about humanity's downfall," Kal continues, lowering his voice. "I only know this because I heard it from the Source. Otherwise, even travelers like you and I would be unaware of the dark forces at play. Humanity is being tested like it hasn't been tested in ages. More pain and suffering are to come, and it will divide us further, unless we act." Kal pauses, his eyes darkening. "Without Estella and the other keys, we're all screwed."

"How do I know you're with the Source and not Cassius? Are you one of the travelers Athena mentioned, sent to help Estella, or are you a half-soul working with Alexander?"

"I told you, I'm on your side," Kal says, frustrated.

Caelum takes a step back, giving him a little slack, but it's only one step. "What do you know about these half-souls? Are there others besides Alexander and Cassius? Athena told me about their plan."

"There's a lot I don't know," Kal admits. "I was told I'd receive important information at the right time. But what I do know is that the more power the half-souls gain, the harder it will be to restore balance to the world. Estella has to complete the work she was sent here to do. I can't let anything, or anyone—" Kal narrows his eyes at Caelum. "—get in the way."

"How am I supposed to trust you? How do I know you're telling me the truth?" Caelum demands.

"I'll show you. Enter my dreams tonight, and you'll see. I'll take you back to the moment the Source gave me my orders."

There's silence as Caelum considers Kal's offer. Then Kal continues, "But I must admit, as I've been carrying out my orders—following Estella in her dreams and hiding in the shadows, waiting for the right time to step into her life—I've fallen for her. Still, the fight against the half-souls must take precedence over our feelings. You must let her choose. If you are each other's destiny, she'll choose you. If not, perhaps *I* am her destiny."

Kal, her destiny? The thought is an unwelcome guest in Caelum's head, and he pushes it out immediately. "*I'm* her destiny," Caelum insists. "I've seen it. Travel to find her in times past, and you'll see me by her side. Travel to the future, and I stand by her still." Caelum gets back up in Kal's face.

Kal doesn't budge. "Both you and I know very well that the future you've seen can change."

*Kal doesn't know anything about Estella and me,* Caelum thinks. But if Kal's telling the truth about the Source giving him orders, then the fight against the half-souls is bigger than all of them. A mix of dark emotions burns in Caelum's chest. He vowed he'd never let anything get between him and Estella ever again, but now this new threat looms over him like a storm. It feels as if everything is unraveling.

"We'll see," Caelum says. "But I'll take you up on your offer to meet tonight. See you in your dreams."

# Chapter 29

*Estella*

At Estella's first lesson after the show, Caelum praises her for the great job she did. Estella looks down, blushing at her lap. She's terrible at accepting compliments. When she finally returns her gaze to Caelum, she notices the tattoo peeking out from under the sleeve of his shirt. There it is again, whatever it is. During their lessons, she's been trying to figure out what's tattooed on him. She only ever sees a small portion of it whenever he wears a T-shirt.

As Caelum plays a rudiment on the snare, Estella tilts her head to try to get a better look at his tattoo—and almost falls out of her chair.

"You okay?" Caelum asks.

He noticed. How embarrassing! What the hell? She decides to just ask him about it.

"What's that?" Estella asks. And then she can't help herself; she touches him. The touch lasts maybe one second, but the feel of his skin rattles through her like a

California earthquake. He's wearing a black short-sleeve shirt that highlights his arms, with snappy little buttons down the front. He pulls up his sleeve as far as it will go, but to reveal the rest of his tattoo, he unsnaps the top buttons on his shirt, exposing his chest and the intricate ink that extends up his shoulder.

Words dry up and disappear in Estella's throat. He looks so good that she can't find her voice. If only he would wrap those arms around her, maybe all the bad in the world would just disappear.

Caelum's tattoo features many elements, including celestial symbols and what looks like a raptor. It's … familiar. He describes it in detail, but Estella is so consumed by her desire for him that she can't think straight. Distracted by the overpowering desire to touch him again, she struggles to absorb what he's saying. Still, she catches snippets about the sun, moon, and stars and our connection to humanity—being present in the moment with one another, without distractions.

The meaning behind the tattoo echoes in her mind, making it the sexiest thing she's ever seen. Its message is to cherish the moments they share and not let anything destroy that connection.

Trying her hardest to play it cool, Estella whispers, "It's nice." When Caelum buttons his shirt back up, it's like he's blowing out a candle in her heart. When he unbuttoned it to show her his tattoo, it felt so intimate, as if he were undressing for her. Now, all she can think about is ripping every single one of those snappy little buttons back open.

Estella asks Caelum if he was raised to be present in the moment, or if he was surrounded by distractions.

He tells her he had a relatively distraction-free childhood filled with music, reading, fishing, and family time.

"I spent a lot of time doing this," Caelum says, showcasing his skills on the drums.

He obliterates her. She falls back into her chair. Words couldn't escape her if her life depended on it. She clears her throat and tries to get it together. Estella doesn't tell Caelum how much she likes his tattoo and its meaning, because when he plays music for her, she forgets who she is.

When Caelum finishes the song, he looks at Estella, and she doesn't know what to say. Instead, she lets the silence settle, simply gazing into his eyes.

Caelum puts down his drumsticks, grabs her chair, and as if she weighs nothing, effortlessly pulls Estella close.

They sit in their chairs, legs intertwined. As they lean in, their faces move closer. They look into each other's eyes and then down to each other's lips, their eyes fixated on what they both want. Pulled in by mutual gravity, they crash into each other like they knew they would.

Caelum pulls Estella into him, kisses her harder, and she could swear the ground beneath her vanishes. She's stunned by the novelty of Caelum's kiss, but at the same time, there's a riveting familiarity to it. She pulls away, disoriented. Losing her balance, she tilts to one side like a listing ship, but pulls off a smooth recovery.

A quiet sob escapes Estella. At that moment, it hits her: she's kissing a man who isn't Lucas, and her husband is gone for good. Was Lucas supposed to be Estella's one true love, her soulmate? Now that he's gone, is it game over? Is that how it works, or is her mind simply fairy-tale-twisted?

Caelum backs away immediately and says cautiously, "I don't want to do anything you don't want."

But all Estella feels are the inches between them, and she can't stand the distance. Ignoring his words, she pulls him back in and kisses him like it's the last chance she'll ever get. There's no going back now. It's too late, and no matter how hard she tries, she won't be able to stay away from him—not after a kiss like this.

Caelum and Estella continue to kiss, teetering on the edges of their chairs. Their bodies move closer and closer as his hands, heavy and warm, glide over her legs, moving higher and higher up her thighs.

"I want you," Caelum murmurs, like he's drunk on her.

Estella pulls back just enough to look into his eyes, which articulate what he wants as clearly as his words. In them, she takes in every color, every detail, and all he's feeling. She brushes the stubble on his face and melts back into him, guiding his hands back to where they were headed. She is overwhelmed by her feelings, and it quickly becomes too much. Not only will she be unable to stay away from him, she'll probably end up falling in love with him. The thought stirs panic in her, igniting a desire to run.

Quickly gathering her things, she uses every ounce of her willpower to exit the room. They don't say anything; the intensity of the moment is written on their faces as Estella races out the door.

# Chapter 30

*Caelum*

Caelum is still buzzing from Estella's kiss as he slips into bed, anticipating the journey into Kal's dreams. Hours pass, his mind racing as he tries to come down from the high. When he finally surrenders to sleep, he closes his eyes to the world and opens them in Kal's dream.

He finds himself on a cozy couch, facing a familiar wall lined with guitars. Recognition hits him. He's back at the music shop.

"What's up, man?" Kal's voice cuts through the silence. Caelum turns to see him standing at the front register, in his usual spot, looking as he does on any workday.

"Why here, Kal?"

"It's as good a place as any," Kal replies, shrugging.

Kal leads Caelum down the hall to the lesson rooms, stopping at a door marked with the number eight—Caelum's room. But when Kal opens it, they're not in his lesson room at all. Instead, they step into a dark, frozen landscape, the air filled with a faint, eerie static.

What Caelum sees stuns him, despite all the other-worldly things he's encountered before. After a quick study of his surroundings, he notices a massive glowing orb dominating the sky, much larger than the moon ever appears from Earth. Above him, ribbons of vibrant light twist and ripple, an otherworldly dance across the sky. There are no signs of life. This world is barren.

"Awesome," Caelum whispers, captivated by the light show above.

"Yeah, those are the auroras of Ganymede," Kal says, his head tilted back, mouth slightly open as he watches the auroras shimmer.

*Huh.* Caelum had no idea. That large glowing orb must be Jupiter, then. He's passed by Jupiter before, but in all his travels, he's never thought to stop on the moon of Ganymede. The vastness of space and time continues to amaze him.

"I didn't know auroras occurred on Ganymede," Caelum says.

"They sure do," Kal says. "Ganymede's the only moon in our solar system with its own magnetic field. It's also the largest moon we've got."

"Why Ganymede?" Caelum asks. The Source could have spoken to him anywhere—any one of the vibrant, complex worlds beyond our solar system, or even on Earth. So, why here, on a desolate, lifeless moon?

"It's as good a meeting spot as any," Kal repeats. "Come, follow me."

They begin trekking across the frozen, barren ter-rain, heading in the direction of where Jupiter looms. The frigid ground is dimly illuminated by the giant planet's soft glow, casting shadows across the rugged landscape. In the distance, Caelum spots a figure kneeling, head tilted up toward Jupiter. He realizes it's Kal—a past vision of him. We're all visions, really.

"Great—two Kals, as if one isn't enough," Caelum jokes. As they approach, he spots another figure beside Kal. "Who's that?" he asks, moving closer. Then he notices the long blond hair and immediately recognizes who it belongs to. "Darin?" he says, baffled. "What's Darin doing here with you?"

Kal shrugs. "What else would he be doing here? Obviously, he's a traveler."

"No kidding! So, Darin's one of us. Where's Valentina, then?"

"Who?"

"Valentina. The other traveler sent to protect Estella."

Kal looks confused. "I don't know a Valentina."

"Athena told me about the travelers sent to protect Estella. I assumed it was just Valentina, and now you and Darin," Caelum says, trying to piece it together. "Valentina must have been given her orders at a different time," he reasons.

"Listen," Kal interrupts, his voice low.

They fall silent.

A voice unlike any other comes from above through the light of Jupiter. It isn't masculine or feminine, and it doesn't speak in any language. It's more of a sound that transcends words, reaching them like pure understanding. The information transferred from the Source to Kal and Darin is exactly as Kal had said. They're guardians of Estella, who is a key.

Kal reaches out in thought. *"Will I hear from you again?"* The Source affirms this. *"What will I learn?"* he inquires.

The Source gives nothing away and vanishes.

At one point or another, some are chosen to hear from the Source. Caelum hasn't had his own encounter yet, but witnessing Kal's communication with it stirs a newfound respect for him. He can't help but wonder, *When will the Source come to me? What will I learn?*

Caelum and Kal turn to look at each other, sharing a quiet moment—the kind that only happens after witnessing something profound.

Finally, Kal breaks the silence. "We cool now?"

Just like that, Caelum is pulled out of Ganymede and back into his bed, the weight of what he's seen sinking in. This changes everything. It means Kal will be a part of Estella's life, whether Caelum likes it or not. He doesn't have to like Kal, but he can't force him out of her world, either—not if he wants to stay in it himself. Interfering with the Source's plans could cost him his place beside Estella. And that's a risk Caelum isn't willing to take.

# Chapter 31

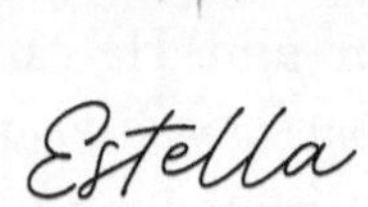

# Estella

Estella takes a tiny bite of her fried fish taco. The fish is hot, fresh, and perfectly crispy on the outside, while tender inside. The cabbage slaw is crisp, and the avocado crema adds just the right amount of tanginess. She places the taco back down beside the other two, still untouched on her plate.

Her daughters chat animatedly across from her, and though she tries to stay present, her mind keeps drifting. They're at their favorite spot in downtown Danville, surrounded by the lively lunchtime buzz they usually enjoy. The street taco trio is her go-to, but today, her heart just isn't in it.

"Mom, why are you so quiet?" Mina asks, pausing between sips of her horchata. "You're acting strange."

Perceptive and intuitive, just like Estella, her mini-me is quick to pick up on any change in her mood. *When will my daughters come into their powers?* she wonders.

She's tired of hiding magic from them. Maybe it's time they learn about the legacy that awaits them.

"Oh, it's nothing. I'm okay. Just tired," Estella says as an excuse. This is not good. Her intuitive child, her little witch-in-waiting, can sense something's off—and Estella knows exactly what it is. It's not her husband she's been thinking about, but Caelum. Guilt consumes her. Because of him, she's lost focus. Her daughters and her writing—that's what she needs to be focusing on right now, not Caelum.

In search of distractions later that afternoon, Estella spends hours working on her book while the kids play in the other room, darting in periodically to tattle on each other. Writing helps keep Caelum off her mind, so she's made good progress. But when she wraps up her writing session, Caelum seeps back into her thoughts, so she looks for the next distraction.

Gathering ingredients to bake a cake, Estella rummages through the kitchen cabinets and calls on her daughters to help her whip up some frosting. The precision baking demands keep her wandering thoughts in check.

Once they've prepared the vanilla frosting, Mina snatches a whisk covered in it from the hand blender. "I get to test-taste!" Mina teases, dashing into the other room with the frosting-covered whisk held high like a victory torch.

"No fair!" Kaitlin's voice echoes as she chases after Mina.

"Cool your jets, kids. There are two," Estella shouts after them, holding the other whisk in her hand. The girls hurry back into the room. Mina meticulously licks the frosting off her whisk while Kaitlin eagerly plucks the other one from Estella's hand. Quiet returns as Mina and Kaitlin savor every last bit of frosting from their whisks.

Kaitlin hands back a polished whisk and gives Estella a hug. Little Kaitlin is a hugger. Mina, on the other hand, shows Estella her affection by mimicking her. Mina's too big for mommy hugs, but Mom is cool enough to copy. Estella leans over to kiss the top of Kaitlin's head, catching a little whiff of shampoo fragrance in her curly ginger hair.

As Estella fills a bowl with flour, she thinks of Caelum. As she cracks eggs into the batter, she thinks of Caelum. As she stirs in sugar, she thinks of Caelum. So much for her distraction. Estella finds herself daydreaming about what it would be like to be with him—his hands gliding over her skin, their mouths pressed together, his arms wrapped around her, their bodies intertwined... Caelum hijacks Estella's mind like a powerful drug.

"Hey, Mama," Mina says. Worried that Mina can read her thoughts, Estella instantly wipes her mind clean of Caelum. "What are you thinking about? It looks like you're thinking a lot." Mina's intuitive abilities are so sharp that Estella wonders if she already has her magic.

"I'm thinking about Daddy."

Estella is officially an asshole.

It's time to tap the brakes a bit and maybe cancel a few drum lessons. Things with Caelum are getting hot and heavy too fast. Time will set Estella straight and give her some clarity and perspective. She'll take a break from music and work on finishing the first draft of her book. That will be best.

Alone in bed at night, Estella is faced with the time it's most difficult to keep Caelum off her mind. Eventually, she dozes off into a dream—and he shows up in it. While she tries to get Caelum out of her head during the day, he pushes his way into her dreams at night. She's losing this battle.

In her dream, Estella and Caelum are lounging in a living room when an earthquake hits. Though minor, it's strong enough to knock out the lights. The pitch black is more terrifying than the earthquake itself. Abruptly, the lights blaze back on, far brighter than before. The intense light emanates from everything, making the air around them turn wavy like heat rising off pavement.

A mysterious figure appears—a woman with brilliant red hair who looks ethereal, like a spirit. It's the woman from the forest. Why does Estella keep dreaming about this stranger?

They converse, but Estella only recalls fragments: *"your fears," "the enemy,"* and finally, *"your destiny."*

Behind stained-glass doors, another woman in a blood-red dress appears, her identity obscured. Estella never gets to see her clearly before the dream ends.

In the morning, Estella wakes feeling defeated for allowing Caelum to invade her dreams. She's also unsettled by the dream itself—another vivid one, like that forest dream, seeming random, yet deeply significant.

Estella knows she needs to snap back into reality, and taking a break from Caelum feels like the first step. With enough time, she's sure her sanity will return, and they can take things slow. She dials her mom, hoping for a for a step-by-step guide on forgetting someone, as if her mom is an all-powerful Wiki-like being with all the answers.

When Estella asks Hannah what she can do to get Caelum off her mind, Hannah replies, "Very simple: don't think about him." Not exactly the brilliant advice Estella was looking for. Hannah adds, "I don't like how much power he has over you. You were never that way with Lucas. You're getting carried away. It's not like you."

"I don't know how to explain it," Estella says. "It's Caelum's energy or something. I swear I manifested him."

Hannah sighs. "I know you worry about the girls, and you feel guilty because of Lucas. Don't. There's no reason to feel guilty. It's time for you to be happy. Lucas would want that for you. But that doesn't mean you shouldn't be careful with this guy. Cool it, get to know him, and maybe give that other guy you mentioned—Connor? Kal?—a chance, too."

"You're right, Mom. I should take a break from Caelum. Maybe even go on a date with Connor or Kal." They end up at the same conclusion Estella already came to, but hearing it from Hannah confirms that it's the best course of action. Mom always knows best.

"You know," Hannah teases, "I could whip up a spell to make you forget Caelum real quick. That is, if you want me to."

"Mom..." Estella warns.

"I'm just kidding." Hannah laughs, but there's a hint of something almost sinister in that laugh.

"Have you cast any spells on me that I should know about?" Estella asks, only half joking.

"Don't be silly. Now, I have to get going. We'll talk soon," Hannah says and hangs up.

Estella is left wondering if there might actually be some unknown spells Hannah has up her sleeve. At least for now, she's not thinking about Caelum.

Estella calls Diablo's Music and cancels her next lesson. She's determined to focus on writing, not music or Caelum. That means avoiding the coffee shop, staying home to write, and steering clear of the DVC, too. She can't risk running into him during her "Caelum detox."

# Chapter 32

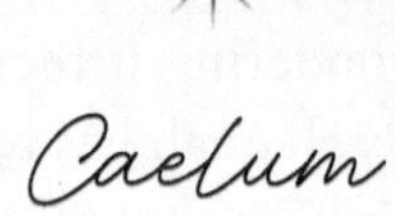

"Travel much?" Caelum asks, his voice low as he steps close behind Darin.

When Darin turns around, he finds Caelum right in his face. Startled, Darin takes a step back. "Oh, hey. I didn't see you come in," he says, surprised.

"I know," Caelum says, holding his gaze, making it clear he's not talking about simply entering Diablo's. "I *know*," he repeats.

"Know what?" Darin asks, brows furrowing.

"Do I have to spell it out for you?" Caelum glances around the empty music shop, then lowers his voice. "Been to the *other side* lately?" He keeps his eyebrows raised in question.

Darin's face breaks into a wide grin. He grips Caelum's shoulders. "You talked to Kal. Finally, brother," he says, letting go of him. "He told me about you chasing him down in one of his dreams." He chuckles. "It's good to have another traveler on our side. We travelers are like family. Kal tells me you know of another?"

"Valentina. You know her?" Caelum asks, watching him closely.

"No," Darin says, shaking his head. "But there's one more in our family you haven't met—Ryoko Hoshino."

The bell above the entrance chimes as a father and his young son walk in, the boy looking wide-eyed at the rows of guitars. Darin nods at them. "Looks like the kid's here for his first guitar," he murmurs to Caelum, then steps away to help.

Darin shows them a couple of beginner models and lets the boy try one out. As the kid clumsily strums, Darin returns and leans in close to speak quietly. "Be at Kal's tonight. Enter through the back gate bordering the trail. I'm heading out soon, so I'll see you there. We're meeting Ryoko."

The kid rakes his hand across the strings in rough, uncoordinated motions, and the guitar makes an ugly noise. Darin takes Caelum's hand and stuffs a folded piece of paper into it. Caelum opens it to see that it's Kal's address. He recognizes the street. From Caelum's house, Kal's place is a short bike ride down the Iron Horse Trail.

Later in the day, Caelum finally leaves the shop, grateful to head home. Estella canceled her lesson for some reason, so the hours he spent at the shop felt stretched. By dusk, he hops on his bike and follows the trail to Kal's house. Moonlight illuminates the path, and with autumn at its peak, it's littered with dry leaves. Foot traffic has died down to only a couple of other bikers and the occasional dog walker. As the night air sharpens, Caelum pulls his hoodie over his head and zips it up, pedaling faster to ward off the chill.

As Caelum cruises down the trail, he scans each house number, searching for Kal's place, until he realizes he must've passed it. He backtracks, and where Kal's house should be, he spots a wooden gate painted a faded pea green, blending in with the foliage around it. Pushing aside encroaching shrubbery, he finally sees Kal's house number. He tries the gate, and it creaks open.

As Caelum scopes out Kal's backyard, he drops his bike by the gate, where it lands with a clatter on the lawn. Past the overgrown grass and the pool, he can see straight through the sliding glass door into Kal's living room. The TV is on, but Kal isn't watching; instead, he's pacing back and forth. Caelum taps on the glass. Kal startles, then rushes over to slide open the door and let him in.

"Hey, you find the place okay?" Kal asks, dressed in a T-shirt, shorts, and flip-flops as though he's just come from the beach, even though it's not beach weather.

"Took some effort," Caelum replies, glancing around. "Do you ever do any trimming or mowing around here?"

Kal ignores the question, instead asking, "Want something to drink?"

"I'm okay, thanks," Caelum says, ready to get down to business.

"I have whiskey," Kal says, disappearing into the other room. He returns with Darin and a clear glass bottle filled to the brim with golden-amber liquid. Darin nods at Caelum in greeting while Kal hands him the bottle.

Caelum eyes it, admiring its contents like it's liquid sunshine. It's a bottle of Scotch single-malt whiskey—distilled in 1990. This is good stuff.

"Whiskey it is," Caelum says as he and Darin take a seat on Kal's couch.

Kal sets out glasses on the coffee table in front of them and pours a measure into each one. Darin raises his glass, saying, "Here's to new family." They clink glasses, and Caelum takes a sip. The whiskey slides down his throat in a spicy, toasty trail and settles into a warm feeling at his core.

"So, where's Ryoko?" Caelum asks.

"Oh, she's not here. She just got back from visiting family in Tokyo," Kal says.

"We're going on a dream trip tonight!" Darin says as he refills his already empty glass. With just a couple of sips between them, Caelum and Kal eye Darin warily. "What? I'm getting over another breakup," Darin uses as an excuse.

"I didn't know this was a sleepover," Caelum says and takes a bigger sip.

"She's not far. She's in Truckee, by Lake Tahoe, but she's jetlagged. So, we're meeting at her place in a dream tonight," Kal says.

"We camp out at one another's places quite a bit, so it'll be good for you to get acquainted with the cabin," Darin says. "I'm usually between Kal's and Ryoko's most of the time." The whiskey has turned his eyes glossy, giving their turquoise color a glow.

"Do you even have a place?" Kal asks.

Darin turns to Caelum and says, "He's just kidding. My house is two blocks from here, but I'm never there, especially now that I'm single again." He flicks his hair back over his shoulder, pours Caelum a refill, and says, "Drink up, partner."

As the whiskey makes its way through Caelum's bloodstream, they trade stories of past lives and travels. They have more in common than Caelum thought, and Kal almost grows on him … almost.

As the clock ticks, the whiskey disappears. With a bottle of whiskey under their belts, consciousness escapes Caelum for a moment. There's a new weight to his eyelids, and he works harder to keep them open.

When he does manage to open his eyes, they're greeted by pandemonium. He's floating amidst supersonic winds.

"We're on Neptune!" Kal yells over the howling wind.

"What's with you and the boonies of our solar system? Can we skip the detour and get where we're going?" Caelum yells back. This is going too far.

"Just keeping you on your toes." Kal spreads his arms wide and continues inspirationally, "We can do anything and go anywhere we want in our dreams."

Distracted by the chaos around them, Darin stares with his mouth slightly open, but no words come out. His glossy eyes dart in every direction.

"Next time, I'm taking the lead," Caelum yells.

"Come on!" Kal shouts. "Let's descend to the core and find a door."

They fall through violent storms in complete darkness, lit only by brief bursts of lightning. The flashes give way to diamond rain until they reach a kind of surface.

"That was rad!" Darin exclaims.

"Gnarly, right? See, I know what I'm doing. There's nothing wrong with having a little fun along the way," Kal says.

On the core of this ice giant, Neptune, Kal opens a door that isn't visible. Doors come in all shapes, sizes, colors, and transparencies. You have to be a seasoned traveler to know where the invisible ones are hidden.

"That's the last time I let you take me anywhere," Caelum tells Kal. He smooths his hair into place, even though it's perfectly untangled and intact. The sheer force of the cosmic nether region throws Caelum for a loop, and he forgets he's in untouchable dream form. He wouldn't have chosen to feel that madness.

The door opens to a dimly lit, cozy cabin. The floor-to-ceiling chalet-style windows are black, blending seamlessly with the night sky, unpolluted by artificial light. The dark, empty canvas makes Caelum wonder what view is painted on it by day. A gentle fire crackles in a steampunk-style fireplace in the corner. The cabin is awash in shades of orange: a rust velvet couch, a raw wood table with a vase full of orange flowers, an orange tea kettle on the stove, and a fuzzy orange cardigan draped over a chair.

Unsure of how to proceed, Caelum whispers, "What should we do? I feel like we're trespassing."

"She has to be here somewhere," Kal says and calls, "Ryoko!"

"There's a light coming from the bedroom," Darin says.

Down the hallway, there are two adjacent rooms at the end, one lit and the other dark.

"Ryoko," Kal calls out again. Nothing. "She knows we're coming, so..." He treads lightly down the hallway towards the room. Caelum and Darin follow behind him.

"Ryoko," Kal says louder as they approach. "I've got Darin and Caelum with me. I hope you're decent."

They reach the door, and the room is empty.

"Hey!" someone yells from behind them, and Darin shrieks. Caelum's heart pounds in his chest. They turn around to see a woman standing in the doorway of the dark room. She erupts into laughter. "Decent," she says through her chuckles. "Hardly," she adds. "The look on your faces..." She sighs. She has a baby face and electric-blue hair, black at the roots and styled in a bob.

"Always a joker," Kal says. "This is my friend, Caelum."

A *friend* of Kal's? That sounds so unnatural, Caelum thinks.

"He's the traveler I told you about," Kal adds.

"Follow me," Ryoko says. She marches down the hallway, picks up the fuzzy orange cardigan, and swoops it over her shoulders. "Tea?" she asks.

"Yeah, I'll have some," Darin pipes up. "What kind do you have?" he asks, then adds, "Can you put some whiskey in it?"

"Let me guess: orange spice," Kal says.

"You know me," Ryoko replies, putting the orange kettle on the stove. "Have a seat, guys."

Caelum and Darin sit on the rust-colored velvet couch while Kal lingers by the stove, chatting with Ryoko. The cabin looks warm and inviting, so Caelum chooses to feel the scene. His corner of the couch is heated by the fireplace, and when he runs his hand over the soft fabric, it's warm. He reclines onto the cushions and sinks into the atmosphere. Darin talks about his love life problems, and Caelum doesn't say a word, simply listening, until they're interrupted by the whistle of the tea kettle.

Ryoko and Kal return to the room with tea. As Kal sets the tea on the table, Ryoko plops down next to Caelum. He bounces slightly from the force of her landing.

"So, Kal filled me in on your story. Darin, Kal, and I were sent here to help Estella. You're here to…" she says, sliding Caelum's tea in front of him with a soft clink.

"Stalk her," Kal interjects.

Ryoko snorts and laughs.

"I wouldn't put it that way," Caelum says, shaking his head.

"I have just the perfect thing," Ryoko says, jumping off the couch. She makes her way over to the crate of records next to the record player beside the couch and flips through the collection. She dusts off the record with the sleeve of her fuzzy orange cardigan before putting it onto the player. As the needle drops, the haunting melody of "Creep" by Radiohead fills the room, its eerie, obsessive tone lingering in the air. Everyone laughs but Caelum.

"I'm so glad you guys are entertained," Caelum says sarcastically, crossing his arms over his chest.

"Oh, I'm just messing with you," Ryoko says playfully. When she returns to the couch, Caelum bounces from her force again. "So, you know another traveler, Valentina? What's her mission?"

"Same as ours, I guess," Caelum says.

"Wonder why Athena didn't tell us about her," Ryoko says. "Maybe she's new. But speaking of Athena, tell me about your last meeting with her."

"She told me that you guys are travelers sent to ensure that Estella fulfills her purpose," Caelum says. "Athena also said Alexander is alive, and she was about to reveal his identity just before I woke up."

"The same thing happened to me," Ryoko says. "Athena was going to give me the four-one-one on Alexander, but then my dream was interrupted, and then she just vanished into another life. Don't you guys find that strange?"

They all agree that there could be more to it, but don't want to jump to conclusions.

"Athena told me something else the last time I saw her," Ryoko adds, staring directly at Caelum without finishing her thought.

"Well, what is it?" Caelum prods.

"Alexander is lurking around Estella," she says, drawing it out for dramatic effect. She then adds, "And … it's possible that Cassius is alive, too. Athena believes he borrowed someone."

"I thought only the Source could do that—you know, possess a person," Kal says.

"That's what I said," Ryoko says, "but Athena thinks Cassius has somehow gained the ability."

"Shit," Caelum mutters. "He could be anyone, then."

Souls move from one life to the next, but they retain a similar appearance. Estella doesn't look exactly like she did in her prior life, but she looks similar. That goes for everyone. Caelum may have some difficulty recognizing Alexander, but he'll find him if he looks hard enough. But Cassius… If he snatched a body, there's no telling who he could be.

"So, we need to get to work," Kal says. "We should split up. Darin and I will stand guard. We'll make sure

Alexander doesn't get to Estella. Caelum, you and Ryoko track down Valentina and see what else she knows."

"Good idea," Ryoko says, locking her arm around Caelum's and theatrically batting her eyelashes at him. "Now, take a sip of my orange spice tea. It's getting cold."

# Chapter 33

Connor pulls up to Estella's place in a black Tesla. She's going on this date as a distraction, a way to take her mind off Caelum. That, and she sort of agreed to it when she ran into Connor at the coffee shop a while back.

Estella fumbles with the untraditional door handle, unsure of how to open it. Connor quickly gets out and comes around to help, his expression serious. He's wearing aviator sunglasses and a pair of brand-new hiking boots. Estella has her own hiking boots on, too, but they're beat up in comparison. She hasn't hiked Mount Diablo yet, but she's no stranger to the local trails.

"I packed some sandwiches and water bottles," Estella says and pats her backpack to indicate where the goods are hidden.

Connor takes a thorough look at her and fixates on her hands, now grasping the backpack like a child cradling a teddy bear. "Nice nails," he says, eyeing her shiny black manicure, which matches his Tesla, gleaming as if freshly waxed. "I'll take that," he adds, grabbing Estella's backpack and tossing it into the back seat. With her buffer confiscated, she feels exposed; there's something about him today that makes her feel oddly vulnerable. He seems more serious than usual.

"Thanks, it's for Halloween," Estella says, glancing down at her nails. After their hike, she'll be prepping for an evening of fun with her daughters and a few friends. The pre-trick-or-treat party is at their house. Halloween spells witchy season. She'll put on one of her various witchy dresses, and this year, her daughters will join her. She isn't ready for the "magic talk" with them just yet, but when the time comes, they'll have an official coven.

"Let me guess: you'll be a witch," Connor says.

"How did you know?"

"Just a guess."

It's a good guess; black nail polish could go with almost any Halloween costume. But the way he said "witch," like it's an insult, gets under her skin. She had decided to give Connor a chance, to get to know him better, but now she's already second-guessing this day of hiking they've planned. A quick lunch date would have made for an easier escape.

They set out on the drive through Danville toward the mountain, passing rolling hills dotted with oak trees. Connor stays silent as they wind up the road to Mount Diablo. Finally, he breaks the silence. "Do you like classical music?"

"Sure," Estella says.

He rolls his thumb over the volume knob on his steering wheel, and the music that had quietly played in the background moves its way to the forefront. Its heaviness fills the car's cabin like a thick fog. The rather large display screen between them reads, *Totentanz – Liszt.* The music begins dark and foreboding, then shifts to a maddeningly whimsical piano. Estella can't help but chuckle. It's the kind of music she'd picture in a movie right before a character's demise—not exactly date music.

"You don't like Franz Liszt?" Connor asks. "I thought you would. He was a Hungarian virtuoso pianist and composer, one of the best." His tone is slightly reprimanding, making Estella feel almost childlike. She considers reaching for her backpack, maybe pulling out her phone as a lifeline.

"No, I mean, I do," she says. "It just feels a bit gloomy for the occasion."

As the song continues, it turns soft and melancholy.

"*Totentanz,*" Connor says. He has a chokehold on the steering wheel as he looks intently at the road in front of him. It's for good reason; the road up to the summit is barrierless and bordered by steep drops. "It means 'dance of death' in German."

A group of cyclists suddenly whizzes past, and she startles. She's uneasy, unsure of whether it's Connor, the dark music, the treacherous drive, the cyclists buzzing past, or all of it.

They come to a stop at the Mount Diablo State Park entrance, and Estella asks, "Is everything all right? I mean, are you okay?"

He hands money to the attendant at the gate and turns to Estella. "Yeah, I'm good," he says. He takes off his aviators, revealing blue eyes that are soft and apologetic. The air of seriousness he had carried up the mountain with him dissipates. "I'm sorry. Maybe I was trying too hard to impress you with my knowledge of Hungarian composers. And I can get this way on All Hallows' Eve, remembering the dead and all," he says, turning his attention back to the road.

Past the gate, the two-way road up to the summit stretches on for miles, growing even more winding. They twist and turn their way higher until they finally reach a large structure that resembles a lighthouse.

"The Summit Building," Connor announces.

They park in the lot at the front of the building and climb the steps to the viewing platform. The 360-degree views stretch for miles in every direction. The air is cool, but the sky is clear, except for a few long, flat clouds drifting like ribbons across the horizon. They stand in quiet awe, taking in the vastness. The only sounds are the wind and the call of a hawk gliding overhead.

"I like coming here during the week, when there aren't that many people," Connor says. Aside from a couple of hikers eating sandwiches at the entrance when they arrived, the place is empty.

"See that rock?" Connor says, pointing into the distance. A large rock stands out against the vista, not far from the platform. "It's a short hike, and the views are great from there. Follow me," he says.

They descend the Summit Building's stairs, retracing their steps back to the entrance. Connor climbs over the railing bordering the parking lot, and Estella follows, navigating down some steep terrain covered in loose rocks. She moves slowly, using her hands to steady herself against the large boulders lining the trail. As they near the giant rock formation, the ground flattens. Beyond it, steep drops lead to a breathtaking view that stretches to the horizon.

"It's tarantula mating season, so maybe we'll get lucky and spot one," Connor says, his tone brightening with the most enthusiasm he's shown all day.

"It's what?" Estella scans the ground around her.

"Mount Diablo is a mecca for tarantulas," Connor says, as though this is something good.

"What?!" Estella shrieks, bolting to his side.

He laughs and says, "Don't worry. They're harmless."

"Are you serious?" She's sure he must be joking; he's just trying to spook her because it's Halloween.

"Yes, I'm serious. Mount Diablo is covered in tarantulas, but they're harmless. No one's ever died from a tarantula bite. Well, almost no one."

"I don't believe you."

"Okay, don't believe me," Connor says, shrugging his shoulders. He looks just past Estella's feet and says, "Oh, there's one!"

She shrieks again and takes off, running back towards the Summit Building. He chases after her and then tries to regain his breath between laughs. Tarantulas and Estella's fear have apparently brightened his disposition.

They make their way back to the rock and settle near a bluff to take pictures. Estella pulls her phone from her backpack, snapping a few shots while Connor hovers close to her. In need of some elbow room, Estella shifts closer to the edge of the ridge.

"I wouldn't want you to fall," Connor says, his voice flat.

They exchange a lingering gaze, and Estella senses a shift in him. He seems to have regressed into a sullen mood.

"I'll be careful," she says, taking a few more photos before tucking her phone away. "Are you doing anything for Halloween?"

"I'm lighting candles for the dead." He looks at her again, but this time, there's a flash of something in his expression that wasn't there before. It's hard to place, but it feels cold.

"No Halloween parties?"

"I don't like parties," he says in a dusky voice, and then she sees it on his face again. It's fleeting, but clear as the sky they're under: contempt. She can see it in the corners of his mouth. She moves away from him, but he draws closer.

"Are you okay?" he asks.

"Yeah, I'm fine. I just got dizzy for a second. It's the heights, I guess." They both look into the distance again. "It's like you said at the coffee shop—you can see into eternity from up here," Estella says.

"To the other side," he says, approaching her again, this time crowding her against the ledge.

"The other side of wha—"

She loses her footing, and he grabs her arm. Her backpack, which was loosely strung over one shoulder, tumbles to the ground. The only thing preventing her from plummeting off Mount Diablo is Connor's grip. As Estella dangles on the ledge, expecting Connor to pull her to safety, more time passes than she's comfortable with.

Wondering what the holdup is, she gazes into Connor's face for answers—and who she sees doesn't look like Connor at all. The contempt in his expression has deepened, no longer lingering at the corners of his mouth, but spreading like a sickness across his face. The look in his eyes terrifies her more than the prospect of certain death should he loosen his grip. Are his eyes filled with terror because of the situation, or is there some other more sinister reason? She can't tell anymore.

Estella's head buzzes, and her eyes cloud over in black. She's hit with a vision. The faceless man appears in rapid, disjointed flashes, like quick cuts in a film. Estella sees Connor, then the faceless man, the images alternating with each passing moment. She can no longer distinguish what's real and what's vision. Is reality interrupting her vision, or is Connor the faceless man?

A hand grabs her other arm. "I've got her," says a familiar voice.

It's Kal—and Darin is with him.

"What are you guys doing here?" Estella asks, her relief palpable.

"You dropped this," Darin says, picking up her backpack, dusting it off, and handing it to her. She hugs it against her chest tightly.

"We hike up here all the time," Kal says, his gaze narrowing as he eyes Connor.

"Small world," Connor mutters.

"Is everything okay here?" Kal asks, his tone shifting as he focuses on Connor. Darin steps up beside him, both now standing in solidarity, their eyes locked on Connor. The way they stand together, like a pair of guardians, reminds Estella of the stone lions guarding the Chain Bridge over the Danube River in Budapest.

"Yeah, everything's fine," Estella says. "I just lost my footing."

An awkward silence ensues as the men assess each other.

"Kal, Darin, this is Connor," Estella says.

The men exchange less-than-warm greetings.

"Do you mind if we join you guys?" Kal asks, and Estella hurriedly responds, "Please do."

Just then, Connor's phone rings. "If you'll excuse me," he says and disappears down the trail.

When he returns, he tells them he has to go. "Something came up," he says, looking at Estella in anticipation, as if he's expecting her to leave with him.

"That's okay," Estella assures him. Really, it's more than okay. She doesn't want to be left alone in his presence for another moment. "I can ride back with Darin and Kal."

"If that's what you want," Connor says, frustration and an undertone of anger woven through his words.

The four of them hike back to Connor's car, and as he drives off, Connor peels out of the parking lot, leaving a cloud of dust in his wake.

"What's with that dude?" Darin asks.

"I don't know," Estella says, shaking her head. "He seemed all right at first, but today … he gave me the creeps."

Connor is zero for two in the date department, and after today, Estella has no plans to let him try for a third.

# Chapter 34

✳

## *Caelum*

Caelum, Darin, and Ryoko are getting waterlogged in Kal's pool, which is heated to an inviting eighty-five degrees, making the thought of stepping into the cold November air the last thing they want to do. Light spills from the sliding glass door of Kal's house, mixing with the soft, colorful LED pool balls floating in the water.

Caelum swims over to the shallow end, where Ryoko and Darin are hanging out, deep in conversation about Ryoko's latest project. She's been writing code and creating different phone apps as a hobby, and her excitement is contagious as she explains her newest idea.

"Another one?" Darin asks, leaning an elbow on the edge of the pool. His slim torso forms an exaggerated curve as he takes a sip of his IPA. "Isn't there an app for everything already?"

"Probably, but so what? That's never stopped me. Now, get this…" Ryoko says, grabbing the red pool ball light. She holds it under her chin like a camper using a flashlight to tell a scary story, casting diabolical shadows on her face. "An app that will predict when and how you die." She laughs maniacally, and Caelum splashes her. A water fight erupts between them.

Darin watches coolly while sipping his beer. Ryoko and Caelum have fallen into this playful kind of friendship, constantly picking on each other, but always in good fun. It seems to have started the day Kal called Caelum a stalker, and Ryoko teased him for it—pretty much the moment they met.

Caelum and Ryoko are dripping wet when they call a truce. She pouts, "I didn't want to get my hair wet, you century-hopping, dream-lurking snake in the grass."

Caelum splashes her again, and just like that, the water fight picks up right where it left off.

"All right, children," Darin says, just as the door to the house slides open. Kal barrels out toward the pool, his long hair, usually tied back, loose and trailing behind him. "Cannonball!" he yells, plunging into the deep end. The pool ball lights toss their colors around as they slosh in the waves. Kal disappears under the water, then reemerges with a big gasp of air.

"Your hair has gotten long," Ryoko tells him, watching as the bottom half of his hair, submerged in the water, fans out in every direction, creating the illusion that he's floating in a dark cloud.

"I've been meaning to cut it," he says.

"Don't," Ryoko says. "Your hair is godlike. It's like your superpower."

"One of them." Kal chuckles. He pulls his hair into a bunch, twisting it behind his head to show how he'd look with short hair. "Will you cut it for me?"

"I don't even know who you are right now," Ryoko says. "I absolutely will not cut it."

"Oh, come on. Why not?"

"First, because I like the way it is, and second, I don't cut hair. Ask me to hack into a mainframe, and I'll gladly do it, but trust me, you don't want me cutting your hair," Ryoko says.

With Ryoko a no-go, Kal eyes Caelum and Darin.

"Don't look at me," Darin says.

"Don't you have a place you get it cut?" Caelum asks.

"Not really. I don't get it cut often, and the last few times, my mom cut it. She left her shears. We can use those."

"Okay, but don't get pissed if you don't like the results." Caelum doesn't tell Kal he knows how to cut hair. Caelum's aunt, Vittoria, tried to cut his uncle Tommaso's hair once, and it was so bad he had to shave his head. Caelum cut Tommaso's hair after that. It turns out he's pretty good at cutting hair.

After everyone gets out of the pool, they disperse into different rooms to shower and get dressed. It seems that Ryoko and Darin keep a complete wardrobe at Kal's, and since Kal and Caelum are about the same size, Kal lets Caelum borrow some of his clothes. He hands Caelum a pair of gray sweatpants with a matching zip-up hoodie and a faded T-shirt with *Aloha* on it. Kal then goes looking for his mom's haircutting shears while the rest of them gather in the kitchen to prepare some refreshments.

Kal shows up with a towel draped over his shoulders, brandishing the shears. "Grab the snacks and follow me," he says. They end up in his multi-car garage, which is spacious, nicely finished, and has a shiny epoxy floor. Not all spaces are used for parking cars; one of the side stalls is set up as a chill spot. In one corner, there's a table with a computer and a few wood-carved art pieces with elaborate, ornate designs. The area also includes a weight bench that looks straight out of the eighties, a TV mounted to the wall, and a smaller table with additional chairs.

"Those are cool. They look like Viking carvings," Caelum says, pointing to the art pieces. Kal's home is scattered with what look like wood carvings from his Hawaiian and Norwegian ancestors—totem poles, face masks, ships, and other items.

"They are. My mom brought these back from her last trip to Norway." He hands Caelum one of the carvings. It's solid wood and feels heavy in Caelum's hands. He runs his fingers over the countless grooves, tracing what looks like a canoe or ship. One end is carved into a serpent with its tongue out, and the other end into its tail.

Kal grabs the chair from the desk with the computer as Darin and Ryoko settle into the other chairs.

"Do you have a comb?" Caelum asks, and Kal pulls one from his back pocket.

"Let's do this," Kal says, sitting down.

"What am I doing here? A couple of inches?" Caelum asks.

"Let's go chin-length."

"No, not your beautiful hair!" Ryoko says, exaggerating a frown.

"Chin-length it is," Caelum replies.

As Caelum combs Kal's still-damp hair into sections, Darin and Ryoko start talking about music. Darin comes to life, going on about some band Caelum's never heard of. Caelum knows Darin's excited because he catches glimpses of his hair bouncing as he moves around, playing air drums and making all kinds of sounds to voice his drum solo. Caelum stays focused while cutting Kal's hair.

"So, while we were keeping an eye on Estella, there was an incident," Kal says.

Caelum stops. "What do you mean by 'incident'?" he asks.

"We had to intervene," Kal adds.

"She was with some tool," Darin says through a mouthful of chips.

"Can you get on with the haircutting? We're going to be here all night," Kal says.

"Okay, okay, but someone tell me what happened, already."

"So, we tracked Estella up Mount Diablo," Darin says, and Caelum makes the first snip. *Krrr...* Caelum loves the sound scissors make when cutting hair. "She went hiking with this guy," Darin continues. *Krrr...* "I guess it was a date."

Caelum stops again. "What do you mean, a date?" he demands, his voice rising. "Who is he?" The heat within him leaves his extremities and goes into his core. His hands are no longer steady. He puts the scissors down.

"Why'd you stop?" Kal asks. On one side in the front, his hair is short, and the rest is long. He looks ridiculous and lopsided, but Caelum is too angry to laugh.

"I need a minute, and you need to tell me about this guy." Caelum starts pacing. "Hand me one of those beers," he says, and Darin grabs one for him.

"Relax," Kal says. "She said his name's Connor, and she doesn't want to see him again."

Caelum takes a substantial sip of beer. After a couple more gulps, he picks up the scissors.

"You good, bro?" Kal asks.

Caelum takes a deep breath. "Tell me more," he says as he works the comb through Kal's hair. *Krrr... Krrr...*

"They were hiking Mount Diablo, and they got close to a ledge at the summit," Darin says.

"Estella stumbled. She was too close. It was too dangerous, so we had to intervene," Kal says.

"Okay, I'm going to need another minute." Caelum puts the scissors back down, and Kal sighs loudly. "How could you guys let her get into that position in the first place?" Caelum demands.

"She's okay, isn't she?" Ryoko says, her voice tinged with hesitation, as if trying to convince herself as much as Caelum.

After polishing off his beer and a few more minutes of fuming, Caelum resumes working on Kal's hair. *Krrr... Krrr...* Caelum can't believe Estella would go on a date with some jackass after their time together.

"Something was off about that guy, though," Kal says. "I didn't get the feeling he was trying to help her." He pauses for a moment. "To keep her from falling off the ledge, I mean."

"What?! That's it." Caelum tosses the scissors on the table. "Who the fuck is this guy?"

"Careful with those," Kal says. He picks up the scissors, inspects them, and snips at the air a few times to make sure they're intact.

"He's right," Darin says. "We need to keep an eye on that guy and find out more about him."

"So, let's agree to look after him," Kal says. "Now, do you two have any updates from Valentina?" he asks Caelum and Ryoko.

"We tried to track her down, but had no luck," says Ryoko.

"I'm thinking we go the dream route. Are you guys up for a trip tonight?" Caelum asks.

"I'm in," says Kal, and everyone nods their approval. "Now, can we get back to my hair?"

Caelum cleans up the cut with a few more snips. "What do you guys think of my work?" Caelum asks, looking at Darin and Ryoko in anticipation.

"Looks good, dude," says Darin, playing air drums and barely glancing at Kal's hair.

"Less godlike, but pretty dang good," Ryoko says. She licks her finger, places it on her hip, and says, *"Ssst!"*

Kal's smiling like a fool. "Whoa. It's so short!" he says, running his hands through his hair. "Do you think Estella will like it?"

With that, Caelum makes one more snip in the back. *Krrr.* This one breaks the clean line.

Later in the evening, the crew opts to watch a movie in the living room and pulls out the sofa bed instead of retreating to the guest rooms. Darin and Ryoko take up the sofa bed. Caelum stretches out on Kal's rock-hard couch, while Kal sits in his recliner, resting his glass of whiskey on his stomach.

"Let's see what's on streaming," Kal says, pointing the remote at the large flat-screen TV mounted to the wall. Movie titles whirl across the screen.

"Ooh! *Bram Stoker's Dracula*! One of my favorites," Ryoko says.

"Gary Oldman does a great Dracula," Caelum adds.

"I just want to watch Keanu Reeves," Ryoko says.

"Same," Darin says.

"How about *Contact*? Any Carl Sagan fans in here?" Kal asks.

Given his fascination with the cosmos, his choice isn't surprising. Caelum likes the movie, too, but doesn't add anything to the conversation, leaving it up to the others.

Ryoko and Darin chant "Keanu, Keanu!", and they get the winning vote based purely on enthusiasm.

Towards the end of the movie, Kal falls asleep, and one by one, the others follow. Caelum is the last to cross into a dream.

"Took you long enough," Ryoko says, tapping her foot.

"It's not my fault. Blame it on Kal's couch. It's not what I'd call comfortable," Caelum grumbles.

"Don't talk trash about the couch. It was a screaming deal," Kal says.

"That makes sense."

Location-wise, they're in the present at Kal's, but in the dream world. It's the meeting point they previously agreed upon.

"We're waiting on your direction, given Valentina is your contact," Kal says. "Unless you'd like me to take the lead. There's this interesting cluster of stars I've been meaning to check out…"

"That's quite all right. I've got this one," Caelum says. Is that what Kal does every night while he's sleeping—float around the cosmos like the *Battlestar Galactica*? "We can get to the point and step into Valentina's dreams, or make an interesting pit stop. The last time I went looking for her, she found me at her upcoming speaking engagement in New York. She auctions off an insanely expensive book, and I think you guys need to see it."

This time, there's no detour through Central Park. They arrive in the Colonel's Room, and the auction is already underway.

"Regal," Ryoko says, glancing around the room.

"That's Valentina," Caelum says, motioning to the woman standing behind the microphone.

"Wow. She's beautiful. I'd kill for those cheekbones," Ryoko says.

"That ancient-looking thing she's holding… Is that the insanely expensive book you were talking about?" asks Kal.

"Yeah. It's called *The Book of Origin and Fate*." The others exchange glances, but none of them have heard of it. "I guess this could be nothing, but something about this scene struck me as significant. I thought you guys might know something about this book."

"One million dollars!" yells a man in the back.

"One *million* dollars?!" Darin yells even louder. "Are you kidding?"

Everyone turns to look at the winning bidder.

"Connor!" Kal says, his voice sharp. "That's that dirtbag, Connor!"

"Who's Connor?" says a newly arrived version of Valentina. Her façade is perfect, not a hint of emotion to betray anything. Either she really doesn't know Connor, or she's that good.

"Valentina, you found me here again," says Caelum.

"You brought friends," she says.

Caelum twists his head, trying to get a glimpse of Connor through the crowd, but it's impossible. He wants to see the man Estella chose to go on a date with after their kiss. Darin, Kal, and Ryoko have already drifted over to him.

"How do you know Connor?" Caelum spits out.

A flicker of fear dances in Valentina's eyes as she meets his gaze. "I … I don't," she says, her voice barely a whisper. "I told you, I have no idea who that guy is." She draws her arms close to her body, suddenly small and vulnerable, like a meek bird at Caelum's feet. She drops her head, dark hair falling forward to shield her face. After a moment, she lifts her chin and meets Caelum's eyes again. Her eyes, their usual icy blue, have turned into gentle pools of water. "I swear," she says, "I'm here to help Estella with her book. Go look in the future, and you'll see that."

The sincerity in her tone is almost irresistible, and for a moment, Caelum wonders if she's cast a spell on him. He turns away, trying to shake the effect, and his eyes land on Kal. The crowd has thinned out, and Caelum sees Kal swiping his fist at Connor. Of course, his fist passes straight through the future hologram of Connor, but he keeps swinging anyway.

"So, who's Connor?" Valentina asks.

"He's a suspect," Caelum says. "At best, he's a douche-bag. At worst, he's a half-soul, Alexander, or even Cassius."

The group returns, and they descend upon Valenti-na, interrogating her about Connor. She makes them weak, like she did Caelum, and Ryoko even gives her a hug. Valentina tells them the same story she gave Caelum about her mission, Athena, and the Source. After

Valentina's story checks out, Caelum introduces her to the family.

"There's something about that book you auctioned off. What do you know about it?" Caelum asks.

"Nothing, really. I know it's old. It's just a job I was hired to do."

"Where does a guy like Connor get a million dollars to spend on a book?" Darin asks, rubbing his stubbled chin.

"That's what we're going to find out," Kal says.

# Chapter 35

Estella is stepping out of her solitary retreat to meet Kal for coffee this morning. After the disastrous date with Connor, she's been tucked away at home, working on her book, though little writing has happened. Instead, she's been spiraling into self-doubt. The encounter on Mount Diablo has shaken her self-esteem, and she hasn't fully recovered.

Before that day, Estella had begun to feel strong for the first time since Lucas's passing. She felt in control, determined not to let herself get swept up in Caelum, or let her emotions run wild. She planned to make thoughtful, practical decisions—the kind she used to make when Lucas was alive. But realizing how wrong she was about Connor has left her questioning her own judgment.

Estella thought she had Connor figured out. He seemed like a decent guy, but now she realizes she doesn't know him at all. Intuition is supposed to be one of her greatest strengths; she's a witch, after all, with the gift of vision—or so she thought. But Connor has made her doubt her powers. Was he just in a mood, or was there something darker beneath the surface? She felt it in his face, his eyes, his voice, the grip of his hand. Whatever it was, it left her feeling uneasy around him. There was a hint of something that made her feel unsafe, but it was so subtle that she wonders if she was losing her mind.

When Estella enters the coffee shop, she scans the room and realizes she's arrived before Kal. With few open tables left, she decides to get in line to order before they fill up. The man in front of her teeters on his flip-flops, his hands stuffed into the pockets of his jeans. This deep into November, even in California, Estella wouldn't be caught dead in flip-flops; her toes go numb in anything below sixty-five degrees, and it's definitely in the fifties today. Her gaze drifts from his flip-flops to her own feet, toasty in fleece-lined booties.

"Medium coffee, oat milk, one packet of raw sugar," the man in the flip-flops says. Kal's subtle surfer accent rides on the words.

"Kal?"

"Oh, hey, I didn't see you come in," he says.

"You cut your hair! I was standing right behind you and didn't even recognize you."

"You like it?" he asks, tucking his dark, lush, chin-length hair behind his ears. When he does this, Estella notices the few strands of silver, mostly at his temples.

"I love it," she says.

Estella places her order, and they wait for their coffees at the counter where she first met Caelum. It's as if a hologram of him stands there, looking just as he did the first time she laid eyes on him. His ghost haunts her. It doesn't matter that she hasn't seen him in weeks, or that Kal looks like a snack standing before her. Caelum's hold on her is stubbornly strong—which is precisely why she must push him out of her mind.

Kal and Estella settle at a table, and she turns her attention to him as they talk about their holiday plans. It's a difficult time of year for Estella and the girls—Christmas without Lucas. She mentions that she and her daughters are heading to Seattle to spend Thanksgiving with her family, though she's still uncertain about Christmas. Kal tells her how his parents host a Christmas gathering every year, going into detail about the familiar traditions and warmth of the party. He invites her to join, and she promises to think about it.

"Have you been writing?" he asks.

"I'm trying to, but I keep getting distracted. Maybe this is what they mean by writer's block … or maybe I just don't know how the story's supposed to end."

"That's okay. You'll figure it out as you go. Just keep at it, and before you know it, you'll have your story. I'm sure of it." His words are encouraging, but it's the way he says them that makes Estella believe him. He sounds so certain, as if he's seen the future and come back to reassure her.

"You're right, Kal. I've been overthinking it. I need to get out of my own head. Sometimes, I'm my own worst enemy."

"Go have fun in Seattle with your family," he says. "Take a break from everything. Don't even think about writing on your trip. And when you come back, I bet the words spill right out of you." He places his large, warm hands on Estella's, and the comfort of his touch makes her believe that maybe, just maybe, he's right.

Upon returning from Thanksgiving in Seattle, Estella locks herself back into a prison of overthinking, trying to make sense of the major changes in her life. She eventually comes to a clear conclusion: her job at the firm was never meant to keep her. Her true purpose has always been to tell a story when the time was right, when she had what she needed—and now, that time has come. And so, Estella writes. The floodgates open, and the words spill out, just as Kal said they would.

Missed calls from Caelum, Kal, Connor, and family pile up as the words—sentences, paragraphs, pages— keep pouring out of Estella. Pictures of Caelum still flash through her mind like flickering shots from a film reel, but she's no longer consumed by him. She's living and breathing her work, day and night, only pausing for time with her daughters.

Writing has become an all-consuming obsession that steals Estella's hours. Concepts of time and reality are increasingly blurring. She spends most of her time in a world of her own making. The days slip away too quickly, and her mind never rests. She's been in this state since late November, and now it's Christmas Eve.

The children are asleep, and Elvis's Christmas album plays, dredging up childhood memories. As "Blue Christmas" fills the room, Estella clings to her laptop, the story inside it feeling like the only thing keeping her tethered to reality.

Estella makes the necessary phone calls, sending her holiday wishes to family and friends. After speaking with her relatives, she rings Kal to let him know they won't be making it to his parents' Christmas party. She even texts Caelum, telling him she'll be back for lessons soon.

This Christmas, it'll be just Estella and her girls, along with Lucas's memory. That's how she wants it. Well, and Estella's story. Nearly complete, it now exists like a separate entity. It took her over a year to write the first half, but only one manic month detached from the world to finish it. What went into it, though—that took a lifetime.

The hours tick closer to Christmas Day as Estella types feverishly. Her glasses are smudged, her eyes are bloodshot, and her hair is twisted into a frizzy mess on top of her head. It's a good thing her children are asleep; she wouldn't want to scare them.

Estella doesn't have another word to give, like a climber reaching the top of a mountain with no more breath to spare. Before she types *The End*, a thought crosses her mind: what in the world will she do now? She looks for ways to change the story, add to it, eliminate parts, and further edit it. She searches for ways to delay the inevitable conclusion, but she can change nothing. The story is complete—minus the title. The truth is, she doesn't want it to end, because she wants to exist in it. Maybe it's real as long as she continues to write it.

After a bout of dreams—dreams of writing, dreams of words, dreams of dreams—Estella awakes before sunrise with a title streaming on repeat in her mind. She can't wait for the world to wake. She must type it out and mark it forever like a tattoo, for fear that if it's not recorded right here and now, it'll be lost forever. She stumbles over to her laptop sitting on the table where she left it, and stubs her toe in the process. Trying her hardest not to disturb her sleeping children, she muffles the curses she wants to scream into the darkness.

Awake as ever, with urgency and a little bit of pain, Estella flips open her laptop, squinting as the screen's light blasts her face. She gives her eyes a moment to adjust before typing out, *Generation Humanity*. It's the ribbon on the package, as complete as it'll get.

Never mind that it's 5:00 a.m.; Estella is calling her mom. It's too monumental a moment, and Hannah can never sleep, anyway.

"Mom," Estella whispers into the phone.

"What?" Hannah replies, much louder.

"Merry Christmas."

"Are you crazy?"

"Sometimes."

"What?"

"Nothing. I know it's early, but I have to tell you—I finished my book!"

Wearily, Hannah says, "That's wonderful, but you could've waited for the sun to come up."

Estella hesitates. "Also, I think I'm in love with Caelum."

There's a long silence. Finally, Hannah sighs. "I know."

"What do you mean, you know?" Estella demands.

"I'm a witch, too, remember?" Hannah says. "We can see love coming, and there's nothing we can do to stop it."

"Then why did you encourage me to take a break from Caelum?"

"Oh, you already had your mind set on that," Hannah says.

"And so, why didn't *I* see love coming? What kind of witch does that make me, then?" Estella asks.

"Maybe you did, but you just haven't realized it yet."

# Chapter 36

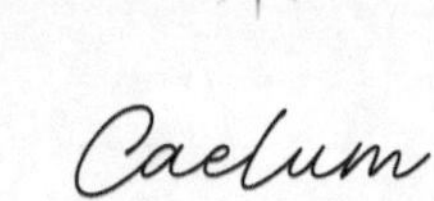

"Your hair looks crooked in the back," Darin tells Kal.

Kal looks at Caelum with narrowed eyes, and Caelum laughs.

The bell at the front of Diablo's chimes, and Caelum is shocked to see Estella walk in, even though it's her usual lesson time. New Year's Eve has come and gone without a word from her, except for a text before Christmas saying she'd be back for lessons soon. Estella hugs Darin and Kal, but offers Caelum only a shy wave.

"I thought you were coming back soon," Caelum says, trying to keep it light, but adds, "It's almost February."

"A month is soon. I assumed you'd save my spot," Estella says.

Caelum raises an eyebrow. "Since when do lawyers assume?"

Estella dips her chin, trying to hide a smile, but when she looks up at him, she's still smiling. "I don't practice law anymore. I'm a writer, and writers create all the rules and assumptions in every world they dream up," she says with a grin. "Speaking of which, I finished writing my book." She says it casually, as if it's an everyday thing.

Darin and Kal cheer and hoist her onto their shoulders like she's just scored a game-winning touchdown. A couple of people enter Diablo's, looking bewildered by the commotion. Caelum laughs and explains, "She wrote a book," and the newcomers offer polite if less enthusiastic nods.

When Kal and Darin set her down, her cheeks are flushed. She looks embarrassed.

"Aren't you excited? It's a big deal," Caelum says.

"I am," she says, though Caelum's raised eyebrow says he's unconvinced. "Really, I am. I've just had a while to process it. I spent the last month figuring out how to market it—and working up the courage to promote it at all. You know, the thing I wasn't brave enough to do when I released my poetry book." She takes a breath, then raises her hands in mock announcement. "Hear ye, hear ye! Novel forthcoming. Hear ye, hear ye! Poetry book available!"

"That's the spirit!" Caelum says, and they laugh. "Really, it's a big step, and I'm proud of you," he adds sincerely. Estella blushes. "About promoting your book… I know an agent. Her name's Valentina," Caelum offers.

"*We* know an agent," Kal says, weaseling his way into another hug from Estella. When she's not looking, Caelum jabs him in the ribs with his elbow.

"Thanks, guys, but I'm an indie author. I'll figure it out," she says.

"Come on, will you at least see what she has to say?" Caelum asks.

"Do I still get my lesson today?" Estella dodges the question. Does she even have to ask?

Caelum's lesson room glows with a warm candlelight-like hue. It's not actual candlelight; there's no drama of a flickering flame. But he's set the dimmer low for a steady mellow light that comes close to the real thing. He's setting a mood. The way the light softens Estella's features, making her eyes glimmer, pulls Caelum closer to her.

"So, when can I read your book?" Caelum asks.

"I'm not ready for anyone to read it yet," Estella says, like he's just asked her an inappropriate question.

"What do you mean? I thought you were getting comfortable with the idea of sharing your work. What better place to start than with me?" Caelum says.

"What I mean is that I'm not ready for anyone *I know* to read it."

"I know you," Caelum says.

She looks at him like he's said something magical—like all she's ever wanted is for someone to understand her, because no one ever has—but maybe Caelum is the one person who will.

"And I believe in you," he adds.

She doesn't say anything, just looks down at the drumsticks she's holding.

"Not to mention, I have a copy of your poetry book, *thunder and daisy*, and I've read it about ten times," he adds with a smile.

Estella looks horrified, and Caelum laughs.

"Now, let's practice your triplets," he says, hoping to shift the focus and ease the tension. He demonstrates the rudiment on the snare in front of him, his movements smooth and precise. Estella copies what he does, but her beats aren't as even, not quite matching the flow of Caelum's.

Caelum inches his chair closer to hers, guiding her hand to the proper grip on the drumstick. It's the slightest touch, not even as intimate as a handshake, but it stirs something in him that feels almost sinful. Estella keeps her gaze focused on her drumsticks, not noticing him pulling back to study her face.

"You look nice," he says, his voice laced with a desire he can't hide. She didn't go out of her way to dress up—baggy clothes, minimal makeup—but to him, that effortless look is irresistible.

"You think?" She looks up into his eyes, her voice also carrying an undertone of desire. She lets out a nervous laugh, glancing away before asking, "Is that your guitar—the one you played at Jack's?" She nods toward the guitar propped up in the corner.

"Yeah," Caelum says softly. "It belonged to my dad."

"Oh, your dad's a guitar player?"

"He was. He … died in a car accident on the Amalfi coast, along with my mom and brother."

The mood shifts instantly, and so does the expression on Estella's face.

"I'm so sorry, Caelum. I had no idea," she says.

"It was a long time ago. I was only sixteen. After it happened, I stayed with my aunt and uncle. We lived in a fishing village, so I made my money on the boats. And when I had enough, I left for the US. I've been on my own since I was eighteen."

What happened to Caelum's family is not something he could have predicted. Travelers see destiny, but there are unforeseen events that can disrupt the future they've seen. An accident is what it was, just like what happened to Lucas. It wasn't supposed to happen.

Caelum wants to keep things light, not burden Estella with sad stories, especially since it's been so long since he's seen her. But he's compelled to share every bit of himself with her. It's not like him. As a traveler, he's learned to stay quiet and hold things inside. It's made him an outsider—at least, until he found his people: Kal and the gang. In their company, he doesn't have to worry about slipping up. But though she's not a traveler, it's different with Estella. He wants her to know everything—which is why he needs to watch it. She can't know about his travels.

To lighten the mood, Caelum gets back to playing rudiments, and they turn their attention back to the drums. Estella works on her triplets, and they practice together in silence. They're connected by sound, and it feels complete in the way that every formula has an outcome. Connections between people are like equations, each with its own unique solution. Caelum and Estella's equation is complex and elegant. Its truth is beautiful.

*Did Estella feel that?* Caelum wonders. The sound connecting them humbles him. He doesn't want lesson time to end. And she has to see his place; after all, its blueprints are based on her dreams, and it's her place, too. He's hesitant to ask, worried he'll scare her off again by overstepping the boundaries she keeps putting up. But today is too perfect to let it end so soon. The worst she can do is say no, so he asks if she wants to come over.

"I don't know if it's a good idea," Estella says, glancing away. "I have to run some errands before picking up the kids..."

It takes a bit of gentle persuasion, but eventually, she agrees.

Estella trails Caelum as he steps out the back door of the music shop, following him across the parking lot until he stands in front of his motorcycle.

"Where's your car?"

"It's at my place. We'll take my bike," Caelum says, pressing a spare helmet into Estella's hands. "Weather's nice for January—I figured it's a good day for a ride. I don't live far."

"Getting on this motorcycle is definitely incompatible with my current level of risk tolerance," Estella says, gripping the helmet. It looks like she's calculating the risk in her head.

Caelum swings onto the bike, while Estella stands with her feet planted firmly on the ground in her Birkenstocks and fuzzy socks.

"Are you going to get on, or what?" Caelum asks.

"I'm getting there," Estella says, stalling for time. Caelum revs the engine, and she yells, "The noise level is only adding to the sense of impending danger!" He revs it again, and a thrill stirs in her expression. Finally, she climbs onto the bike and squeezes him tightly. It's sweet, this step outside of her comfort zone, just for him. They take off with her Birkenstocks clinging on for dear life.

After the short ride to Caelum's house, they pull into his tree-lined driveway and park by the front door. Estella takes off her helmet, and it looks like she's just had an experience. Her hair is tousled, and her eyes are bright with excitement. "That was so much fun!" she says, smoothing her hair back, her gaze drifting to Caelum's house. It's a single-story modern design with clean lines, painted a soft gray with white trim—simple, yet inviting.

"Your home is so charming. I swear I've dreamed about a place like this," she says.

Once inside, Caelum takes her on a tour. As they make their way through each room, she trails behind him, observing quietly until she says, "I like the décor. It's giving modern bohemian vibes—so artsy and relaxed. It's tidy, but not so tidy that it doesn't feel cozy and lived-in. I just love it!"

There are four bedrooms: the master, a guest room, the music room, and the library. When she steps into the library, her energy shifts like a sudden change in the weather. Lighter on her toes, she glides past the shelves, her fingers brushing the books as she marvels at the high ceiling. The space is small, but the big windows flood it with light, and every inch of the floor-to-ceiling mahogany bookshelves is packed with books. There are big, comfortable chairs to settle into, a table where they could set their tea, and a few houseplants to keep them company while they read.

"I can't believe you have a library! Your place couldn't be more perfect," she says, settling into one of the chairs, her hands running over the fabric of its arms.

"I had a feeling you'd like it," Caelum replies, sitting next to her in the other chair. For a moment, it's as if he's sitting on a throne, his queen finally beside him.

Caelum then leads Estella into the music room, which is filled with an array of instruments—guitars, drums, violins, and all kinds of other gear. Cables and pedals pattern the floor in an intricate web.

"Grab that Gibson Les Paul and follow me to the kitchen," he says.

Estella picks up the guitar and says, "It looks vintage."

"It's vintage, all right," Caelum replies. "I like vintage things." He had to do some traveling—*his* kind of traveling—to find it. It's Eric Clapton's "Beano." It was stolen in 1966, and to this day, it is one of rock's most famous stolen guitars. Why not use his gift to satisfy his musical obsessions? In how many lives does a person get to be a traveler? One, or maybe two, but almost always none. Might as well make the most of it. Getting his hands on the guitar was difficult, but somehow, Caelum managed to track it down and recover it. What's the person who had it going to do—report it missing? Caelum will return it to its rightful owner with an anonymous drop, but not before he enjoys it first.

In the kitchen, Caelum grabs drinks—a beer for himself, and tea for Estella—then leads her and Beano to the backyard.

"Wow, you have an amazing view of Mount Diablo!" Estella says.

Caelum is reminded of Estella's outing with Connor on the mountain, and it momentarily darkens his mood. He needs to track Connor down, and soon.

"Are those oranges?" Estella asks, cradling Beano as she surveys the garden. "And lemons!"

"Yeah, that's about all that's left this time of year. I had blackberries in the summer." It took him longer to get Estella here than he'd hoped. She'll have to wait for her blackberries. Caelum relieves her of Beano's weight, and they sit facing Mount Diablo.

"How about some Clapton?" Caelum asks.

Estella agrees, not knowing how fitting a Clapton song would be.

Halfway through the song, Caelum looks up to see if Estella's enjoying his guitar playing. She smiles, then looks away as soon as their eyes meet. But the next time he glances at her, she doesn't look away. She looks at him like she undeniably wants him.

# Chapter 37



Estella isn't sure how she let Caelum convince her to come over to his place, or get on that motorcycle. But now that she's here in his backyard, with Mount Diablo stretching in the distance, she can't imagine leaving. His home has it all: a garden brimming with fruits and vegetables, a music room, and a library she's dying to explore. But all she can focus on right now is his hands moving over the guitar—and how she imagines they'd feel beneath her sweater.

"I have to get going soon," Estella says after he stops playing. "But can I see your library again before we go?"

They return Caelum's Les Paul to the music room, and he gives her a brief story about each of his guitars. One he bought at a guitar shop in Naples when he was a kid and has carried with him ever since. Another, he found in a pawn shop during a search for a necklace that had been stolen from him. He figured if he was going to find the necklace, he might as well start by checking all the local pawn shops. He never found it, but he did discover a Koa top Taylor.

"What about this Les Paul you played for me?" Estella asks.

"Maybe I'll tell you about it another day," Caelum replies. "Let's go to the library."

Back in the library, Estella takes in the scene. The room is bathed in light pouring through the tall windows, and the walls are lined with bookshelves. It's a bookworm's dream. Trying to gain deeper insight into Caelum's mind, she gets closer and browses the bookshelves. What does he like? What does he think about? What kind of person is he? The shelves are filled with everything—philosophy, art books, sci-fi, classic literary works, and everything in between.

"Have you read all of these?" she asks.

"Over time, yes," he replies, his voice casual.

He's well-read, then. Too good to be true. Then, a book catches her eye. Printed on its binding: *Kama Sutra*.

"Hmm, I'm unfamiliar with this one," Estella says, pulling it from the shelf. She teases, "Would you recommend it?"

Caelum smiles innocently, shrugs, and says, "Definitely a must-read."

Estella flips open the book and takes a quick glance. "Oh—it's illustrated," she says, snapping it shut.

They laugh, and Caelum steps closer. He takes the book from her hands and reaches behind her to place it back on the shelf, his eyes never leaving hers.

"We should probably go," Estella says, without conviction. Despite the slight quiver in her voice, she hides her emotions well, but her heart is now racing, turning the previously calm waters of her blood into a storm, threatening the coolness of her façade.

Estella is pressed between Caelum and the bookcase when he whispers, "Please stay." The words sound soft, but feel heavy. "Come here," he adds, his voice carrying a hypnotic, ethereal quality, like the sound of a harmonic ringing out from a guitar. And Estella is powerless to do anything other than what he asks.

Caelum kisses her, and a handful of books tumble to the floor. They leave them where they land, irrelevant now, like everything else around them.

*Oh, no—not now!* Estella thinks frantically, feeling the familiar buzzing in her head as her vision darkens.

"Are you okay?" Caelum asks.

The faceless man appears in her vision, moving closer than ever before.

"Estella?!" Caelum calls out in alarm, gripping her shoulders.

The faceless man is right in front of her now. The shadow slides from his face. He wraps an arm around her back and pulls her close. Green eyes. Estella's gaze trails over his features before she steps back. As the vision fades, she gasps, exhaling the breath she didn't realize she was holding.

"It's *you*," she whispers.

Caelum stares at her, awkward, and Estella realizes how crazy she must seem.

"I mean, whenever I close my eyes, I keep seeing you," she says, trying to explain.

Caelum doesn't say a word, and the weight of his silence only makes her feel worse.

"How do you feel about witches?" she asks, laughing nervously. *Definitely crazy now,* she thinks.

Caelum moves closer, pressing his body into hers. "Witches are sexy," he says, his lips so close that they almost touch hers.

"Good," she says and displays her crescent moon. "Because this isn't a tattoo."

"Looks like a tattoo to me," Caelum teases, and Estella laughs.

"Yeah, it is, but that's not all it is."

"Witches' mark?"

Estella squeaks out an uncertain "Mm-hmm."

"I know," Caelum says softly. He sweeps her up into his arms, adding, "Like I said: sexy."

Effortlessly, he carries her to his bedroom. She stops resisting, letting him take the lead. This is what she wants. Caelum, the faceless man—he's what she wants.

Once they're in Caelum's room, everything around them blurs into the background; he is all she sees. They kiss at the foot of his bed, and Estella feels his hands under her sweater, just as she'd hoped. The warmth, the energy, the sensation—it's even better than she imagined. She slips out of her sweater and tosses it on his bed. Her modest breasts, covered by the thin lace of her bra, disappear under his rugged hands. She places her hands over his, letting him know they're exactly where she wants them. After he unbuttons them, Estella's loose-fitting pants fall at her feet, leaving her in only her underwear.

Caelum consumes her, kissing her, touching her, guiding her onto his bed until he's above her. His kisses travel lower, and with a quick tug and unhooking, her bra falls away. His mouth trails over her breasts, fueling a rising heat in her. It's soft, warm, and somehow cool all at once. She presses her hips into him, tugging on his shirt, urging him closer. It's hardly fair; Caelum is fully clothed, while Estella has only her panties for cover. They fumble together, tangled in each other as she works to lift up his shirt. Their kisses deepen as Estella struggles with the button on his jeans, and after a moment, he helps slide them off. They fall silent as their bare skin finally meets, separated only by the thin fabric of their underwear.

Now, Estella takes control, pushing herself on top. As she moves over him, she feels the strength of his desire. All she wants is to strip away the last barriers between them and feel the soft and hard of them collide.

There's no getting enough of him, and she's back at it, kissing him again. His hands are all over her, one on her breast and the other on her behind, like he's trying to hold all of her at once. Every second with him feels like perfection, and she feels held as if she's never been held like she needed to be held.

In a dizzying moment, Estella pulls Caelum back on top, and they toss aside the last of their clothes. The feel of him against her, without anything in between, takes her breath away. They lock eyes, and she sees the weight of his desire.

He fills every part of her soul. They make love—the kind that could drive a person to do anything, to risk everything. All the heavy want and need rushes to its limits, then dissipates into a new beginning.

They rest on their backs under the crumpled covers, the sides of their bodies touching like paper people.

# Chapter 38

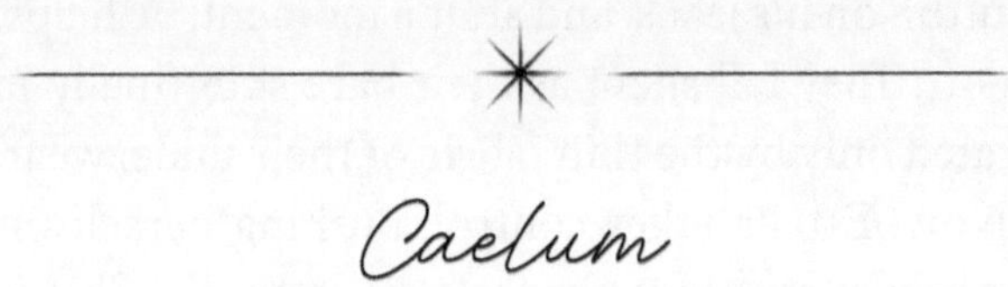

The chalet windows, blackened by night the last time Caelum saw them, now frame a sweeping view of snow-dusted trees stretching across endless peaks and valleys. The sky looks big in Tahoe, especially from the perch of Ryoko's cabin.

Caelum and the crew are spending the weekend here, planning to meet Valentina in a dream tonight. She's at her place in New York, so it's the easiest way to connect. They'd agreed to meet in the nether regions of the galaxy Proxima b, mainly because Caelum let Kal have this one. After his time with Estella, Caelum was feeling generous. That, and Kal was selling the place like an intergalactic travel agent.

The day has been spent carving up the mountain with Kal and Ryoko on snowboards and Caelum and Darin on skis. It has been a while for Caelum, so after dinner and a hot shower, he's unable to move from his spot on Ryoko's orange couch. He's draped over the cushions in the toasty nook by the fireplace, watching the sunset through the cabin's magnificent windows. Just as he's about to nod off, Ryoko gets in his ear and says, "Hey, cut my hair."

"What? No," he says, shifting slightly, but not moving from his cozy spot. "Next thing, Darin will be asking for a cut, too. I'm not your Edward Scissorhands."

"You're not getting scissors anywhere near these strands of gold," Darin says, gathering his hair into his hands and holding onto it protectively.

"Oh, come on, you did such a great job with Kal's hair," Ryoko says. "Don't you think it's about time we cut off this blue?" Her roots were only an inch long when Caelum first met her, but now the blue appears to sprout from her earlobes.

"You want a pixie cut?" Caelum asks.

"Why not?" she says, determined, though the crinkle between her eyebrows tells Caelum that she's more nerv-ous about the prospect of short hair than she lets on.

"I'll do it," Caelum sighs, tearing himself away from the cradle of comfort. "But after this, I'm crashing."

Darin and Kal chill in the living room while Ryoko and Caelum disappear into her bathroom, where he finds she has every toiletry known to humankind. Her combs come in every color of the rainbow, and she owns more than one pair of shears.

"How does one person need this many combs?" Caelum asks, holding up a colorful handful.

"You never know what can happen. It's good to be prepared."

"So, you're a traveler, a computer hacker, and a prepper?"

She swats at Caelum before handing over the scissors, and he cuts her a damn good pixie—tight on the sides, longer on top, side-swept just right. The new hairstyle, paired with her baby face, makes her soft and sophisticated. Without the edgy blue tips, she doesn't look like the Ryoko Caelum knows; she's someone entirely new. As soon as he makes the final snip, she bursts out of the bathroom to showcase her new hair. Caelum, meanwhile, is left to sweep up the former Ryoko's blue strands littering the bathroom tiles.

Spent after the day's activities and playing the group's designated hairstylist, Caelum heads straight to bed as promised. One by one, he, Darin, Kal, and Ryoko slip into their dreams and reunite.

Caelum's feet sink into sand as water washes over them. He scans the surreal sky, where multiple suns shine down on him. *Hello, Proxima b.* The largest of the glowing suns is Proxima Centauri. It appears far more immense than Earth's sun, but emits a gentle glow, like a burning ember.

Valentina materializes not far from them and approaches. There's nothing casual about her. Her walk is more of a strut, and even in her dreams, it looks like she's dressed for the runway.

Ryoko leans close to Caelum's ear and whispers, "She's so hot. You think she'd be interested in me?"

"I thought you had a thing for Caelum," Darin says casually.

"She does not have a thing for me," Caelum says quickly, the notion making him uneasy. He's only ever thought of Ryoko as a friend—or at most, the pesky little sister he never had.

"Yeah, but he's taken," Ryoko jokes.

"He is *not* taken," Kal cuts in defensively and returns his focus to the terrain, kicking at loose rocks and sending puffs of dust into the air.

"How do you know I'm not taken?" Caelum says, his voice rising in challenge.

"What do you mean?" Kal says, peeling his eyes away from the landscape and setting them on Caelum. He looks fully engaged now.

"Nothing," Caelum says, unable to wipe the smile from his face.

"Yeah, right. You expect me to believe you have that dumb look on your face because of nothing?" Kal's eyes narrow. "You better tell me what happened."

"What happens between Estella and me is none of your business," Caelum says.

Kal grumbles, storms off, and kicks up another cloud of dirt.

"What are you two arguing about?" Valentina asks. "And whose idea was it to meet here?"

Caelum motions to Kal with his eyes. Kal stands with his back to the group, arms crossed, gazing up into the warm light of the suns.

"There's nothing wrong with this place. Am I the only one around here who appreciates the beauty of the cosmos?" Kal says, still looking into the sky.

"Okay, I've had enough. I'm pulling you guys into my place in Manhattan," Valentina insists, and from one hot second to the next, they're in a high-rise luxury apartment.

Valentina's place looks modern, and so clean that it could be used as an operating room. Everything is some shade of white, from the quartz kitchen counters to the pale herringbone hardwood floors to the couch Caelum is hesitant to even sit on. Darin and Kal have already claimed space on the spotless couch, though they don't need to worry about dirtying it with their dream-form bodies. Still, they look like stains on a wedding dress.

"Nice digs," Ryoko says, peering out the window at the twinkling lights of New York City. She stands close to Valentina as they both gaze out the window. Ryoko is more hip-hop dancer, Valentina more ballerina.

"You look different," Valentina says, glancing at Ryoko over her shoulder.

"You noticed," Ryoko says. "I cut my hair. Well, Caelum cut it for me."

Valentina's eyes move between Ryoko and Caelum before settling back on Ryoko. "Cute," she says flatly, then turns and walks away.

Ryoko's gaze trails after Valentina. Long legs, exposed by a miniskirt and further lengthened by high heels, carry Valentina toward a drink cart in her living room.

"I'm making drinks," she announces. "It's silly, isn't it? Drinks in dreams—as if we even need them. Let's say it's for ceremony," she says, pulling the cap off a clear bottle containing equally clear liquid. She doesn't ask the others what they'd like. Instead, she hands them vodka martinis with a twist.

Darin knocks his back like a shot and sets his empty glass on the coffee table.

With mild irritation, Valentina eyes Darin. "Thirsty?"

"Dreams are what you make of them, and I'm getting toasted in this one," Darin replies.

He's right: the rules of reality don't apply in the dream world. Drink a little and get drunk, or a lot and not; it makes no difference. With enough will, dreams go where the dreamer wants them to, or take them on an unexpected ride. Travelers possess a greater level of control, but that's not to say they don't get surprises.

"Help yourself to another," Valentina says.

Darin does just that and returns to the couch. He sips this one.

"Did you get Estella's manuscript?" Caelum asks Valentina, making himself another stain on the couch.

"I did, but I haven't had time to look at it yet. I'll dedicate some time to reading it in the next few days."

"I'm having a Valentine's Day event at my club. You've spent some time there, I hear," Kal says. "It would be a perfect opportunity for you to meet Estella and discuss her book," he suggests.

"Isn't Valentine's Day next week? I'm not sure I'll be available," Valentina says, lifting her martini to her lips.

"Oh, will you be spending it with a special someone?" Ryoko asks, genuinely interested.

"No... Well, let me check my schedule." Valentina pulls out her phone, holding her nose high with lips pursed tight as she scrolls through it. "Okay, I suppose I can make that work."

"So, it's a date," Ryoko says and gives Valentina an *"I'll take you now"* stare.

As she sits on the adjacent white loveseat, as immaculate as the sofa, one of Valentina's rare smiles slowly spreads across her lips. "A date," she repeats as she returns Ryoko's come-hither stare.

Ryoko, still standing by the window, answers the call of Valentina's gaze and glides toward the loveseat, holding her martini stem between delicate fingers. Valentina's posture makes the others look like weeping willows, but not Ryoko, who sits down next to Valentina on the loveseat with more grace than Caelum's ever seen her pull off. Above average in height, but not as tall as Valentina, Ryoko mimics Valentina's posture, but doesn't quite attain the same stateliness—difficult to do in Ryoko's oversized anime T-shirt and flannel pants. As Ryoko and Valentina admire each other, the three couch stains sip their martinis until Kal's patience runs out.

"Let's get to the point of this meeting, shall we?" Kal says. In the wake of the silence, he adds, "Connor."

"Let me handle Connor," Valentina asserts. "Because I worked the auction, I have a good reason to contact him."

"Okay, but we need to know what's so special about that book, and why he wants it," Caelum says.

"And where he got the million dollars to buy it," Darin adds and takes another sip from his almost-empty glass.

"Yeah, it just doesn't add up. Most people don't have a million dollars lying around to spend on some obscure old book," Caelum says. "Maybe he's working on behalf of someone with cash. More importantly, him showing up there in the first place can't be mere coincidence."

"I don't know," Valentina says with a shrug. "People from all over the world come to that event. Maybe he's working for someone, like you said, or maybe he has family money. There are lots of explanations."

"Maybe, but as far as I'm concerned, he's our number one suspect. And if he is a half-soul, he's dangerous. We should work together," Caelum insists.

"You don't think I can handle Connor on my own?" Valentina says, her tone a mix of hurt and pride. *"Pfft,"* she adds, crossing her arms.

"What is it with you men?" Ryoko comes to Valentina's defense. "You think we can't handle one stupid half-soul?"

"That's not what I meant," Caelum says with a sigh. "Fine, but approach him with caution, and I want to know everything."

"Don't worry. I'll get the dirt on Connor and report back," Valentina says.

Darin eyes his newly empty glass. "Toasted, I am not. My dream escapes me."

# Chapter 39

The Valentine's Day operation Kal is running at the DVC is off the charts. Various shades of red and pink dominate the scene. Love songs, conversation, and perfume intermingle in the air. A blur of champagne bubbles and magenta sequins whizzes past Estella as she scans the crowd for a familiar face. The club members, usually clad in yoga pants and gym clothes, have been replaced by movie star look-alikes. The event is taking place in the club's large open space, usually reserved for group classes. They've opened the retractable glass wall to the adjacent patio, where the band is set up, creating the impression that the place was designed for parties.

Caelum promised Kal he'd help set up, so instead of arriving with Caelum, Estella is meeting him at the party. She'd gotten the impression that Caelum wasn't fond of Kal, but now, it's as if they're best friends. Estella had hoped to see Caelum last weekend, but he took off with

Kal and Darin to stay at a friend's cabin in Tahoe. She'd be lying if she said she wasn't bummed about missing out on spending time with Caelum at his place. Still, she likes the idea of him being part of her group of friends.

Not only is Estella meeting Caelum for a Valentine's Day date, she's also meeting Valentina, the literary agent, to discuss her book. Though she'd been preparing to self-publish it, she promised Caelum she'd send Valentina a copy of her manuscript. Valentina requested the meeting, so she must've liked it. This is a big moment for Estella.

Trying to dazzle Caelum and impress Valentina, Estella carefully chose her dress for the evening. Opting for the safe bet, she went with black; nothing says vixen author like a black silk dress. While she feels comfortable in it, she can't shake the awkwardness of showing up alone. To give her hands purpose, Estella searches for a mocktail to fill them.

On her way to the bar set up in the corner, Estella spots Kal holding a tray of drinks, looking sharp in a suit instead of his standard uniform of T-shirt, jeans, and flip-flops. She's never seen him look so dapper. While she's a fan of typical Kal, she can't help but appreciate this new look on him. When she catches his eye, the drinks on Kal's tray begin a slow slide, but he steadies it before a drop is spilled.

Kal looks at Estella like she's some exotic sea creature that's washed ashore. She realizes it's the first time he's seen her in a fancy dress. Estella tells him how sharp he looks, and Kal says, "Don't get used to it." He explains that wearing a suit brings back bad memories of his venture capitalist days.

"I was just getting drinks for everyone," he adds. "Follow me. I know just what you'd like."

Kal leads her to the bar, and within a few shakes, the bartender whips up a nonalcoholic concoction. It's the color of ballet slippers and smells like a flower.

"Hibiscus spritzer," Kal says. "You like?"

Estella takes a sip and tells him, "It's love in a glass."

Kal takes off with his tray of drinks, and Estella follows behind with her tasty pink fizz, savoring sips along the way. He leads her to a private nook away from the band, where the noise level drops a few notches. A group of partygoers stand around a high-top table, and the first pair of eyes that Estella locks onto are Caelum's. His eyes show surprise, then quickly shift to desire as they trace the length of her body. He rushes to her side.

"You sexy witch," Caelum whispers into her ear, and she shushes him.

Much less obviously, Estella then scans the length of Caelum. He's dressed all in black, from his suit to his shirt, his hair slicked back. He looks Bond-like. They get lost in each other, until Darin interjects with a hello. He doesn't look like his usual self, either; his hair is restrained in a ponytail, he's clean-shaven, and though he's not in a suit, his shirt is buttoned and collared. Between Darin less rock and roll and the boys in suits, the party is a classic cinema time warp.

"This is our friend, Ryoko," Caelum says.

"I can introduce myself." Ryoko pushes past Caelum. "Ryoko Hoshino," she says, extending her hand to Estella. She takes Ryoko's hand, and they exchange introductions. Estella's first impression of Ryoko is that she's a force to be reckoned with—dainty in appearance, but undeniably bold with her daring hair and neon-orange dress.

"We're going to be good friends," Ryoko tells her with certainty. She clasps Estella's arm, claiming her for conversation, while Kal runs off to oversee the party. Caelum and Darin begin debating the band's performance, and Ryoko gives Estella a crash course on her life.

"So, it's official? You two are a thing?" Darin suddenly asks, his gaze moving between Caelum and Estella.

Estella doesn't respond, instead looking to Caelum, waiting for his response.

He steps closer, sliding his hand to the small of her back and pulling her into him. "We're a thing," he confirms, studying her eyes before pressing his lips to hers. Enveloped in Caelum and his kiss, Estella fails to keep her glass level, and some pink drink makes its way out of her glass onto the floor.

Kal clears his throat, and Caelum and Estella separate. He's back, and his expression has shifted, his eyebrows lower, his tone sharp. "Get a room, you two," he mutters.

Estella feels a pang of guilt. She knows Kal likes her. She likes him, too. But Caelum is the constant in her mind, the name always on her tongue.

"Valentina's arriving any minute. I'm going to greet her at the entrance," Kal says and jets.

The last thing Estella wants is to hurt Kal, but she knows she has. The joy of being with Caelum is always tinged with guilt for disappointing people she cares about, like Kal and Lucas. While Lucas is gone, she knows it would hurt him to see her with Caelum.

Filling the awkward silence Kal left behind, Estella turns to Darin and asks, "No Valentine's date? Where's your boyfriend—the one I met at Jack's that time?"

"It didn't work out," Darin says, his tone clipped. Estella realizes she's hit a sore spot. Darin straightens, clasping his hands in front of him as he stares off toward the band. The tension is clear, so she doesn't press. After a pause, Darin adds, "I don't have much luck in that department."

Creating one awkward moment after another, Estella turns to Ryoko and asks, "How about you? No date?"

Before Ryoko can respond, Kal appears, accompanied by someone who looks like a goddess.

Ryoko replies slyly, "I'm working on it," walks over to the goddess, and plants a kiss on her cheek.

Now that Estella sees Valentina in person, she recognizes her as the woman Caelum was speaking with by the water fountain that time he didn't notice her in the gym.

"Estella, I'd like you to meet Valentina," Kal says.

As Valentina steps into their circle, Estella suddenly feels smaller and underdressed. While she and Ryoko are about the same height, Valentina towers over them, easily pushing five-ten or five-eleven. Their dresses are equally elegant, but on Valentina, hers looks like high fashion.

"Guys, let's give Estella and Valentina some time to talk," Caelum says. He flashes Estella an encouraging look, one that seems to say, *You'll do great.* But it does little to calm her nerves. Valentina might hold the key to what comes next. And yet, everything about her—her height, her striking beauty, her composed demeanor—feels utterly intimidating.

"What did you…" Estella's voice catches in her throat, which went dry at the first sight of Valentina. "… think of my manuscript?" she squeaks out. There's not a pink drop left in her glass to offer relief. Estella peels her shoulders back and lifts her chin, trying to show the confidence her voice failed to convey.

Valentina doesn't answer right away. Instead, she holds up the martini glass she's been carrying, inspects its contents, and takes a sip. Her glass is full. Estella's is empty. Valentina lets out a heavy sigh, and Estella's heart sinks with it. The woman holds a royal flush, while Estella feels like she has nothing but two of a kind.

"I loved it," Valentina says.

Estella breathes a sigh of relief, her heart floating back into place.

"I'll send you my full review in a couple of weeks, and we'll set up a time to chat then. Sound good?"

Estella blinks a few times.

"Great. Now, where did Ryoko go…?" Valentina says before Estella can articulate a response, then saunters off.

Estella smiles into the bottom of her empty glass.

Moments after Valentina leaves, Caelum and Darin return, looking like blackbirds with ruffled feathers. Their earlier polish is gone, replaced by a frantic, disheveled energy.

"Where's Kal?" Caelum asks, his voice tight.

"I don't know. I've been chatting with Valentina. Is everything okay?" Estella replies, concern sharpening her tone.

"I have to go. I'm sorry. I'll explain later," Caelum says, already moving, Darin close behind him.

Before she can think, Estella's feet carry her after them. She weaves through the crowd, on the verge of bumping shoulders and tipping drinks. Over the sea of heads, Estella sees Caelum and Darin catch up with Kal, who's standing by the band. The band drowns out their words with the blood-stirring beat of the drums as they transition into a new song. Whatever Caelum tells him transforms Kal. He looks activated, just like Caelum and Darin. Before Estella can reach them, the boys take off running. Pushing forward, Estella watches them disappear through the entrance, and they're swallowed by the night.

With the guys gone, Estella goes looking for Valentina and Ryoko. After taking a lonely wander through the crowd of slow-dancing couples and intimate whispers for a few love songs, she calls it a night. Valentina and Ryoko are nowhere to be found. Everyone has left. Estella is the last loveless lover standing.

# Chapter 40



*Caelum*

Caelum and Darin slip into the DVC men's lounge for a quick break from the party, leaving Estella to meet with Valentina. The lounge is stocked with practical amenities—mouthwash dispensed from large bins into tiny paper cups, single-use shavers, and other essentials. The air is thick with the sharp blend of mint and cologne.

Darin pours himself some mouthwash, swishing it around while Caelum lathers his hands with pink liquid soap. Darin inspects his reflection and spits the mouthwash into the sink, rinsing it away with water before he sucks in a breath for that clean mouthwash sting.

"Not sure about this clean-shaven look on me. What do you think?" Darin asks, running a hand over his smooth face.

"Huh?" Caelum asks, glancing up from the sink to the mirror.

His breath catches. Athena's face stares back at him instead of his own. Is he losing his grip on reality? He's had a couple of drinks, but he's nowhere near drunk. "Dude, are you seeing this?" he asks, turning to Darin.

One look at Darin's wide eyes gives him his answer.

Athena appears vividly, her flaming red hair and brown button eyes sharp against the mirrored surface. From the other side of the glass, she pounds her fists, her voice urgent. *"Caelum, is that you? Can you see me?! Help!"*

"Yes, it's me. And Darin," Caelum calls back. "We can hear you, we can see you."

But Athena doesn't seem to hear him. Her voice breaks through again, distant. *"If you get this, please help! Alexander trapped me in the in-between!"* she cries, her image flickering. *"Alexander is Connor!"* she declares, then fades away.

Caelum turns to Darin, their shock mirrored in each other's expressions. "Let's go," Caelum says, and they bolt from the men's lounge. They need to get Kal—but first, Caelum has to tell Estella they're leaving. How will he explain this one?

Caelum's shoes clatter against the glossy tile as he races toward the club's front doors, the sound echoing in his ears, loud and frantic. Darin and Kal are right behind him, their footsteps pounding in rhythm with his own. The slick bottoms of his dress shoes make him unsteady, and he reaches out, grabbing Kal's shoulder for balance. The brief pause slows their momentum, and Darin crashes into them, sending all three into a momentary tangle.

With a few hurried pats on shoulders and taps on backs to steady themselves, they regroup and push forward, heading for the parking lot. That's where Kal said they'd find Valentina. On their way out, Ryoko and Valentina had mentioned to Kal that they'd be in the parking lot, checking out Valentina's new car.

"There," Darin says, pointing into the distance. In the far corner of the parking lot, Valentina and Ryoko are tangled up against a gleaming black Mercedes sports car, illuminated by the glow of an overhanging light. Shoes now tapping on the concrete, the group's approach draws their attention. Ryoko and Valentina hear them coming and quickly unravel from each other. Subtlety might have been better, but Caelum's fancy shoes aren't built for stealth.

Valentina looks directly at Caelum, and even across the lot, he can see it in her eyes. It's not the eyes themselves, but something behind them—the sickening emptiness of someone consumed by the in-between. Her face twists into a mask of fury as she pushes away from Ryoko, who throws up her hands in confusion.

"Valentina!" Caelum yells, and her hand disappears into her purse. The silver glint under the lamplight reveals that she's pulled a blade. In a dangerous dance, Valentina slashes at Ryoko, who pulls her torso into a deep curve to dodge the blade. Then, with a fluid roundhouse mo-tion, Ryoko's rhinestone-studded shoe sweeps up and connects with Valentina's hand. The knife drops to the ground with a clink and a spin.

As the men close in on Valentina, she scrambles over the hood of her car, tears open the door, and gets in. Kal is the first to reach her, slamming his fist against her driver's side window. The crack of the impact echoes, but the glass holds. With a screech, Valentina throws the car into reverse, narrowly missing Caelum and Darin as she skids away.

"You bitch!" Ryoko screams, her voice rising over the roar of the engine. She clutches her side and lifts her hand to check the damage. Her bright orange dress is torn near her ribs, a dark red stain spreading across the fabric. The others rush to her aid.

"It's just a nick," Ryoko says, smacking Caelum's hand away as he tries to inspect the wound. "What the fuck just happened?!"

"Cassius just happened," Caelum replies. "Valentina is Cassius, and Connor is Alexander."

"What?! How do you know?" Ryoko demands.

"Athena—"

"Athena? You found her?"

"She found me," Caelum says. "Darin and I were in the men's room freshening up when she appeared in a vision. At first, I thought I was dreaming—I've never had a vision before—but then Darin saw her, too."

"Caelum and Darin caught up with me and filled me in," Kal adds. Caelum's attention shifts to the blood dripping from Kal's hand, a splatter marking the concrete.

"You're hurt, too. Let's get out of here and clean you guys up," Caelum says.

"My place," Kal says.

But Darin presses the question. "Wait. Athena said Connor is Alexander. She didn't say anything about Valentina being Cassius. How did you know?"

"I didn't. It was a hunch," Caelum replies. From day one, he knew there was something off about her. "When I found out Connor was Alexander, I figured Valentina had to be the body Cassius used to get here. The book auction—they were both there. I saw the way she looked at him."

Ryoko exhales heavily. Still clutching her side, she slips off her heels and dangles them by their straps. A couple of inches shorter now, she stands there, weary and defeated. "Why couldn't Cassius snatch someone less attractive?" she growls.

"Let's get to Kal's. We have work to do," Caelum says, reaching for Ryoko's shoes. This time, she lets him help.

Before leaving, Darin bends down to retrieve Valentina's switchblade. He folds it, slides it into his back pocket, and says, "Might come in handy."

At Kal's, they clean and bandage his hand and the slice to Ryoko's side. Thankfully, the wounds are superficial. The attack on Ryoko's emotions, however, cuts much deeper.

Ryoko changes into the oversized overalls she keeps at Kal's and sulks around his man cave in the garage, where they've retreated to devise a plan.

"We have to go there," Caelum says.

"Where?" Darin asks, quietly plucking pentatonic scales on a guitar.

"The in-between," Caelum says grimly.

Darin's fingers falter, a stray note hanging in the air before silence falls. Everyone stops what they're doing.

"Uh-uh," Darin says, shaking his head as the others likewise voice their disapproval.

"How else are we going to rescue Athena?" Caelum insists. "We can't leave her there. One of us should stay behind, just in case … you know, in case we get stuck."

Travelers rarely venture into the in-between, for good reason. It's an abysmal void, a place of danger and despair. Those trapped there leave their human forms in a trance, in limbo. Stay too long, and that traveler is as good as gone.

"Stuck," Darin echoes, his opposition to the plan growing.

"If we end up turning into sleepwalkers, we need a babysitter," Caelum continues. It wouldn't do any good if one of them wandered off in a daze and met with peril. "Besides, if we're gone long, we'll need help with basic things, like using the bathroom and hydrating. We'll need someone to direct us in our semiconscious state."

"I'm not up for a trip to the in-between. I'll stay back and take care of you guys," Ryoko says. She tugs at the straps of her overalls and cracks her first smile since finding out her crush is Cassius. "I promise I won't peek when you're in the bathroom."

"Can we trust someone who's been seduced by the devil?" Caelum asks, and Ryoko's smile vanishes. "Too soon," she says flatly.

"Sorry." Caelum stretches his arms out for a hug. Ryoko swats them away. She's already starting to seem more like herself. Caelum has hope that they'll rescue Athena unscathed.

"Here," Darin says, pressing Valentina's switchblade into Ryoko's palm. "You might need this if they come looking for us."

Ryoko quickly drops it into the large pocket of her overalls. She doesn't want to see the knife, a reminder of Valentina's betrayal.

"Don't we need a special key to get into the in-between? Our usual keys to the other side won't work," Kal points out.

"I'll take you to the key," Caelum says. "It's the same key I used the last time I helped Athena out of there. I hurled it into an awful moment I never planned to revisit."

The crew spends the rest of the evening making careful preparations for the journey—hopefully short, but possibly long. It'll be a two-step process: first, retrieve Caelum's key to the other side, then get the key to the in-between. No one reaches the in-between from the dream world; the only way to that cosmic shithole is through the other side.

Instead of their usual separate guest rooms, Caelum, Darin, and Kal have to bunk together in Kal's room. It'll make it easier for Ryoko to keep an eye on them and stop any sleepwalking wanderers.

Kal's room looks like it belongs in a beach house. Surf photos line the walls, and a glossy black-and-white surfboard rests on a rack, reflecting the glow of a nearby lamp. The faint scent of coconut tanning lotion lingers in the air. Kal's California king bed offers plenty of space, but still, it'll be a tight squeeze with the three of them.

"I have dibs on one of the sides," Caelum says.

Kal catches air when he throws himself onto the bed and says, "My side."

"I don't mind sleeping in the middle," Darin says as he lays down to rest.

"Keep your hands to yourself," Kal jokes, giving Darin a playful shove.

Once asleep, the guys appear in Caelum's room in Positano. They're sprawled on the floor in the same positions they occupied on Kal's bed, like they've been beamed up. Kal glances around, taking in Caelum's space. He examines the room as though searching for clues to Caelum's psyche, his gaze lingering on the open balcony door before stepping outside.

"Nice place," Kal says over his shoulder.

Darin, meanwhile, hones in on a stack of old vinyl records near the bed. He's already thumbing through them when the past version of Caelum stirs in his sleep. Startled, Darin jumps, sending a record flying into the air. Caelum catches it mid-spin and hands it back.

"Didn't see the other *you* there," Darin says with a nervous chuckle, jerking his thumb toward the bed.

A sudden loud thud interrupts them as the balcony door slams shut. Darin flinches, and the record is airborne again. This time, it falls to the floor, but doesn't break.

"Give me that," Caelum says, picking it up. He's done playing Frisbee with his records.

"Valentina!" Kal yells from outside.

The past version of Caelum is already up inspecting the door when Caelum and Darin hover over to Kal.

"I thought we'd pick up my key to the other side when Valentina paid me a visit here," Caelum says. "In case I missed something."

"I saw her," Kal says. "She kicked your door shut with her pointy black heel and bolted."

"Of course," Caelum says. "That was the last night I spoke with Athena. Valentina must have caused the diversion so Connor could trap her."

"Same thing happened to Ryoko," Kal says. "She was talking to Athena in a dream, and it was cut short just before Athena was about to share something important. After that, Athena disappeared."

"They were doing everything to keep Athena from exposing them," Darin says.

"It's time we stop them and bring Athena home," Caelum says, leading them to the drawer holding his key to the other side. Pausing, he turns to Darin and Kal. "Wait… If you two know where I keep my key, what's stopping you from coming here and taking it any time? Can I trust you?" Caelum stares into their eyes with enough intensity that they each take a step back. Every traveler is given one key to the other side, and every traveler guards it with their life.

"I'll show you mine if you show me yours," Darin quips.

"All of us, including Ryoko, should know where all the keys are hiding. We're *ohana* now, and family shares," Kal says.

Caelum hesitates, but he knows they're right. Strength in numbers. He retrieves his key and places it in his palm.

"Yours looks different from mine," Darin says, picking it up and examining it closely. "A four-leaf clover. Interesting. Mine has a heart. Ironic, isn't it? I get the heart key, yet I never find love I can hang onto."

"Mine is a circle," Kal says, glancing at the others. "Gets you to the other side just the same."

"Right," Caelum says, pocketing his key. "Let's do this."

# Chapter 41

The pastel yellow of the music shop is the only splash of color on an otherwise gray day. Rain soaks Estella's clothes as she hurries from her car to the shop. At the entrance, the sign on Diablo's simply says *Temporarily Closed*—no explanation, nothing more. That's all they left her, too: nothing. No answers.

She's called about her lessons, about their whereabouts, but no one has picked up. She knew the shop would be empty, yet here she is, hoping she might catch them returning from wherever they disappeared. They have to come back eventually, don't they?

Someone is still running the DVC, but it's not Kal. She hasn't seen any of them come into the coffee shop, either. They're nowhere to be found. Worry gnaws at her, and she wants answers. It's now March—nearly a month since they all disappeared without a word.

It's been crickets from Valentina, too. She had promised Estella a full review of her manuscript within weeks of their meeting, but now it's as if she's vanished, too. When Estella called the number Valentina had given her for follow-ups, her assistant said she was on leave with no return date in sight. That's when the last shred of hope Estella had left evaporated—just like her friends.

Windshield wipers squeak against the glass as Estella drives the short distance from Diablo's Music to the coffee shop. She's been stopping there almost daily—not just to pour her heart into writing, but in the faint hope of running into one of her missing friends.

After weeks of medicating with romcoms, she's turned to the comfort of writing. All is well in the worlds she creates, and it's where she spends most of her time. A new story is percolating in her mind—a new story, new chances. There is always a new story to be told, but she's not ready to leave the one she's just written.

After parking her car, Estella flings open the door, only to step ankle-deep into a puddle. Rainwater seeps through her sock in a cold, unwelcome shock. Tempted to abandon the mission and head home, she wrings out her sock, wrestles it back on, and pushes herself to go inside.

The tables are all full, so Estella doesn't pull out her work. Instead, she wraps both hands around her coffee cup, savoring its warmth and scent. The creamy, rich taste soothes her nerves, taking the edge off her damp, chilled foot. As she sips, she scans the faces in the room, hoping to spot someone familiar, but she finds no one. Her thoughts drift, as they always do, to the past month. Every day, she wonders why Caelum disappeared, why he hasn't contacted her—and every day, she comes up empty. Like the rainwater soaking her sock, the cold truth is sinking in: she may never hear from him again.

The thought destroys her. Maybe he wanted only one thing, and now that he got it, he's gone. So what if she fell in love with him? It's entirely possible he never felt the same. Maybe it was all in her head. She had created a character, made him into everything she ever wanted, and made him walk on water. He was just a dream.

As soon as Estella finishes her coffee, she leaves the crowded shop, her missing friends nowhere to be found. She gets another soaking on the way back to her car. At least there's still time to write at home before her daughters get out of school.

Estella starts the engine, and music blasts from the speakers. It's a favorite, but the song is like a knife through the heart. "Just Like Heaven" by The Cure takes her back to the last time she heard it—the night they disappeared. The band had played it as they all ran out of sight, the last moment she saw Caelum and her friends. And Valentina, too.

Maybe Caelum is with Valentina now. After all, they vanished together. Estella remembers seeing them at the DVC, talking by the water fountain. She wonders if something has been going on between them this whole time. She should've trusted her gut. They're probably in his library at this very moment. Maybe he seduces lots of women with his library.

Estella feels like a fool for trusting him. Blinded by attraction, she threw all reason out the window. She made herself vulnerable in the worst way, like a lamb cornered by a wolf. Caelum took full advantage of it, moving in for the kill. Anger builds heat, and the chill of rain-soaked clothes fades. All the secrets, stories, and dreams she shared with him blew through him like a gust of wind, something intangible he never intended to keep. If he ever truly felt anything for her, she would've heard from him by now.

Over the weeks, she's cycled through disappointment, anger, sadness, and loneliness—but there's still love. Even if Caelum is a wolf who uses his library to charm women, a mad desire for him lingers. Hate or anger can't seem to stick. Whenever she remembers the pain he caused, animosity builds in her like thunderclouds. But then, she'll think of the way he looked at her in his library. The clouds disappear as fast as they came, and sunny skies return.

That sweet look on Caelum's face—Estella could have sworn it was the look of love, but she must have been wrong. He had looked at her like his eyes held all the truth in the world, telling her, *"I know you."* How cruel of him to wield those words so recklessly. Doesn't he know that no one really knows her? Doesn't he know that she believed him?

Estella is barely through her front door when she kicks off her shoes and peels off her socks, the waterlogged one coming off first. She rummages through her sock drawer for the coziest pair and slips them on. Restored to baseline comfort, she taps out some sentences on her laptop, periodically checking her phone like it's an itch. Immersed in the new world she's creating, she forgets about Caelum for a while. Time slips by too quickly, and before she knows it, she must leave to pick up her daughters from school.

By the time Estella and her daughters are on their drive home, the rain lets up, and a break in the clouds allows light to spill through. Her mood must be solar-powered, because as soon as the sky shifts from gray to blue, she suggests a detour to her daughters.

"How about we stop for cupcakes?" Estella asks.

Mina and Kaitlin respond with an enthusiastic cheer, and just like that, Estella is a hero. It's easy to forget about her problems when she takes a trip to Storyland, or when she's with her daughters.

As they enter the cupcake shop, they're greeted by a rush of sugar-sweet air and smiles from the people behind the counter. Smiles come easy to those who deal in cupcakes. Nope, no problems in here.

The girls press their hands and noses to the glass separating them from the cupcakes as they browse the colorful selection. Kaitlin picks strawberry, as usual. It's been her favorite flavor ever since Estella told her that her hair is the color of strawberries only because Estella ate so many of them when Kaitlin was in her belly.

Estella goes for vanilla with rainbow sprinkles, because nothing says happy like rainbow sprinkles. The first bite is bliss—soft, dense sweetness with the crunch of sprinkles for added pizzazz. Nope, no worries in here.

After taking the longest time picking a flavor, Mina settles on vanilla cake with chocolate frosting, then licks all the frosting off first. Nope, no broken hearts in here.

But once it's night and Estella is alone in bed, watching TV, she loses the battle of trying to keep Caelum out of her head. His Trojan horse invades her thoughts—glimpses of his hair grazing the corner of his lips, his hands covering her body... When she closes her eyes, she's with him, his body is pressed against hers, touches on her skin, kisses on her mouth.

There's no escaping Caelum, even while she sleeps. In a dream, she's greeted by the hauntingly beautiful sound of a violin. It plays a song of longing, love, and everything blue. Tonight, they're together for a brief moment in a dream set in an endless desert. All Estella can see are dunes of sand stretching across the horizon. They're alone in a sea of sand when a massive storm kicks up, sending rivers of dust into the air, blowing it into a vortex around them until the light of the sun all but disappears. Estella and Caelum both wear white, gauzy fabric—hers in the form of an unblemished, flowy dress tossing in the wind, and his clothes torn and dirty like he's been to hell and back. He looks beaten down and defeated, his thin shirt only emphasizing what's underneath.

As he glides the violin bow over the strings, Estella can't help but imagine sliding her hands under his threadbare shirt, feeling what it barely conceals. Caelum lowers his violin and looks at Estella against the sandy neutrals they're drowning in, his blazing green eyes a refuge of color.

"I'm coming for you," he says.

# Chapter 42

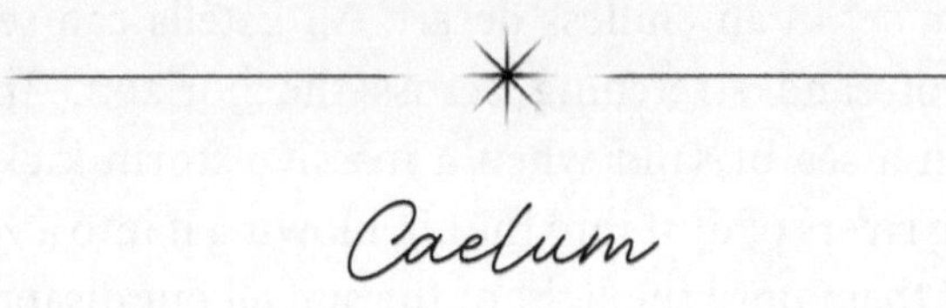

*Caelum*

"Have you taken us straight to hell?" Darin asks as they float in a raging inferno.

The fire closes in around them, obscuring their surroundings, whistling, screaming. Caelum forgot how frightening and loud fire sounds are when one is in the thick of it. There's no point in explaining their location here; they won't hear him through the deafening howl of the flames. In a dream world hover, Caelum leads them away from the burning fire, smoldering wooden beams crashing down around them, and through the rubble of what once was Rózsa Castle.

"I threw the key into the night that Estella and I died in our last life together."

"What is wrong with you, man?" Kal asks as burning ash blows through his form, burning a little brighter just as it passes through him. "Are you a glutton for punishment or something?"

"The point was to hurl the key into a place no one would find it, a place no one would ever think to look. The point was to never revisit this burning hell."

"Yet here we are," Kal says.

"Let's just get the damn key," Caelum mutters. "The less we see here, the better."

"I hear screaming," Darin says, drifting toward the voices.

"No, don't!" Caelum calls out, racing after him, with Kal close behind.

But he is too late. They hover over the former versions of Caelum and Estella. Estella's leg is pinned beneath a fallen beam, and Caelum strains with all his might to lift it. But he knows their fate. The words they exchange will be their last. Their hands are smudged with soot, clasped together, when the realization that Estella is trapped sinks in. Caelum turns back to the beam, wrestling with it until blood seeps from the scratches it carves into his arms. But he can't bring himself to look into her eyes again—eyes that know the end is near, but don't understand what the end brings, that don't know the beginning beyond the end—eyes filled with utter finality.

"Save yourself!" Estella screams, and it shakes Caelum to the core, just like it did the first time. Though Caelum can't bear to look, he's compelled to. He knows he couldn't save her then, nor now, but he can't help but try. Her chest heaves in her torn, singed gown made of lace, now covered in soot as the smoke thickens the air around them.

No, Caelum did not save himself. He did not leave Estella. He could not.

"I'm coming with you," Caelum says instead, choking on the dense smoke. "To the other side," he adds, his voice barely a whisper. "I'll find you. I'll always find you," he promises as they're overcome by smoke, washed away by flames.

Caelum made Estella a promise, and in every life he's lived, his word is good.

When the fire subsides, Darin and Kal stand before him. They don't speak, just hover close in a kind of spiritual hug. *"I'm sorry"* and a new understanding are written on their faces.

In search of the key, Caelum floats off, his head drooping and his body limp, like a coat left hanging on a hook. Just outside what's left of the castle walls, they arrive at a large well, its mouth paved in stone. Buried under ash in its depths lies the key.

Darin and Kal wait at the entrance as Caelum begins his descent. The bottom of the well spans roughly fifteen feet across, the area he must sift through to find the key. On his knees, he presses his hands into the layers of ash and soot, searching blindly until something catches his eye—a glimmer of gold in the faintest nook, illuminated by a shaft of moonlight.

He reaches out and pulls out a key, half buried in the ash. But as he examines it, confusion creeps in. It's not the key to the in-between. It's too pretty. It looks just like his key to the other side. But how could it be? That key is safe in his pocket.

Caelum hesitates, then pulls out his key to the other side and holds them both up to the single beam of light piercing the depths of the well. They're identical. After a moment's pause, he pockets the second key. Now he has two.

Caelum continues sifting through the ash until the tip of his finger connects with something hard. It makes the kind of scraping sound against the rocky bottom that something metal would make. He fishes the object out of the soot and rubs it clean. This is it. The key to the in-between is decayed and rusted. Its teeth are rough and jagged like a predator's teeth, and the key's bow is a circle with an X in the middle. The key itself looks like a warning sign—a warning Caelum would like to heed, but can't. Not if they're to rescue Athena.

Caelum bursts from the well, and Darin and Kal follow, no questions asked. While they may not like it, they know where they're going. Dark doors—they're unmistakable. Rare and scattered, they are the only passages to the in-between. Their presence is felt before they're seen, a deep unease that settles in the pit of the stomach, the air heavy with sorrow and decay. They repel most, driving a primal instinct to flee, but the lost are irresistibly drawn to their quiet malice. These doors lie in the darkest periods of history, and Caelum knows just where to find one.

First, they arrive at a door, its edges shimmering faintly, a well-traveled threshold to the other side. Caelum hovers before it, pulling all three keys from his pocket.

"Three keys?" Kal asks, eyeing the golden pair and jagged one.

"Two of the same," Darin says, nodding at the matching four-leaf clover bows.

"Found them both in the well," Caelum says. He examines them, frowning. "Shit—how do I know which one is mine? They're identical."

He inserts the first golden key into the lock, turns it, and pushes the door open. The vacuum of time blows through like a powerful gale. Pulling the door shut, Caelum then tries the second key, and they're hit with another blast of time when the second key works.

"Guess I really do have two," Caelum murmurs.

When they set foot on the other side, familiar energies rush to meet them, lighting them up with understanding. Without a word, the spirits know their mission and send them on their way. The energies' light carries them to the edge of darkness. They must make the journey through this door on their own.

The door to the in-between seethes and pulsates with hate, and it isn't far. It's here, on the other side, in the now. The current time is already bleak, a moment that will only darken if they fail.

"I'm not going in there," Darin says, doubled over, clutching a fist to his stomach.

"I know the feeling, but we must carry on. We can do this," Caelum assures them.

"He's right. We got this," Kal says, gripping Darin and Caelum's shoulders like they're one unit, one weapon.

The door, inky steel, shifts like liquid, humming an unintelligible, sinister prayer understood only by the in-betweeners. When Caelum turns the key in the lock, the hums morph into bone-chilling howls.

"Shut out what you can. Don't absorb too much, and don't listen too closely," Caelum warns.

He puts the words into practice, bypassing the handle and bursting through the door with a swift kick. They are sucked in with a shriek, the force of it sending them tumbling. Their lights are dimmer in the in-between, and there's no light to guide them. Darin swats at his face as if fending off a bee, his hands tangling in his long hair.

A low groan escapes Kal, followed by panicked screams that quicken Caelum's pulse. They settle when Caelum grabs them, pulling them into a huddle. Unlike Caelum, Darin and Kal are newcomers, virgins to the in-between. Their shells need toughening.

*"Cassius, Cassius, Cassius."* It is both a twisted greeting and a recognition of their presence.

"Don't listen to them," Caelum says. "Hold tight to what's good, and they won't corrupt us."

The in-betweeners scour for cracks in their souls, any point of weakness where they can seep in like malevolent tar.

"Where are we going?" Kal asks, gritting his teeth.

"I don't know," Caelum says, his voice low.

Growls rumble from Darin and Kal's clenched jaws.

"*Yet.* I don't know yet. We must…" His words trail off as he pauses, gathering focus. "We must listen for Athena—tune out the voices of the in-between, and listen for Athena's voice."

In the in-between, time collapses on itself, stretching, slowing to a trickle, and then rushing in waves. Caelum can't say how long they've searched for Athena before they find her. It could have been mere seconds, the time it takes for a fallen star to blaze a trail, or it could have been an eternity. A few times, they counted themselves among the lost, only for their lights to flicker back to life, glowing brighter. It was in one of these moments that Athena's voice cut through the emptiness.

They follow her song until they see her light. While it's dim, it is still brighter than the in-betweeners. It ignites her fire-red tresses, and like a lighthouse, guides them to her. She weeps as she sings in a murmur, and when Caelum speaks, she doesn't hear him.

"Athena," Caelum says, his hands on her shoulders, but her eyes don't connect with his. He's invisible to her. She's been trapped in the in-between for too long, perhaps fighting it so relentlessly that she's unable to let anything in—not even him. "Athena!" Caelum repeats, shaking her shoulders gently. A flicker of recognition sparks in her eyes. "It's me, Caelum."

"Caelum…" She murmurs his name slowly.

"Yes, and Darin and Kal." They surround her, their lights intermingling in a synergistic blaze that pushes back the hungry souls of the in-betweeners. She burns ever brighter.

Without letting the in-between steal another moment, they merge into one blinding force and make their escape. Untouchable, they crash through the gates of hell and emerge on the other side.

The first dawn after an endless night blinds them momentarily with its light. The refuge of the other side restores their wholeness, and an almost forgotten strength awakens within them.

Just as soon as the euphoria of returning settles into their bones, Athena says, "I'd be lost for eternity without you, but now you must listen. My message is urgent, and I fear time is slipping away. You must have seen me in the vision; I used the last of my energy to send it. You know now that Alexander is Connor, but Cassius walks among the living, too. He's occupied a woman…"

"Valentina," Caelum says. "Thanks to your warning, we figured out her true identity through her connection to Connor."

"We almost had her," Kal says, rubbing the fist he smashed against Valentina's car window, "but she got away."

"You don't understand how important it is to stop them," Athena says, stepping closer and gripping Caelum's arm. "Not only is their mission to silence Estella, but they also seek to spread a dark message." She buries her face in her hands, crimson hair spilling over like curtains closing on a finale. "There is a text," she then says, looking up at them, her expression tortured, "its words foretold to usher in the end of times."

"*The Book of Origin and Fate,*" Caelum says.

"You know of it? Is it too late?!" Athena cries.

"I hope not," Kal replies, his tone urgent. "But we have to act fast. We saw Connor buy it at auction. They must be working on distributing it to the masses as we speak."

"No wonder they shelled out a million bucks for it," Darin says. "It's priceless evil."

Suddenly, a brilliant flash fills the space around them. The Source, in the form of a powerful light radiating an intense energy, comes to them with a message.

*"There is power within words. Just as they heal, they can poison. Just as they repair, they can destroy. Words, whether spoken by the light or the darkness, may hold great influence. They have the capacity to ignite a movement of salvation, or become a weapon of unimaginable magnitude. This text, its words, will stir a hate the world has never known. It must be erased from time, and those who speak its words must be silenced,"* says the Source.

"You must go now," Athena tells them.

*"There's something else,"* the Source says. *"Estella is to be a traveler. My consent is all you need to transform her. Her key..."*

Caelum feels a strange warmth and reaches for his pocket, where heat is slowly building. It's where her key burns. He retrieves the keys, and one of the two identical keys begins to glow.

*"Meet her in a dream, and take her on a trip. Show her truth,"* the Source says, before the other side fades away.

When Caelum wakes from his extended slumber, he's sandwiched between Darin and Kal, whose heavy arm is draped over him. In a swift toss, Caelum flings it off and sits up.

"How the heck did I end up in the middle?" Caelum asks, not expecting an answer in the quiet darkness.

But then Ryoko says, "Well…"

"Never mind," Caelum says quickly. "I don't want to know."

There's a soft clink as Ryoko tugs the lamp chain, revealing herself slouched in the adjacent chair. Her eyes are dull, not their usual rich brown, and the light casting shadows on her face reveals that she's exhausted.

"Were we any trouble?" Caelum asks.

"You three are a handful," Ryoko says, rubbing her lower back as she twists her torso, grimacing at the crack of her spine. "Like three big babies needing around-the-clock care. One of you gets up for water, and you all get up. One needs to eat, and the other sleepwalks into the door. It was a nightmare. I'm like a sleep-deprived mother of triplets."

"Did they come looking for us?" Darin asks. He yawns big, muffling it halfway through with his hand.

His face, shaved clean the night they went to sleep, is now covered in a short beard.

"No, but Estella did. She rang the bell, but I didn't answer. I didn't know what to tell her," Ryoko says.

That extinguishes the last trace of sleep in Caelum. He can't imagine what Estella must be thinking, but it can't be good. It's damage control time.

"I have to get to her," Caelum says, rolling over Darin to get out of bed.

"It's late," Ryoko warns. "She's probably asleep, and you need to gather your strength. You'll have to wait until tomorrow."

Before she even finishes, Caelum's legs give out, and he collapses back onto the bed, catching himself on Darin, who groans when Caelum's elbow connects with his gut.

"See what I mean?" Ryoko says.

"Tomorrow…" Kal says, propping himself up to sit. His gaze drifts to Darin. "You look different," he says.

Darin touches his face and discovers his beard. Caelum and Kal follow suit, also finding that their facial hair has grown. Darin moves his hands to his hair and encounters two braids, his fingers gliding over the plaits.

"Pigtails," Ryoko says with a smirk. "It made your hair easier to manage."

Checking to see if Ryoko took liberties with their hair, Caelum and Kal quickly run their fingers through it. Then Kal hooks his thumb into the waistband of his boxer shorts, stretching them to peek inside.

Ryoko rolls her eyes. "There's nothing interesting in there."

Kal grins, flopping back onto his pillow. "Tomorrow," he starts again, this time serious. "We put an end to Alexander and Cassius."

# Chapter 43

*Estella*

Estella pops in her earbuds, and when the music starts playing, she pedals a little faster and feels a little freer. After days spent locked inside, working up the courage to publish her novel and crafting new poems, she's finally out, riding along the Iron Horse Trail. Much of her poetry draws from the life she lived before Lucas, but lately, Caelum's name lingers, unwritten, yet ever present in her verses. When a sad love song comes on, she slows, the lyrics cutting through her like they were written for her pain. She thinks of Caelum. *Damn him.*

While she feels the promise of a new chapter, she can't fully let go of the last. She craves the closure people yearn for when someone vanishes without a word. He could have at least said goodbye.

The trail is an obstacle course. Estella weaves from side to side, dodging joggers, kids, dogs, and other bikers. About a mile in, a buzz from the pocket of her sweatshirt catches her attention. Like a tightrope walker, she struggles to keep her balance, gripping the handlebars and keeping her eyes on the path while sneaking a glance at her phone.

Incoming call from Caelum. *Oh, crap!* She swerves off the trail and into the bushes. Emerging with a few scratches and a crown of dried leaves and twigs in her hair, she groans. Where's her phone? She dives back into the shrubbery to retrieve it.

Estella finds her phone, her heart racing. The thought of talking to Caelum after all this time leaves her breathless. What could he possibly have to say now? She takes a shaky breath and answers.

Caelum starts with a simple hello. A matching response would make sense, but Estella remains silent. There are too many words—or none at all—to express what she feels, so she says nothing.

"I'm sorry," Caelum says, his voice heavy with regret, but it's nowhere near enough. "I've been thinking of you. Missing you." Estella exhales deeply, but words still elude her. "And like I said, I'm coming for you."

The call ends.

What did he say? He's never told Estella he's "coming for her." Not once. Well, except in that desert dream...

Estella stands frozen, phone still in hand, mouth hanging open. Tears well up. She's spent weeks on end in the dark, and Caelum's sudden words hit like a floodgate bursting. She is more confused than ever.

She dabs her eyes with her sleeve and gets back on her bike, Caelum's scant words running in circles in her mind. It's like they're connected in a way she can't explain, like he was in her head, or in her dreams.

The wind picks up, and the clouds move in, blotting out the sun. The trail grows quieter as foot traffic thins. Rain is in the forecast, though no drops have fallen yet. Fearing she'll get drenched, Estella pulls her hoodie over her head and picks up the pace.

She quickly reaches the stretch of trail that weaves through downtown Danville, running along the parking lot where the farmer's market is set up on weekends. Suddenly, a guy steps out from the parking lot, squarely in her path. Estella brakes hard, nearly toppling over her handlebars to avoid crashing into him. His hoodie is pulled low, shadowing his face, and he just stands there frozen, like he's stuck in a Jell-O mold, blocking her way.

She yells at him, "Move it!"

He tilts his chin up, the light catching his face—the face that haunts her.

"Caelum?"

He pushes back his hoodie. "It's me."

"How…?" That's all that comes out. "… *did you know where to find me?*" gets lost, but the one word she manages to get out is a start. There are too many how's, what's, and why's to know where to begin.

"I told you I was coming for you." He smiles, looking into the distance down the trail. "Let's walk," he says.

As they stroll down the trail, Estella walks her bike between them, neither of them knowing where to start. An uncomfortable silence fills the air. Caelum acts as if he's about to say something, then Estella looks at him, and he lets out a breath, whatever he was going to say getting lost in it.

"Where were you?" Estella finally asks, dubmfounded.

"It's complicated, but I'll explain, I promise. First, I want to hear about you. How've you been? Are you okay?"

*No. I'm very not okay,* she thinks. But instead, she says, "Yeah… I'm okay. I've been working on getting my book published, and writing poems. I never heard back from Valentina."

"Good," he says.

*"Good?"*

"Uh… I'll explain that later, too."

"Listen, I had this dream about you, while you were … away," she begins hesitantly. "We were in a sandstorm in the desert, and you were playing the violin. In the dream, you told me you were coming for me. So, when you said on the phone—'Like I said, I'm coming for you…' It sounds crazy, but it's like you were really there in my dream."

"It's not crazy. We need to talk about something," he says, stopping in his tracks. They stand alone on the now deserted trail, the clouds overhead near bursting at the seams. "It's about the importance of dreams. There are all kinds of dreams, but every now and then, there are dreams that offer a glimpse of the future, or the past— something bigger than what we see or know in real life. They are gateways to other worlds, other times, even oth- er realities. These are special dreams, ones that shouldn't be ignored—dreams that inspire art and movies, fuel desires, and change lives."

"I know the importance of dreams. I'm a witch, remember?" Estella says, her voice steady, though she isn't sure where he's going with this. "Is there a particular dream you've been having? Like a recurring dream? I have recurring dreams and visions all the time. I had a recurring vision of you." She hesitates, then adds, "Well, I didn't know it was you at first, but—"

Caelum cuts her off, his voice urgent. "No, that's not what I'm getting at." He pauses, his eyes intense, as if he's choosing his words carefully. "There is a world, a reality where we know we are to be born into this world and live this life, without knowing the other boundless reality we come from. On the other side, we know everything."

"Are you talking about life after death?" Estella asks. "I do believe there's something beyond this life, that our energies don't just die." She swallows, but confusion makes it go down hard.

"In these dreams, we can go to the other side. We can go anywhere," Caelum continues. "There are doors. You just have to find them. You almost opened one of them in that one dream—the one where you wore the red dress. On the other side of that stained glass door was you. It was a future you. It was a door to the future. Do you see what I'm saying? There are many, many doors to many, many places and times."

"I didn't tell you about that dream…" she cuts in, the words coming out shakier than she'd like. A mild panic settles in. As Caelum talks in riddles, Estella's thoughts spiral. Does he have some kind of magic himself that he's been keeping from her? She knew he was too good to be true…

"Don't you understand?" Caelum says, his voice low and insistent. "Each life is but a mere speck in an unending state of being, and your dream about meeting me in the desert—it was real. I was trying to reach you from the in-between."

"Caelum, what are you saying?" Estella whispers. Mild panic turns to disbelief. *How is he getting into my dreams?* she thinks. *Is he getting into my head, my thoughts...?*

A knot forms in the pit of her stomach. She stares at him, the man she thought she knew, and suddenly, he's a stranger. Is he some kind of witch, too—the powerful dark ones her mom and dad warned her about? Estella descends into a place darker than the despair she felt when Caelum went missing as her perception of him shatters.

"Maybe if I explain it better…" Caelum offers. "At the intersection of this world—" He motions towards the ground. "—and the other side—" He moves his hands up to the sky. "—we may catch a glimpse of something that is not completely known to us in our current life. These glimpses can come in dreams, life passions, people we meet, and the unexplainable. It's when someone seems familiar, but we don't know why. It's like when *we* first met. Did you feel the unexplainable?"

"Okay, you're not making any sense." Estella thinks of excuses to leave. She needs time to process.

"We've been together before," Caelum continues, "in another life, and on the other side."

"Who are you? I don't even know you," Estella says, stepping back from him.

"When you fall asleep tonight, I'll show you. I'll explain where I've been, tell you about Valentina, everything. Then you'll understand," Caelum says, his eyes wild, the different shades of green twisting and bending into one another like the mad brushstrokes of Van Gogh's cypresses.

The clouds tear loose, and it begins to pour. It's a timely and welcome excuse to escape. Estella hops on her bike.

"I have to go," she says, pedaling away quickly, putting distance between her and Caelum.

"Estella!" Caelum yells after her. "You'll see, I promise!"

The faster Estella pedals, the sharper the sting of the rain against her face. She tugs on the strings of her hoodie, pulling it tighter over her head, but it's no use; she's drenched. Besides, Estella doesn't feel the cold or the wet. She feels nothing.

# Chapter 44



Cold, wet, and anxious, Caelum strips off his rain-soaked sweats, tosses them in the laundry hamper, jumps into a quick shower, and gets dressed. He rushes through the motions to do nothing but wait for sleep. Bedtime is still hours away, but getting into a dream to meet with Estella is urgent. He doesn't dare imagine what she must think of him now, and she'll feel that way until she learns the truth. Tonight's dream can't come fast enough.

To pass the time, Caelum wanders into his kitchen, but he doesn't feel like eating or drinking. Instead, he calls Kal, who, along with the rest of the crew, has gotten a head start on tracking down Connor and Valentina.

"She thinks I'm nuts," Caelum says the moment Kal picks up. "There was no way around it. I had to tell her about everything—the other side, dreams, our history… So, I laid it all out, like a royal flush, but she just looked at me like I'm crazy. She didn't get it."

"Why would she? It defies all earthly logic," Kal reasons. "Even witchy magic. You know that witches can see things, but they don't have access to the kind of knowledge we have."

"The only way to get her to understand is by showing her, so that's what I'll do tonight," Caelum says, leaning against his kitchen counter. "And then, hopefully, we'll catch up with you guys."

"Good plan," Kal says hurriedly, then shifts, his tone sharpening. "Now, here's the deal. We had no luck getting to Connor and Valentina in reality, so we had to track them in the dream world. I slipped into a dream, combed through the last week or so, completely unnoticed, and found out they're working with a local publisher, San Francisco's aptly named Diablo Press. They've struck a deal to distribute the text." He pauses. "But it's worse than we thought. They plan to create an ebook and embed something in both the ebook and the text that manipulates people the moment they read it. We're not just dealing with some book. This is mind control."

Caelum's phone slips from his hand and hits the hardwood floor. A muffled *"Hello?"* comes from the speaker as he scrambles to pick it up. Expecting a cracked screen, he hesitates to look, but the sturdy case holds up. "I'm on my way," he says, pacing around the kitchen island. "Tonight's meeting with Estella will have to wait."

What if they're too late? The fate of humanity rests on their shoulders, and here he is, anguishing over what Estella thinks of him.

Kal's voice cuts through his spiraling thoughts. "Not so fast. There's good news. It hasn't gone to print yet, and we know where the text is locked away."

Caelum stops pacing. "The plan?" he says, gripping his phone tighter.

"Break into Diablo Press and take it," Kal says, his tone steady.

"I can handle that," Caelum offers quickly.

"No need," Kal replies firmly. "We have everything under control. We're going to execute tomorrow night."

"Look, I'm doing this," Caelum insists. "If I can track down and confiscate Beano, I can certainly snatch that decrepit book."

"Beano…?"

"Never mind. I'll just be there to get the book, okay? Tonight, Estella becomes one of us. Tomorrow, that book becomes a heap of ashes."

"You should also know we've found Valentina's local hideout," Kal says. "She's got a place in Blackhawk. Ryoko insists on handling Valentina, but Darin and I refuse to let her go alone. She wouldn't have it, though; she's determined to be the one to bring Valentina down. You know, it's personal for her."

"I know, but don't let her go it alone," Caelum replies, his jaw tightening. "Valentina is too dangerous, and she's probably got her puppet, Connor, right by her side."

"Darin and I are doing what we can, but you know Ryoko. She does what she wants, when she wants. We're trying to get ahold of her now, but she's gone offline," Kal says.

"You and Darin better get on it, then. I'll be at your place tomorrow, and we'll make our move on Diablo Press after dark."

"Okay. Good luck tonight, man," Kal says. "You know, with Estella. Just say the word, and we'll pay a visit in case she needs convincing."

"I may need all the help I can get," Caelum says grimly.

Two a.m. approaches, and still no sign that Estella has entered the dream world. She must be having trouble sleeping. Caelum's anxiety builds by the moment. Then, like a wave, it washes over him; Estella has finally stepped into the dream realm. Caelum's eyelids grow heavy, the pull of the dream world taking hold, and soon he slips into that space. The first stop is to retrieve the keys—the ones that, when dreams end, always return to the same place they were found. With the keys in hand, the next destination is Estella.

California poppies blanket the field where Estella stands. She wanders barefoot through the flowers, her tresses flowing in the gentle wind. Caelum calls out to her. She turns her head and peers at him over her shoulder, tossing her head back in a playful laugh, the sun infusing her brown hair with a golden glow. Through the poppies, she runs towards Caelum and jumps into his arms.

"Caelum, I've missed you so much," she says, wrapping her arms around his neck.

"I've missed you, too. You don't even know how much." His voice is thick with emotion. "Now, there's something I must show you. I'd like to take you to the other side."

"Oh, right. I forgot," she says—and in an instant, all traces of happiness vanish from her face. She withdraws her arms from around his neck like water pouring down a drain. "You're not who I thought you were. You're a dark witch, aren't you? Have you been reading my thoughts—my *private* thoughts? They're not yours to read, you know?" She pushes him away, her eyes filled with hurt. "Why can't you be the person you were before you disappeared—the person I had dreamed of?"

"I am that person," Caelum says, his voice soft, but firm. "If I were you, I'd think I was a dark witch, too, but you have to trust me. Take my hand." He extends his arm toward her, his palm an invitation hovering in front of her. She looks at it skeptically, hesitant. "Please," Caelum adds, his voice tinged with urgency.

When she looks up at him, her face softens. She hesitantly places her hand on his.

Through the field of poppies, Caelum leads Estella to a barely visible outline of a transparent door suspended among the flowers.

"What is this?" Estella asks, her voice filled with wonder and suspicion.

"It's where our travels begin," says Caelum.

"Is this a door? Where did this come from?" She inspects the door closely, placing her hands on its surface, feeling its cool, solid existence. "This appeared out of nowhere. How strange."

"It's been here all along. You just have to look closer," Caelum says, pulling two identical golden keys from his pocket. They're indistinguishable at first, but one begins to glow, brightening with a warm, radiant light. "This one must be yours," he says, handing her the glowing golden key. She gazes at it in wonder as it smolders in her palm. "Go ahead, unlock the door," Caelum encourages.

After some trial and error, the key clicks into place, and Estella pushes the door open. She doesn't step through, but stays put, peeking into the other side.

"It's okay," Caelum reassures her. He takes the first step, and she follows him into endless time.

"Where are we?" Estella asks, his voice filled with amazement as she searches the expanse around them.

"We're home," Caelum says. It's light and dark at the same time. It's more a feeling than anything else, a completeness. On the other side, we're reunited with everything and everyone we've ever known in life and in death. We stand in truth in its purest form.

Tears spring to Estella's eyes, her mouth moving, forming words that don't come out. After a moment of struggling, she manages a strained whisper. "I can feel it. I feel the unexplainable." Through a mix of laughter and tears, she says, "Yes, we are home!"

"You're a traveler now. You know what this means, right?" Caelum says.

"I do. I can feel it." Her eyes widen with realization. "Oh! We never really die, do we? I mean, our energies. And I can use my dreams to go anywhere, can't I?"

"Yes," Caelum says with a nod. "Remember your dream in the forest? Travelers walked through you. When we travel, we can choose to pass through anything or anyone—unless it's another traveler. When you wrapped your arms around me in the field of poppies just before you became a traveler, I could've let your arms pass through me. But I chose to feel you."

"And now that I'm a traveler, you have no choice but to feel me," Estella says. She puts her hands on Caelum's chest, grounding herself in this new reality.

Caelum motions to what's in front of them, another vision of Estella. He's taken her to a point in the past.

"Is that me?" she says, moving closer. She stares at her younger self lounging on her bed, wearing skinny jeans and holding a smartphone. She studies the face of her younger version and the screen of the phone she's holding. "I must be fourteen or something," Estella says, recognizing the moment. "I'm on that app I used to play Tetris all the time. There was just something about every Tetris piece having its place, all the pieces fitting together."

Having traveled to multiple points in Estella's life, Caelum knows she just wanted to be a Tetris piece. But she's never been a Tetris piece—not really.

"I brought you here to show you how we travel in time," Caelum says.

"My room at my parents' house in Seattle," Estella murmurs, inspecting her surroundings. "My old drum set!" A wave of nostalgia hits her when she hears footsteps. Her mom walks into the room, and Estella's jaw drops. "Is that my mom? She looks so young!" Estella moves closer, inches from Hannah's face, studying every line and contour with wide eyes. "This is too weird," Estella whispers.

She follows Hannah out of the bedroom and down the hallway. The walls aren't decorated with family portraits; her family wasn't one for those types of photos. But when they reach the living room, adjacent to the kitchen, Estella sees a display of Hannah's paintings, including some of the portraits she had painted of Estella throughout the years.

"It's time to move on," Caelum says softly. "There's much to see, but we could never see it all. That would take an eternity."

Caelum guides Estella through the moments on the other side, teaching her how to navigate the flow of time. He toggles closer to the present, and as they go, they're met by the gentle presence of connected spirits. Each moment they pass through brings more clarity to Estella's past lives, the souls she's known returning to her with increasing familiarity. Her spirit feels like a battery recharging, growing fuller with each connection. The weight of her past—of who she's been, of all the love and loss—becomes more tangible, more real.

Then, a flare of energy erupts within her, like a flame reigniting, and Estella knows instantly who it is: Lucas.

They rush toward each other, spirits intertwined, colliding into a vortex of energy that spins them together in perfect harmony. There's no sorrow, shame, or regret. There is no need for explanations or apologies. On this side, everything is understood, every moment of their shared history is felt, and there is only love, pure and eternal.

They unravel from the vortex, still intertwined in an unspoken connection, standing in a space where time and regret no longer matter. Only love remains—the joy of being together in perfect support and understanding.

"I see you're not here to stay," Lucas says, motioning to Estella's key.

"We'll find a place for that in the dream world," Caelum assures her. "So you can unlock the other side to visit Lucas whenever you like."

As Athena joins them, an unspoken understanding settles over the group. Estella and Athena need no introduction. Their souls resonate as if they've known each other across lifetimes. Athena's very presence seems to pour knowledge into Estella, and in an instant, the story of Alexander and Cassius blooms within her mind.

"It was you," Estella says, her voice edged with recognition, "the spirit in the dream—the woman in red, behind the stained-glass doors. That was me in the red dress, and you said, 'Your fears, the enemy, your destiny.' You were warning me about Valentina." Her expression darkens as she adds, "And Connor."

They sense that Athena has already connected with Lucas, and he knows everything—Estella's mission, she and Caelum's shared past, the truth about Cassius being Valentina and Alexander being Connor. Scenes come at them like blinding camera flashes: a black sports car, an ambulance, and bystanders frozen in shock. Athena sees Caelum picking up on new information.

"Tell them, Lucas," Athena urges.

"It was Connor who sent me home to the other side. He ran me down in his black sports car," Lucas says grimly.

"His black Tesla…!" Estella says, her energy flaring like a brewing storm. Her voice trembles with fury. "Why would he do that?! What did you ever do to him?"

"Why do half-souls do the wretched things they do? Because their spirits have burned out, leaving them hollow. Because they don't know love. Connor and Valentina want to turn people into half-souls for selfish, power-hungry, ego-driven reasons," Athena says. "Lucas was merely an obstacle—one that stood between Connor and you."

Surrounding Estella with his presence, Caelum gently diffuses the flickers of negative energy. "We have much to do," he says. "And that includes dealing with Connor. It's time we continue our journey."

But as the words leave his mouth, a fresh cascade of images crashes into his mind. A woman he doesn't recognize. A bloody knife glinting in dim light. The cold blue of Connor's eyes.

"What's this?" Caelum asks, confused.

"I was Emily Dunn, Connor's wife, and my death was no accident either. I died by his hand," Athena says. Caelum's head spins. "Remember, the Source granted me a life with no traveling rights, but with the promise of a dream—one that would tell me everything I needed to know to find Alexander, to help you and Estella."

Caelum nods in recognition as the pieces fall into place.

"The Source came to me in a dream," Athena continues. "And in that moment, my world changed. I was given a glimpse of the other side and the knowledge of who I had been before. From that moment, I ceased to be Emily. I seduced Connor to get close to him, and we wed. I was on the brink of connecting with you and exposing his true nature when, somehow, he discovered my identity. I'll never forget the moment he breathed my true name, *Athena*—as he drove the knife into me."

"Connor is finished," Caelum says, determined. "We have one more stop on our journey tonight, but by the light of day tomorrow, we'll be working to eliminate that book—and Connor and Valentina along with it."

After parting with Lucas and Athena, Caelum leads Estella through time to when the Source gave Kal and Darin their orders to protect her. Scrolling through time on the other side is a bit different than in dreams, where it's not as clear. Caelum has no trouble finding the moment, but Estella is much too distracted by her surroundings to watch the scene as it unfolds before them.

"What is this place?" Estella says, astonished. Jupiter dominates the sky. She stumbles back when she sees it. New to traveling, she finds Ganymede shocking, unlike anything she's ever seen. The vast alien landscape stretches around her, illuminated by the hypnotic dance of crimson auroras rippling above. Her mouth falls open in awe as she watches the shimmering ribbons of light.

"Kal and Darin are travelers, too? They were sent to protect me?" Estella asks once she realizes what's taking place on Ganymede. "I knew there was something special about them."

"Ryoko, too," Caelum adds. "You know now that Valentina and Connor are not your friends, but remember—you also have people looking out for you. You have an important purpose."

"I can feel that, too," she says, her voice tinged with growing clarity. "My book! In that dream, when Athena said, 'Your destiny,' she was talking about my book!"

"Do you understand now? Why you had to write that book?" Caelum asks.

As the implications of her purpose sink in, Estella feels the weight of it all resting on her shoulders.

"Why me? I've always felt like there were books inside me, but…"

"I don't know," Caelum says. "But what you have to say will help a lot of people. There are others—and your story, and theirs, will create the change the world needs."

"The Source… When can I speak with the Source?" Estella asks.

"I don't know that, either," Caelum says, chuckling. "We may go countless lifetimes without hearing from the Source. Give yourself time. The more you visit the other side, the more will come back to you—and the more you'll understand."

"Ah, Ganymede," Kal says as he admires the other-worldly view. He's arrived with Darin.

"We don't mean to crash the party," Darin says, rubbing his bearded chin with his thumb and forefinger. After their journey through the in-between, Caelum and Kal shaved, but Darin opted to keep his scruff.

Estella blinks, then points at Darin, her finger hovering in the air. "You have a beard," she notices, then she shifts her finger toward the past version of Darin as if playing a game of connect the dots. "But that Darin doesn't."

"That's the old me," Darin says, grinning. "The new me is bearded." He pauses, running his fingers through his scruff. "For now," he adds. "I can never get past the itchy stage."

Just then, Ryoko makes her delayed entrance, appearing alongside Darin and Kal.

"There you are," Kal says.

"Here … I … am," Ryoko says dramatically, spinning around Estella, her energy as lively as ever. "So, you're a traveler now. What a wonderful thing to be."

"Yes, indeed," Kal says. "Now that we're one big, happy family of travelers, it's time to tend to some pressing family business." Everyone stares at him blankly. "You know … like burning *The Book of Origin and Fate*." He motions for the group to follow him. They all move toward him—everyone except Ryoko.

Caelum stops and turns back to Ryoko, the others following his lead. "What are you waiting for?" he asks.

Ryoko hovers higher, and the auroras of Ganymede flare brighter around her. She looks like an edgy angel framed by the fiery red light.

"I can't go with you," Ryoko says. "Let's just say I caught up with Valentina at her place in Blackhawk, and … it didn't end well. It's my dang heart; it always gets me in trouble."

Upon them hearing Ryoko's words, everyone's lights dim a little, and they rush to her side.

"Tell me it's not true," Caelum says, his light dimming further as the truth sinks in.

"You know I could never love Cassius, right?" Ryoko says, her voice heavy with emotion.

"Of course," Caelum says, and the crew voices their agreement.

"The person I loved—or could have loved—never existed," Ryoko says.

"You don't need to explain. I understand," Caelum says, motioning to the others. "We all understand." Valentina had only shown Ryoko a carefully crafted illusion—a face she knew Ryoko longed to see. That version of Valentina—the one Ryoko fell for—was never real.

"You don't have to worry about Valentina—or, you know, Cassius," Ryoko says, her tone brightening. "She may have taken me out, but I made sure to take her with me. I crossed first, and she wasn't far behind. That knife of hers came in handy after all." She raises an eyebrow at Darin, who gives a subtle nod in acknowledgment. "When she passed over, you better believe I was waiting for her, key to the in-between in hand." Ryoko's lips curve into a smile. "I don't think she'll be crawling out of that pit anytime soon. But it's Connor you need to watch out for."

Estella winces at the mention of his name. "We'll work on reuniting him with Valentina," she says. She lowers her gaze and then whispers, "I'm sorry we didn't have the chance to get to know each other better. In life, I mean."

"Nonsense," Ryoko replies, waving her delicate hand through the air as if brushing aside an unwelcome thought. "In dreams and on the other side, we'll know each other better than we ever could in life."

At her words, the crew visibly brightens. They draw closer, their spirits glowing as they spiral around one another, a shared sense of connection and light filling the space between them.

"But I'll miss your jabs, your jokes, and your abundance of orange," Caelum says, his voice heavy with the weight of the loss. No matter how many times he loses someone, even when he knows they're just a dream away, it never gets easier. Though life, in all its beauty, never feels long enough, waking hours stretch long when you're apart from loved ones. "Who's going to give me a hard time now?"

"Eh, you know where to find me," Ryoko replies with a smirk. "Now get going."

# Chapter 45

## Estella

Estella's eyes flicker open to a world forever changed. Nothing about her has changed—except her understanding. Yet this knowledge changes everything. She's been gifted with a higher consciousness, but can't share her insights with anyone beyond her circle of travelers. The hardest part, she realizes, is resisting the urge to shout the secrets of the universe for all to hear. Being a traveler will teach her to be silent. No more spilling tea.

Estella moves through the morning in a dreamlike haze. As she brushes her teeth, she catches her reflection in the mirror, puzzling over it. How strange it is, she thinks, to inhabit a human form—a temporary vessel holding energies for a while. Returning to her body after flying on the other side, her spirit feels squeezed into tight quarters. And yet, what a precious gift it is, this body. There's nothing quite like the connection of energies through touch in the three-dimensional world. That kind of intimacy doesn't exist on the other side.

Estella looks at her children with new eyes. How magnificent they are! No matter what happens, she knows they'll be okay in the end. They'll always reunite. We are all immortals. We are all gods. The endless weight of a mother's worry eases. She longs to share this new understanding with her daughters, but can't. It's not for her to share. Hope and faith are all that is theirs. Her heart is so painfully full that she clutches her chest. How incredible it is to be alive! Can a mortal hold this much love without bursting? And Caelum…

Estella dials him, and as the phone rings, she notices something strange: the fear and anxiety that have always quietly simmered at her core are gone. How much lighter she is with the promise of the infinite! So, this is what it means to be Zen. She's officially chill, and for the first time, she has no reservations about sharing her words with the world. Her art, she now knows, is part of keeping the human spirit alive. That's what matters—not how many books she sells or who likes or dislikes her work, but the energy she gives through it.

Caelum answers, and Estella blurts out, "I love you, I love you, I love you!"

They both laugh at the silliness and inadequacy of the words. They vow to never use them again—a vow they'll certainly break.

"I'm coming with you guys to Diablo Press," Estella says firmly.

"You should stay with Darin. He'll watch over you and the girls," Caelum insists.

Estella shakes her head. "We don't need watching over. The babysitter will stay with Kaitlin and Mina."

They go back and forth, Caelum arguing against it, Estella standing her ground. Eventually, she convinces him to let her join the heist.

"But first, I need to see you," she says, her voice softening. "Come for me when the girls are in school."

Caelum skids up to Estella's place on his motorcycle. This time, she has no hesitation about getting on. She feels freer than she ever imagined, but also more aware than ever of how precious life truly is. She secures her helmet snugly, hops on behind him, and wraps her arms tightly around his waist.

As they pull into Caelum's driveway, Estella sees his house with fresh eyes. For the first time, it hits her: this is the home of her dreams, *their* home.

Caelum removes his helmet and turns to help her with hers. Before she's even free of it, his lips are on hers. The unexpected touch makes Estella's heart race.

They don't stop kissing as they walk through the front door. They don't stop kissing as they make their way to his room. They kiss as if they're trying to merge their souls together. Though they try, their bodies get in the way.

Despite their knowledge of the infinite, Caelum and Estella remove each other's clothes with the urgency of those who know their time is finite. Life, death, and dreams—the veil between them is thin indeed. These are the moments that shouldn't be taken for granted.

Estella glides her hands over Caelum's broad shoulders, then slowly works her way down to his jeans, tugging them and pulling his body closer. Caelum peers down at her with eyes that carry the weight of endless time. She'll do whatever he wants when he looks at her like that.

Caelum's hair falls in a wave over his face, and Estella gently tucks the strands behind his ear. She kisses along his jaw, catching the faint scent of woodsy soap and lingering where it's strongest. The sharp poke of his stubble brushes against her fingertips before she moves her hands back down to his waist to undo the top button of his jeans.

With her newfound enlightenment and heightened energy, Estella pushes Caelum onto the bed, crawling over him like he's captured prey. She begins kissing him, and the desire between them deepens with every touch. She moves lower, exploring new territory, though it's been so long since she's let herself feel this way that part of her would need a guidebook if it weren't for the desire guiding her now. She has all of him, but it's not enough.

All the want builds until it reaches need, and she pulls him on top of her. Their connection builds slowly, euphorically, until everything else fades into nothing but that feeling, growing stronger until it overtakes them both.

They lie in sleepy completeness for a while, and soon, Caelum dozes off. When he wakes, Estella turns toward him, propping her elbow on the bed and cradling her head in her hand. She admires him for a moment before gliding her hand over his tattoo.

"This is the Rózsa family coat of arms, isn't it?" Estella asks.

"You remember now?"

"I do, András Rózsa. It is I, your maiden, Mária Teré-zia," she says playfully.

"We were them lifetimes ago, but our fates won't end the way theirs did. Not if I can help it," Caelum says, taking Estella's hand in both of his.

"Do we know our fates?" Estella asks.

"Working with the future can be tricky. It's not concrete like the past. Futures are more like moving targets, constantly shifting."

"The future didn't come to me on the other side, but I felt a lot of our past," Estella says. "It's like my dreams make sense now. That song you played on the violin in the desert... I remember it."

"Long ago, it was your favorite song," Caelum says, propping himself up to sit. "And on that note, I think there's something you'd like to see."

"Okay, but first, you'll have to excuse me," Estella says, slipping the sheet off the bed. "I'm about to make myself feel at home." Leaving Caelum exposed, she wraps her bare body in the sheet and darts out of the room. Caelum, fumbling with his underwear, stumbles as he gives chase.

She sprints to her favorite room, the library, where the bookshelves overflow with volumes she has read, treasures, or wishes to read. Running her hands over the spines, she pauses, her fingers lingering on the books. Then, a thought sparks: the garden. She takes off again, heading for the glass doors leading to the backyard. Pressing her hands and face against the cold glass, she peers out at the garden, her breath fogging the surface.

"My favorites! You've planted them all, haven't you?" she says as Caelum finally catches up. The fleeting fog fades from the glass once she quiets. Before Caelum can answer, she's off again, this time heading for the music room.

On her way, a flash of faint pink catches her eye when she passes the open door to the spare bedroom. She backtracks a few steps and peers inside. The room is ballerina-themed, complete with a ballet barre and two beds. While the walls are a soft pale pink, the color doesn't overwhelm the space like one might expect. Instead, aside from the pointe shoes hanging elegantly on the wall, the décor features cream, tan, and natural wood tones. It's a sophisticated girl's dream.

"I did some more decorating. Do you think the girls will like it?" Caelum asks, appearing in the doorway.

"Are you kidding? They'll love it!" she exclaims. Too excited to stand still, Estella races to the music room. When Caelum turns up moments later, mildly out of breath, Estella's already holding Beano.

"Be careful with that," he says.

"I know what you did," she teases. "Our past isn't the only past that came to me on the other side. I know a bit about what you've been up to in this life."

"Oh, yeah?" Caelum says, smirking. "But you didn't see what else I tracked down. Before you took off running, I was trying to tell you." He walks to the armoire in the corner, retrieves a key from his pocket—a real key, of course—and unlocks the cabinet. With a triumphant smile, he swings open the doors to reveal a worn violin resting under a glass case.

Estella steps closer, tilting her head. It looks like any old violin to her, but she doesn't know much about violins. Caelum carefully lifts the glass case and cradles the instrument, handling it as though it were a delicate soufflé on the verge of collapse.

Once the violin rests under Caelum's chin, he slides the bow across the strings. Estella's eyes widen in recognition, and as the notes fall into place, her eyes turn glossy. Memories can stir powerful emotions, but the effect is synergistic when they come from another life. Swallowing the lump in her throat, she nods once, silently acknowledging the song that first brought them together. She's still holding Beano as Caelum locks the violin away again with the same care he showed in retrieving it.

"Let me see that," he says, taking Beano from her. He props one foot on the lower rung of a chair and balances the guitar on his upper thigh. The moment he begins to play, the room fills with the soulful sound of blues, his mastery evident in every note. As Caelum looks down at the strings, his hair falls to the corners of his mouth, reminding her of the first time she saw him, and turning her on just as much he did then. The arousal pulls her back into her body, reminding her that it lies bare beneath the sheet wrapped around her. Meanwhile, the guitar covers his briefs, leaving him effectively as exposed as she is. She knows he won't make it halfway through the song looking like that. As he plays, the muscles in his chest, arms, and abdomen tighten with each precise movement, his fingers finding every place they need to be. It's a seduction on every level.

Words, at this moment, feel as useless as a fallen guitar pick. Estella sweeps them up, saving words for another time, and Caelum follows her back to the bedroom in silence.

# Chapter 46

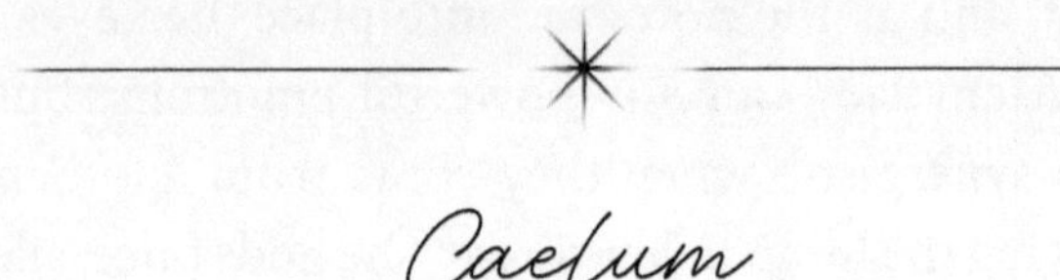

*Caelum*

That's the place. It looks exactly like Caelum saw it in his dream. Diablo Press sits in an unassuming brick building just off the waterfront near Ghirardelli Square. Kal has parked in a dark alley behind the building, and the crew waits for the right moment to make their move.

"Can you help me out, man? I'm suffocating in here," Caelum says, fiddling with the window button. The air feels thick, like he's choking on a million coconuts. They're crammed into Kal's SUV, with Darin and Estella in the back, Caelum in the passenger seat, and the bionic coconut air freshener swinging from the rearview mirror. No wonder Kal always smells like coconuts. Strong fragrances and colognes have never been Caelum's thing; the only scent you'll ever catch on him is laundry detergent or soap.

"Sorry, I had it on lock," Kal says, pressing a button to lower the window halfway, finally letting in a bit of breathable air. The coconut scent weakens only slightly.

The night air has lost its sting as warmer temperatures settle into the Bay Area. But in the city, the air, thickened with the marine layer, is several degrees cooler. With Caelum's window open, a less-than-comfortable chill fills the car. No one seems to mind.

"So, how do we know where to look once we're inside?" Estella asks.

Caelum twists in his seat, turning toward the back to face Estella and Darin as best he can. "Remember how I fell asleep for a moment when we were in my room? I poked around Diablo Press during that power nap," he says.

"Aren't you efficient?" Estella quips.

"Gotta love dream travel," Darin says, tapping out an air drum solo as Led Zeppelin's "Kashmir" pours from Kal's sound system. "It's the easiest way to case a place."

Kal cuts the music, and Darin freezes mid-drum.

"Darin, you're our getaway driver. You move into the driver's seat when Caelum and I go in. Estella, you sit shotgun. When it's time to get out of here, Caelum and I jump in the back," Kal says.

"No way. I'm going in, too," Estella insists, crossing her arms firmly over her chest. She doesn't look like she's going to budge.

"Absolutely not. There's no way you're going in there," Caelum says.

"Caelum's right. We're here to ensure your safety, remember? What good would we be if we let you participate in armed robbery?" Kal adds.

"Armed?" Estella asks, eyebrows rising.

"You thought we'd go in naked, did you?" Caelum says, patting his side. The check tells him what he already knows: the gun is there if he needs it.

Estella doesn't let up. She protests, weaving some kind of witchy magic into her argument, making a compelling case for why she'd be a good asset on the inside.

"Yeah, but…" Caelum starts, then trails off. Caelum and Kal mumble their disagreement, but neither can come up with an effective counterargument. Estella's pulled a witchy mind trick on them.

"Fine, but stick close," Caelum finally says.

Outside Kal's car, they breathe in the cool air tinged with San Francisco grit and seawater. The grimy but mellower smell of the city is a welcome reprieve from the concentrated artificial scent of the tropics. In the distance, the Hyde Street cable car grinds along its tracks, turning the corner. The street behind the building is quiet, with no one in sight—an ideal moment to make their move.

"Pull your hoodie down low, and don't look up at any security cameras. There's one at the entrance in the back. And don't touch anything," Caelum instructs, yanking his beanie lower.

"Don't worry. I've come prepared," Estella says, pulling black leather gloves from her pocket and slipping them on. Has she done this before?

Muffled music comes from the car, and Caelum turns to see Darin playing air drums again. "We're relying on *this* guy to keep a lookout?" he asks the night. Oblivious to everything around him, Darin lets his long hair flap, and his wrists pump in the air. When Caelum taps on the car window, Darin's hair falls flat, and his hands drop to his lap. Using two fingers, Caelum motions for him to keep watch, pointing to his eyes and then the surrounding area. Darin responds with a closed-lip smile and a thumbs-up.

"The windows at the back of the building don't have glass-break sensors. That's our point of entry," Kal says, pulling a hairband off his wrist and wrapping it around his hair. It's just long enough to form a low ponytail, with a few strands falling loose in the front. He raises his hoodie over his head, then points ahead, signaling that it's go-time.

With no one in sight, they make it to the window unnoticed. Caelum takes off his sweater, holds it up over the glass, and with one swift motion, jabs his elbow into it, shattering the window. First, there's the loud crack of the break, followed by hundreds of glass fragments tinkling to the floor. The sweater dampens some of the sound and keeps most of the glass contained inside the building.

Estella and Kal stand with their backs to Caelum, scanning for passersby, but thankfully, none appear. Sharp shards of glass protrude from the window corners, so Caelum wraps his sweater around his fist and knocks them out.

Kal goes in first, then they help Estella through, and then it's Caelum's turn. Glass crunches under their shoes as they make their way through the window. Squeezing through takes some maneuvering, but they manage to avoid getting scratched. As they move deeper into the building, the last remnants of the streetlights fade. The place is pitch dark, smelling of stale coffee and ink.

Caelum knows the book is locked away in a desk on the second floor, so he takes the lead, using the flashlight on his phone to guide the way. It's dead silent, except for the occasional creak under their feet as they tiptoe down the hall toward the stairs.

As they near the staircase, Caelum stops and whispers, "You guys wait here and keep watch." Estella and

Kal exchange uneasy glances and start to protest, insisting that they stick together, but Caelum holds firm. "I'll be in and out with the book in a matter of minutes," he says.

Caelum ascends the stairs carefully, but he doesn't do it quietly. Almost every step of the rickety stairs creaks loudly as he makes his way up to the top. Quiet returns once Caelum reaches the second floor. Peering over the banister, he spots Estella and Kal below. Caelum's phone light flickers in their direction, unintentionally catching their faces. They flinch, raising their arms to shield their eyes. Then, a beam from Kal's phone cuts through the darkness, momentarily blinding Caelum. Dust dances in the light as it settles on Caelum like a makeshift spotlight. Squinting, Caelum sees Kal giving him a thumbs-up. With a nod, Caelum turns and continues down the dark hallway.

At the end of the hallway stands a frosted glass door, its surface glowing faintly orange. Either someone is inside, or a light has been left on. Once Caelum reaches the door, he listens intently for any noise, but all he hears is his own breathing.

Not knowing what he'll find on the other side of the door, Caelum draws his gun before trying the handle. After a few tries, he finds that the door is locked. No matter; locks have never been a problem for Caelum. Within seconds, he picks it, the mechanism giving way with a soft click.

The door opens just a crack, enough for the barrel of his gun to slip through. With his eyes right behind his gun, Caelum sweeps the room as he steps inside. But it's just Caelum and the pounding of his heart. A lamp illuminates scattered piles of paper sitting on top of the desk that holds the book.

Wasting no time, Caelum makes a dash for the bottom drawer and gives it a pull. It doesn't budge. This lock is tougher than the door, but he's prepared. Digging into his pocket, he pulls out his tools and crouches down.

As he works the lock, he hears a thud. He freezes. The sound came from downstairs.

Sweat builds on Caelum's brow as he wrestles with the stubborn lock. A bead of it escapes, slipping down his cheek and disappearing under his chin. The heat and pressure are suffocating, and he tugs at his collar, desperate for air. Then, a scream pierces the silence.

Estella.

Heart racing, Caelum jams his pick into the lock with renewed urgency. *Click.* The drawer slides open, but all he finds are papers—crinkled, disorganized, and useless. No book. He tears through the contents, papers ripping in his frantic hands. Where is it? It was supposed to be here!

With the creak of the steps at a staccato, Caelum makes it down the stairs in a fraction of the time it took to climb them. At the bottom, Kal is sprawled on the floor, and Estella is nowhere in sight.

"Kal!" Caelum shakes him urgently. "Are you okay?"

Kal's eyes flutter open. He moans, reaching for the back of his head. He mumbles something that doesn't make sense. Caelum digs his fingers into Kal's thick hair, searching for any sign of injury. His hand finds a noticeable bump. He pulls his hand back to check for blood. Nothing. Kal's out of it, but he's going to be okay.

"Where's Estella?!" Caelum demands.

Kal's eyes flutter open again, focusing for a moment before closing. "Huh?" he groans as his hand drifts back to the bump on his head. He lets out another moan before collapsing flat against the floor.

Then, another scream—this one from down the hall, near the broken window.

# Chapter 47

Estella

"We could be good together," Connor says to Estella as he presses her against a coffee maker on the counter's edge. The coffee carafe clanks against its base as they knock against it, and Estella catches a stronger whiff of the stale coffee scent lingering in the air.

Connor's hair is wilder than ever, the veins in his neck prominent, almost pulsating, and his dead blue eyes are a whirlpool of madness. Estella can't bear to look at him as he presses himself against her, his gun digging into her side. With the hard metal pressing between her ribs, Estella squirms, trying to move away from the gun, but Connor only squeezes his body tighter against hers.

She looks away, her gaze landing on the broken window they came through. It's so close. If only she could reach it—escape from the man who killed Lucas and Athena, get away from this murderer.

Connor grabs Estella's chin with his rough hand, forcing her to face him again, and her stomach churns as she meets his gaze. Her eyes flick back to the window, a possible escape, but with her chin still gripped in his hand, he jerks her head, pulling her attention back to him. Reluctantly, Estella's eyes are back on Connor.

"Just think of what we can accomplish," Connor says. "Once you read the book, you'll be inspired. You can even write for us," he says and twists his lips into a sick smile, exposing teeth more menacing than Estella remembers.

"I don't think so, Connor," says Caelum, who has crept up behind them, gun aimed at him. "Or should I call you Alexander?" he continues, stepping closer, his gun now pointed directly at Connor's head.

A deep, rolling laugh rumbles from Connor's gut, and Estella feels him tremble with each rasp. "Did you think it'd be so easy?" Connor says. He jabs his gun harder into Estella's side, and she yelps in pain. "I'll kill her," he warns, dragging Estella back a few steps.

Guns are pointed at each other, and now Connor and Estella are face-to-face with Caelum. Sweat stains line the front edges of Caelum's beanie, but his hands are as steady as time on his gun. Caelum's eyes, without a trace of fear or doubt, are green glass under sharp eyebrows. Estella's breath slows as she watches his calm mastery, but she notices the hand Connor uses to aim his gun at Caelum quivering ever so slightly. Inspired by the unshakable confidence in Caelum's eyes, Estella is emboldened to act.

In retaliation for the assault on her ribs, and in an attempt to crack a few of his, Estella throws an elbow back into Connor. Her jab drives into his right side, causing the hand holding his gun to drop away from Caelum. Within moments, Caelum is on Connor, pummeling him. With a brutal pistol whip, Caelum's gun connects with Connor's face, followed by another sharp crack as Caelum slams the hand Connor uses to grip his own weapon. The gun falls to the floor with a heavy clunk, and as they continue to wrestle, Estella quietly steals it.

"Stop!" she yells, and their heads snap towards her. The gun feels heavy and awkward in her hands as she points it at Connor. Trying to hide the fact that she's never held one before, Estella grips it tighter and straightens her arms. Caelum backs away from Connor, raising his own weapon. With two guns now pointed at him, heaving with breath, hands empty, Connor is just another desperate criminal who has run out of options.

The wail of police sirens grows louder until a blinding red-and-blue flash fills the room through the broken window. Within minutes, the back door bursts open, and several officers with guns drawn swarm the scene. Dozens of guns, besides the two Caelum and Estella are holding, are now aimed at Connor. His shoulders slump, but anger still burns in Connor's eyes.

"Hands up!" commands one officer. "Turn around and put your hands behind your back!"

Connor snarls, but complies. As the cops frisk him, Caelum leans in to inform Estella that they've been working with the police to bring Connor to justice. After Athena told Caelum about Connor's misdeeds, he hired an investigator to work the case.

Cuffs dangle from the officer's grip as he says, "Connor Dunn, you're under arrest for the murders of Emily Dunn and Lucas Larsen."

To Connor, it's the sound of freedom slipping away, click by click, as the officer tightens the cuffs around his wrists. To Estella, it's the sound of relief, and justice finally served.

As the police escort Connor out of the building, Kal emerges from the other room, rubbing the back of his head. Estella almost trips over her feet in her rush to reach him. Before dragging Estella away, Connor had snuck up behind them and cracked Kal on the back of his head with the grip of his gun. It was such a violent blow that Kal crumpled instantly to the floor, lying motionless. At that moment, Estella feared Connor would succeed in taking them out one by one.

"You okay, brother?" asks Caelum, massaging his own injury. Connor clocked him good in the jaw during their scuffle.

"I'm totally fine. Just a bump—but maybe I should be the one asking you if *you're* okay," Kal says.

Beanie missing, hair messy, and clothes askew, Caelum looks like he just stumbled out of a bar fight. He smooths his hands through his hair and scans the floor for his beanie. It's lying next to them on the dusty floor of Diablo Press.

Kal bends down to pick it up, whacks it against his leg to release dust and a couple of shards of window glass, and then hands it to Caelum. Before putting it back on, Caelum pulls Kal into a quick hug, giving him two loud pats on the back. It's the most love Estella has seen them exchange, and she feels it in her heart, too. Caelum and Kal then notice Estella reveling in their deepening friendship, and clearing their throats, they step away from each other.

"The book. It wasn't there," says Caelum, kicking around some of the larger pieces of broken glass, which scrape and clink as they collide. "Connor must've taken it. He could've hidden it somewhere else, or it may even be on him."

"It's right here," Estella says, pulling it out from behind her back and presenting it. The book is so ancient that she's surprised it doesn't crumble into dust in her hands. When Connor and Caelum were brawling, it dropped out of Connor's jacket, along with his gun. Estella snatched the book and stuffed it under her sweatshirt, tucking it into the waistband of her pants.

The crunching sound of glass shards underfoot alerts them to Darin's presence. "Right on," Darin says when he sees Estella brandishing the book.

"I told you I could pull off a heist," Estella says with a grin.

After she spends most of the night wide awake, replaying the night's crazy events, the feeling Estella has been waiting for finally takes hold—the one she knew would come, sweeping over her like the dense fog that rolls over the Santa Cruz mountains. She's in a familiar place. She's dreamed this dream before—the one with the two dark figures in the forest, the man with the vivid green eyes and the woman with hair like fire, the ghosts who walked right through her.

Estella is there again, standing in the forest, but this time, she sees it with new eyes. The trees of the Hungarian countryside have a familiarity that transcends this life.

They're the trees she's standing amongst in her dream, and they're also the trees that surround Rózsa Castle. As she takes a closer look at the ghosts' faces, she sees what she hadn't noticed before. She knows these people: Caelum and Athena. Estella is learning that unfamiliar faces in dreams may, in fact, be the faces of loved ones from lifetimes ago.

Everything else is as it was before, except Caelum and Athena don't walk through Estella this time. Like a lover whose heart has been broken more than once, Estella knows what's to come. This time, she steps aside, clearing their path, and she watches them walk by. But rather than ending there, her dream continues. Estella looks in the direction they walk, and sees herself—a version of her from long ago: Mária Terézia.

In the next moments, Estella learns the true depth of Athena's love—the most everlasting kind there is. Athena was Estella's mother in another life. As a newcomer to the other side, Estella hadn't realized that when they first met. Now, she understands why Athena has appeared in her dreams: to guide her, the only way she can, from the other side.

# Chapter 48

Estella finds Caelum just as he's drifting off to sleep, barely a foot in the dream world, halfway between reality and a dream. Caelum was preparing to travel to her, but Estella beat him to it.

"Not even in my dreams can I hide from you now," Caelum says. Estella looks at him in silence, clearly unimpressed. "Not that you weren't in all my dreams to begin with," he adds.

She still isn't amused. "Steering the ship of dreams isn't easy," Estella finally says, frustrated.

"You'll get the hang of it," Caelum replies. "With practice, it gets easier to direct your dreams—to find a particular person, place, or point in time."

"I hoped to see you once I fell asleep, but instead, I found myself in a recurring dream. I've had it many times, but only now do I understand its truth. It was a glimpse of our past—and Athena. Why didn't you tell me she was my mother?"

As if summoned by her name, Athena's vision appears, an angelic hologram. Her hair and gown seem to flow as though she's suspended in water. With out-stretched arms, she beckons Caelum and Estella to follow her to the other side.

"I'll let you take the lead," Caelum says to Estella, and sooner than he expects, they're standing in his library. "You're not as bad at this dream-traveling thing as you think," he says.

The library is steeped in evening stillness, the tall windows charcoal black against the dim glow of a small lamp between two armchairs. It's the perfect refuge for a sleepless night. Given Estella's love for the library, Caelum isn't surprised that she chose it as the place to stash her key to the other side.

"Where did you hide it?" Caelum asks.

"Guess," Estella says, her excitement building as she hovers toward the top shelves. But this is too easy. Caelum doesn't hesitate. He heads straight for the book titled *Kama Sutra*, pulls it from the shelf, flips through the pages, turns it upside down, and gives it a shake. Nothing. As he feels around the far end of the shelf, Estella clucks her tongue. Grounded now, she shifts her weight to one side, crosses her arms, and says, "Way off."

Where could it be? Caelum begins an inventory of his books, flying past the shelves until he gets stuck on Carl Sagan's *Cosmos*. When he pulls it from its place, a gold key glistens behind it.

"Bingo," Caelum says, reaching for the key.

"The cosmos is where stars are kept," Estella says. Caelum smiles, touched that she remembers his earlier observation about the link between their names and stars. "Well hidden, don't you think? It's as random a spot as any. I doubt anyone would look here," Estella says.

"Nothing is random," Caelum replies, holding up Estella's clover-shaped key, a perfect match to his own.

The polished mahogany door to the library swings open, revealing the other side, where their people await. Kal and Darin have already used their keys to enter, and they now stand with Ryoko, Athena, and family. Lucas, along with Caelum's parents, Dante and Aurora, are there, too.

"Mother," Estella says, and Athena's light shines brighter, emanating from her ghostly form.

"Our mothers are many, and we are, in turn, mothers to countless others in the unending circle of time, where all are family," Athena says.

Ryoko clears her throat, cutting through the moment. "Not to be a downer, but even though Connor is locked away, he can still cause trouble in the dream world," she says. Hovering above them, Ryoko suddenly dives, landing beside Estella with a force that sends a ripple through her. "You know what this means, right?" she asks, her excitement mounting. Met with silence, those brown of her eyes flicker with a fleeting spark of orange. "We have more traveling to do," Ryoko belts out before she fades into the morning light of a dream at its end.

It's been a few days since Connor's arrest, but today the crew is celebrating. Caelum is hosting a barbecue at his house, and everyone's invited, including Emma. While the crew gathers in the backyard, Emma is on her way from the airport. Meanwhile, Kaitlin and Mina are practicing pliés in their ballerina-themed room.

In the backyard, Kal and Darin set the table for the party, while Estella is in the garden, gathering vegetables for a salad. With summer approaching, the air is perfectly mild, ideal for dining outside. Mount Diablo stands clear and vivid against the sky, its sharp outline unobstructed on this cloudless, breezeless day.

"Guess what we're barbecuing today," Caelum says, holding up *The Book of Origin and Fate*.

"I thought you took care of that," Estella says, walking over with a fistful of lettuce in one hand, and chubby deep red tomatoes, still joined by the vine, in the other. The knees of her oversized jeans are dusted with soil, and rebellious waves have escaped her ponytail, framing her face in their usual unruly way.

"I was waiting for the right moment—when we're all together," Caelum says. With that, he tosses the text, along with its unimaginably destructive words, into the fire pit before them. The book falls open onto the coals, its pages igniting, bending, and blackening in the fire. The garden produce slips from Estella's hands, tumbling onto the grass, as Darin grabs the bottle of lighter fluid resting on the barbecue.

"Burn, baby!" Darin says, squeezing the flammable liquid onto the smoldering pile.

"Gnarly!" Kal shouts, and everyone steps back as the fire roars to life, sending a shimmering swirl of glowing particles higher and higher, until the book is reduced to ash. They whoop, holler, and dance around the fire in celebration as the book and the dark fate it promised turn to nothing. What remains is true hope, indestructible and enduring.

At the commotion, Kaitlin and Mina rush outside to join the revelry. Mina, dressed in an outfit like Estella's, looks like a shrunken version of her. Mina grabs Caelum's hand, while Kaitlin, who's taken a liking to Kal, wraps her tiny fingers around his pinky. Everyone joins hands, forming a chain and skipping in a circle around the fire.

*"Lánc, lánc, eszterlánc, eszterlánci cérna"* ("Chain, chain, turning chain, thread of the turning chain"), Kaitlin and Mina chant. They don't know much Hungarian, but they sing the Hungarian nursery rhyme that their great-grandpa, Laszlo, taught them as best as they can, their laughter filling the air, until the chime of the doorbell cuts through.

Caelum and Estella head to the front door to greet Emma. When they return to the backyard, Darin, Kal, and the girls rush to greet her, showering her with big hugs. Ready to master the grill, Darin dons an apron and reaches for lighter fluid yet again. When the flame flares up and almost singes his beard, Caelum can't help but chuckle at the sight of him.

As the smoky scent of barbecue fills the air, Kal brags loudly about riding big waves in Hawaii while Caelum rolls his eyes, unrestrained. It's Caelum's cue to bring some music into the mix.

"Any requests?" Caelum asks, holding Beano.

"How about some Clapton?" Estella says and chuckles.

As Caelum plays guitar, the group enjoys the barbecue, and music becomes the only conversation. Inevitably, Kal starts spewing science and cosmology facts, but no one's really paying attention—except for Emma.

Over the quiet strum of the guitar, Caelum listens as the seduction unfolds.

Emma's eyebrows perk up when she says to Kal, "That's so interesting! Tell me more."

Oh, good lord, she knows not what she's done… He'll never shut up now.

With fingers stained purple from picking blackberries, Estella joins the conversation. Kal dives into quasars, talking about them for five minutes straight while Emma and Estella listen quietly, absorbed by the unfolding cosmic ramble. When he pauses for a breath, Emma steers the conversation in another direction, bringing mercy to Caelum's ears.

"So, you finished writing your book?" Emma asks, turning to Estella. "How does that feel?"

"It feels like I'm doing what I'm supposed to do," Estella says, looking at Emma. "It feels like I was lost and got found. Like … I'm *me* again—that little girl in the third grade who just wanted to write a book."

"I remember," Emma says. "You always had a story in your head."

Estella shrugs. "I guess I had some living to do before I could write my stories," she admits. "And if my books help anyone feel a little less lonely, a little less lost, like I was, it'll mean something." She wants the lone Tetris pieces to know they have a place, too—that there's a place for everything and everyone.

Estella and the girls celebrate with fizzy pink drinks that Kal concocted, while the rest of them sip champagne. Caelum glances at Estella, and judging by the expression on her face, he can tell she's about to float away, just like the bubbles in his champagne. *Sors, destino*, fate—call it what you will—is at play, and words are what shape Estella's.

But even with the universe conspiring to help them, they have work to do. Without the distribution of Estella's book, their mission isn't complete. The message of solidarity, peace, and love must be heard. It will take a lot of work, and perhaps some traveling, to get the book into the right hands. But in the end, her words will find their way to the ears that need to hear them.

Mount Diablo disappears into the dark after they enjoy homemade *pan di spagna*—Italian sponge cake, whipped cream, and the fresh blackberries Estella picked from the garden. It's Caelum's mother's recipe, and one of his favorites.

Kaitlin and Mina are now asleep in their room, and Emma has made her way into the kitchen to help herself to another glass of champagne. It's just the travelers sitting around the fire pit, listening to the fire crackle.

"It's not the end of Connor," Kal says, his voice cutting through the quiet. "You guys know that, right?"

They gaze over the fire at one another's faces, shadows and the light of the fire dancing across each one.

"Until he's in the in-between, where he belongs, he can cause trouble. He can use his dreams," Caelum says.

"He can use his dreams to dig up a past copy of the very book roasting in this fire," Darin adds, his eyes widening as he stares into the flames.

"The Source and other energies are working on eliminating the text from time, but you're right, it's possible," Caelum says, his jaw tightening. "Prison will keep him contained for a while, but maybe not for long. If he gets the right half-souls to help him, he may find a way out, and the text could get back out into the world."

"We'll have to get to him first," Estella says, her voice laced with the thrill of the hunt. "Like Ryoko said, we have more traveling to do," she says, pressing in close to Caelum and wrapping her arms around his bicep.

"If we can find him in a dream and trap him in the in-between, Connor will be finished." Caelum says.

"We all know what happens to mortals who get trapped in the in-between for too long," Kal says nervously.

Darin nods, his face darkening as he adds, "What almost happened to us."

"And we need to work urgently," Kal says, his voice taking on an edge. "Before Connor recruits others to do his dirty work."

"To our next trip," Darin says, raising his glass high.

Emma reappears, holding two glasses. "What are we toasting to?" she asks.

Estella's eyes dart to Caelum's. He knows what she's thinking, because he's thinking the same thing. Emma mustn't know a thing about their travels.

"Here," she says to Estella, handing her a drink. "I poured you a glass of this pink stuff."

"We're toasting to us. Together. Here. Now," Estella says.

# Chapter 49

## Estella

A glowing light burns in the night sky, swooping closer and closer to Caelum's backyard. It's not a shooting star or space debris; its movements are otherworldly. Emma's champagne glass slips through her fingers, shattering on the pavers surrounding the fire pit.

"I'm having a vision," Emma murmurs, her voice unsteady. She turns to Estella, but Estella isn't looking at her or the broken champagne glass; her gaze is fixed on the light. "I don't get visions," Emma stammers, as if trying to convince herself. "I move things with my mind. I have telekinesis, not visions." She gestures to Estella. "You're the one with visions. Are you seeing this?"

Emma's eyes dart around the fire pit, searching the faces of Caelum, Darin, and Kal, but everyone is transfixed by the burning light. Estella finally looks at Emma, and Emma winces under her gaze.

"Sorry," Emma blurts out. "I didn't mean to out us." She glances nervously at the others. "It's best if they know," she says defensively. "Because if they're going to be our friends, and if they're not cool with witches..."

"It's okay. They know," Estella says, her eyes not moving from the glowing light.

The vision made of light burns brighter, forcing everyone to squint. It floods Estella's senses—her eyes, ears, heart, and mind—with its energy and message. It is the Source. Warmth and vibrations course through her body, and her ears fill with ethereal music. She knows Emma and the others feel it, too. In this moment, they're connected as they would be on the other side. Emma is one of them now. The Source has transformed her into a traveler; she had to know, and they need her help.

After a final surge of electric buzzing, the light vanishes, leaving behind a cold, dead silence. Estella is met with a chill and inches closer to the fire pit. When she turns to Emma, she sees tears streaming down her cheeks and the purest form of joy on her face. Emma knows everything now. There's nothing Estella needs to explain. She crosses the space between them and pulls Emma into a long hug.

Kal's voice cuts through the quiet. "Can I get in on that?"

They unfurl from their embrace, and Emma laughs, wiping her tears with her sweater sleeve.

"Another secret to keep," Estella says to Emma. "From everyone but us," she adds, glancing at each face around the fire.

"Cheers to that," Kal says, lifting his glass. The others follow suit, raising theirs in the air. Kal's eyes stay on

Emma, and when she glances his way, a smile spreads across his face—one that makes it clear he likes her. Caelum shakes his head and chuckles to himself.

"You know what this means, right?" Estella says to Emma. "We can chill together in our dreams!"

Emma lets out an excited scream, and the two burst into laughter, just like they did as teenagers. "The distance between here and Seattle—or anywhere else, for that matter—doesn't mean a thing anymore," Emma realizes.

"The Source filled Emma with all the knowledge we have for a reason. Did you guys pick up on that, too?" Caelum asks.

The group nods in agreement.

"It's like we talked about. Our fight with Connor isn't over yet," Darin says, his expression serious.

"And I can help," Emma says. "My bookstore—we'll distribute Estella's books through it. We'll raise awareness, work with other stores, and get her words out there." She raises her hand, twirling her finger in the air. The shards of her broken champagne glass rise, hovering above the fire pit. Slowly, they join together, forming a reconstructed glass that glistens in the firelight, held together only by magic. With a flick of her wrist, Emma lets the glass fall apart, the shards tumbling into the flames. "My gift will come in handy, too," she says.

"That was hot," Kal says, grinning.

Emma meets his gaze and smiles back, her expression mirroring the one he gave her earlier, letting him know she likes him, too.

"Wait," Estella says, suddenly serious. She puts a finger to her lips. *"Shhh."* There's a faint cry. "What is that? Do you guys hear that?"

The group falls silent, straining to listen. The cry sounds again, faint but unmistakable.

"Sounds like it's coming from inside," Caelum says.

Estella's mom instincts kick in, dragging her thoughts to the darkest possibilities. She bolts toward the house, the group close behind. As she nears the girls' room, the cries grow louder.

"Mommy, mommy, mommy!" Mina shrieks.

Estella flips on the light to find both Kaitlin and Mina in tears. "What happened?" Estella asks, her voice trembling. It doesn't matter that she knows infinity; she's still a human mother, her heart breaking at her children's cries. "Did you have a bad dream?" she asks.

"No," Mina sniffles. "There was a man in our room!"

Caelum steps forward, yanking the closet door open, but it's empty.

"He disappeared," Mina whispers.

Caelum checks behind the curtains, then under the bed, finding nothing.

"Are you sure it wasn't a dream?" Estella asks, sitting on the bed and pulling Mina into her arms.

"I wasn't dreaming!" Mina insists. "We weren't asleep yet. Kaitlin and I were whispering when he appeared."

Estella turns to Kaitlin. "Did you see him, too?"

"Uh-uh," Kaitlin says, shaking her head and wiping away tears with the edge of her comforter. "I got scared because Mina was scared."

Estella stands and moves to Emma, lowering her voice. "Not dreaming—seeing things. Do you think she had a vision? That she's coming into her magic?"

Emma leans in, whispering back. "Maybe." She turns to Mina. "Is this the first time it's happened?"

Mina nods, her face streaked with tears.

"It might be time for the magic talk," Estella murmurs to Emma.

Emma's eyebrows shoot up. "You haven't *had* the magic talk?" she asks too loudly.

"Magic?" Mina echoes.

Estella sighs. "Girls, we need to talk," she announces.

Emma and the men take the cue and leave the room.

"I think what you saw was a vision," Estella tells Mina. "I get them, too. So does Grandma—and most of the women in our family. It's a part of our magic. And it's not always just the women. For example, my grandpa—your great-grandpa—can read people."

"Magic?" Mina's eyes widen. "We have *magic*?"

Kaitlin drags her blankie over to Mina's bed and snuggles next to Estella.

"Some might call us witches," Estella says playfully, tickling her daughters and laughing a witchy laugh. "But when you have magic, it's important only to tell people you trust." She holds up her pinky. "So, let's pinky-promise to keep our magic to ourselves."

Mina hooks her pinky with Estella's and promises.

Kaitlin hesitates. "But I didn't see anything. Does that mean I don't have visions?" Her face flushes. "Does that mean *I* don't have magic?"

"You may not have your magic yet, but that doesn't mean you never will. It's just not your time," Estella reassures her.

"You mean Mina gets *magic*, and I don't?!" Kaitlin's cheeks are now burning a deeper red, closer to the color of her hair. She clenches her fists.

The lights flicker, the closet door rattles, the curtains billow, and the beds shake.

"What the—?!" Estella braces herself against the bed.

"What's happening, Mommy?!" Mina cries, clinging to her.

"Kaitlin!" Estella yells.

Suddenly, the room goes still as Kaitlin relaxes.

"Well," Estella says, catching her breath. "I guess I was wrong. It looks like you *do* have your own magic." A smile crosses Kaitlin's lips. "It's just different than mine and Mina's." She studies Kaitlin, perplexed. How could it be? All the women in their family have the same gift. Certain gifts tend to run in families.

"Emma!" Estella calls.

Emma steps into the room. "Do we have a new addition to our coven?"

"Two," Estella says. "You won't believe this—Kaitlin has *your* gift!"

"What?!" Emma says in disbelief.

"Yeah. It was like an earthquake just tore through here," Estella says.

Kaitlin and Mina whisper excitedly.

"I thought the rule is 'one family, one gift,'" Estella says to Emma.

"Not always," Emma replies. "New magic appearing in a bloodline is rare, but not unheard of." She twirls her finger, and the curtains sway as if caught by a breeze. "Can you do this?" Emma asks Kaitlin.

"I already did," Kaitlin says proudly. She mimics Emma's movement—but nothing happens. Frustration flashes across her face as she tries again and again.

"Don't worry," Emma says. "It takes time. I'll teach you."

"And I'll teach you everything about visions," Estella promises Mina. "But tell me more about the man you saw. Can you describe him?"

"He's the man who came to our house when the babysitter brought chocolate chip cookies," Mina says.

Rage builds in Estella. If she had telekinesis like Emma and Kaitlin, she'd tear the place apart.

Estella turns to Emma and says one word: "Connor."

# Chapter 50

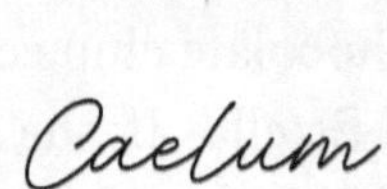

"We'll all sleep here tonight. If anything happens while we're asleep, even the slightest disturbance will wake us, so Kaitlin and Mina will be safe," Caelum says.

"Who gets the sleeper sofa in the living room?" Kal asks, glancing at Emma. She quickly looks down, hiding a smile.

"You and Darin," Caelum tells him, giving him a light shove.

Kal sighs, his shoulders sagging.

"Sorry, dude. You're stuck with me," Darin says with a wide grin.

"I should sleep in Mina and Kaitlin's room tonight, just in case," Estella says, pacing the length of the library, far from the girls' room. They have gathered in the library to plan how to deal with Connor, not wanting the girls to overhear. Mina and Kaitlin may have their powers now, but they're not travelers. "I'll set up the air mattress in their room. We'll share it," she says to Emma.

"I guess I'm sleeping alone tonight," Caelum says.

Estella walks over to Caelum, wraps her arms around his neck, and looks into his eyes. "Just for tonight," she says, then kisses him.

Sleeping alone doesn't bother Caelum so much, knowing they'll be together in their dreams.

"If it makes you feel better, you can join us on the sleeper sofa," Darin offers, grinning.

"Hard pass," Caelum says, sparking laughter from the others.

"Where are we meeting, and what are the plans in Dreamland?" Kal asks as he scans Caelum's bookshelf. He goes straight for *Kama Sutra*.

*What is it about that book?* Caelum thinks, striding over and snatching it out of Kal's hands. "Give me that," he says, shoving it back on the shelf. "You guys track Connor down in his dream while I grab the keys," he instructs. "Try places we've seen the book before, like the Antiquarian Book Fair or Diablo Press. Once we find him, we drag him to the other side and lock him in the in-between."

"Sounds like a piece of cake," Emma says, though there's unease in her voice.

"We can do this," Estella says firmly. "Yes, we've got some searching to do, and a couple of stops to make, but we have strength in numbers." Estella looks Emma in the eye, mischief in her gaze, and adds, "You know, our powers still work in the dream world."

"That was fast," Darin tells Caelum.

"I kept the key to the in-between where I keep my key to the other side, so I only had to make one stop," Caelum says, studying his surroundings. The window they used to break into Diablo Press in the past is intact, which means they're in a moment sometime before they broke in.

"We've already tried the Antiquarian Book Fair, but Connor was nowhere to be found," Estella says.

"I don't see him," Kal says, hovering near the window before drifting toward the stairs.

"Can he pull the book from this dream into the real world?" Emma asks, following Kal. The others hover after them.

"No, objects in dreams don't transfer to reality," Caelum says. "What he's doing is reading it in the dream world and typing out what he can remember when he wakes up. He had begun creating the digital copy before he got arrested, and with enough time, he can recreate the whole book." There's a sudden creaking sound. *"Shhh..."* Caelum puts a finger to his lips. "We should try the office upstairs," he whispers.

They float to the top of the stairs. Caelum sees the frosted glass door to the office glowing orange. The light is on, just like the night they broke into Diablo Press.

"Now what?" Darin asks.

"We bust in," Caelum says, barreling toward the door.

He kicks it open, with the others following close behind. Connor is sitting behind the desk, nearly falling out of his chair when they rush in. He shoves the chair aside and stands, clutching the book tightly in his hands.

"What are you going to do? Take the book from me?" Connor says, laughing. "I'll just keep coming back for my nightly readings."

"We're not going to take the book," Estella scoffs, her eyes burning into Connor. "What good is a book if it's just a dream? It must be made into reality."

"We're here to take *you*," Caelum declares, moving closer to Connor.

"I don't think so," Connor says, flying toward the window.

Caelum almost grabs him, but Connor slips through. With Caelum in the lead and the others close behind, they close in on Connor. Given that travelers can't pass through one another in dreams, Connor will be in trouble if they get their hands on him. The only thing that could save him now is if they can't catch him or if he wakes up.

With great speed, Connor nears the Golden Gate Bridge. Caelum knows there's a door to the other side at its entrance. If only they could get their hands on him and drag him through…

"Emma, there's a door at the bridge. Work your magic!" Caelum calls out.

The night air whips through Emma's long, dark hair. She must have chosen to feel the scene, making it as close to reality as possible. She raises her arms into the air as she blazes through the night sky. Extending her arms toward him, she unleashes her power, and Connor tumbles toward the ground. Caelum grabs him first, followed by Darin and Kal. They each get a hold of Connor, and Caelum gets him in a headlock while Darin and Kal grab his arms, dragging him toward the door to the other side.

"Estella, get my key from my pocket and open the door," Caelum says.

"I have my own, remember?" Estella says, brandishing her key. "I grabbed mine when you went to get yours."

She unlocks the door to the other side, her movements swift and sure.

Connor is cursing and kicking as they drag him through the door. Energy surges around them, ready to greet them, and Connor stills. He is powerless against the force of the multitude of energies that swiftly guide them toward the steely dark door to the in-between. It hums with a low vibration, and Caelum feels a sinking sensation as he nears it.

Caelum steps back from Connor as the others, aided by the energies, hold him still. Connor writhes under their power. The veins in his neck bulge, his jaw is clenched tight, and his eyes are wells of madness.

"Not happy to be going home?" Caelum asks Connor, retrieving the key to the in-between from his pocket. He unlocks the door as it seethes with negative energy. When the door creaks open, a powerful suction from the in-between pulls on them and howls in Caelum's ears. The energies retreat, withdrawing their light.

"Stay back," Caelum tells Estella and the others. He grabs Connor while Darin and Kal let go of his arms. Estella and Emma hold onto each other for support as the force of the in-between tugs at their hair and clothes. Caelum pushes Connor through the door and into the in-between. "Don't ever come out again!" he shouts.

"Won't you be my guest?" Connor sneers, suddenly turning and pulling on Caelum. He struggles to break free, but the mighty suction force of the in-between works in Connor's favor. With a violent tug, Connor pulls Caelum into the in-between with him—and with a thunderous clap, the door slams shut behind them.

# Chapter 51

*Estella*

"Hey, wake up," Emma says, shaking Estella awake.

Estella pops upright, her hair a tousled mess, but her eyes are wide and alert.

"What just happened?" Estella says, glancing around. She's still on the portable mattress in Kaitlin and Mina's room. "Where's Caelum?" she whispers, careful not to wake the girls.

"Let's get Darin and Kal," Emma whispers back.

Throwing off her covers, Estella bolts to Caelum's room. "Wake up, *please* wake up!" she cries, shaking him with all her strength. His body sways under her hands, but his eyes remain shut. "Please," Estella pleads, her voice trembling.

Caelum groans. *He's waking up!* she thinks, shaking him harder. His eyelids flutter.

"You won't be able to wake him," Kal's voice cuts in. He's standing at the door to Caelum's room with Darin and Emma. "He'll stay in a trancelike state until he gets out of the in-between."

"When is that going to be?" Estella demands, her voice sharp. Memories of the last time Caelum vanished into the in-between flood her mind. She gets up from the bed. "I'm not going through this again," she says, storming out of the room.

The others trail after her into the living room and kitchen area. The faint light of dawn filters through the wall of windows, casting soft grays and blacks over the backyard. Mount Diablo looms in silhouette, the sun still hidden behind it. Estella rests her arms on the kitchen island and hangs her head. She needs a moment to think.

"I'll make us coffee," Kal offers, flipping on the kitchen light. He grabs the copper kettle from the stove and fills it with water.

"Let me help," Darin says, opening the cabinet where Caelum keeps the coffee mugs. Darin and Kal have been to Caelum's often enough to know their way around the kitchen—especially his whiskey cabinet.

"I can't just sit around here and wait for him. We have to do something," Estella says. She plops down onto a stool at the kitchen island, and Emma slides onto the stool beside her. "We need to go after him, help him get out of there," Estella insists.

"It's too dangerous," Kal says, scooping ground coffee into the French press. "We don't know the in-between like Caelum does."

"Yeah, we could get lost in there," Darin says. The kettle whistles, and he rushes to turn off the stove. "Besides, we don't have a key to get in."

"What about Caelum's key?" Estella asks.

"I saw him pull it from the lock and put it back in his pocket after he opened the door," Kal says, pouring steaming water into the French press. The coffee grounds bubble and swirl in the glass, fogging it up. "The key is trapped in the in-between with him," he adds grimly as the rich aroma of coffee fills the kitchen.

Darin opens the fridge and peers inside. "There's some leftover sponge cake with berries and cream from the party," he says, pulling out the *pan di spagna* and setting it on the counter. He scoops what's left of it onto dessert plates.

"How can I eat anything right now? I feel so helpless. Caelum is trapped for who knows how long, and I can't do anything about it!" Estella collapses onto the counter. "What if he *never* gets out?" she adds, her voice muffled as her hair falls over her face.

"Are you sure you can't eat?" Darin asks. He places a plate on the counter, the fluffy sponge cake topped with her favorite blackberries, handpicked from the garden, just within reach. Estella catches a whiff of the cake's sweet, fruity scent and straightens in her chair. Kal sets a steaming cup of coffee beside the cake, with milk and a spoonful of sugar, just how she likes it. She breathes in the mingling aromas of cake and coffee and says, "Well, I suppose I could have a bite."

The four of them eat their cake and sip their coffee in silence, the tension lingering in the room. Finally, Emma breaks the silence. "How come Caelum knows his way around the in-between so well?"

Kal swallows a bite of cake. "Well, he's been in there at least two times that I know of. The first time, he rescued Athena from it. That's how he earned his traveling rights. Then Darin and I went with him to rescue Athena a second time."

"There's something else, though," Darin says. He carries his coffee to the big windows and looks out at the view of Mount Diablo. The sun has risen over it, and sunlight pours through the windows, making his blond hair glow gold. "He must have a strong soul to be able to find his way out of there like he did."

"Yeah, I don't think Darin and I could've found our way out without him," Kal says. "I mean, eventually, we would've escaped," he adds, puffing out his chest and glancing at Emma, who sips her coffee. "It may have taken some time, but Darin and I have strong enough souls to make it out. It's the weak ones, the half-souls, that can spend an eternity in there. It's a miracle that Cassius and Alexander—or, you know, Valentina and Connor—made it out of there once. I don't think they'll get out again—not without some serious help."

Darin walks back to the kitchen island and sets his coffee mug down. "Low key, I think Caelum could be a healer, an alchemist of sorts—someone who can transform adversity into strength and help half-souls. Not that there's any helping Valentina and Connor, but maybe that's why Caelum can navigate the in-between."

"What's for breakfast?"

Everyone turns to see Mina and Kaitlin standing in the kitchen. Mina yawns and rubs her eyes while Kaitlin clutches the blankie she drags behind her.

Darin glances at the empty plate where the cake had been, now smeared with cream, only a couple of berries left. "Uh, well … there *was* cake," he says.

"You guys ate all the *cake*?" Kaitlin drops her blankie. Her face puckers in anger, turning bright red. She balls her hands into fists, just like she did last night. Estella hears a clattering—a rhythmic vibrating of the plates on the countertop.

"Stop that right this minute!" Estella warns Kaitlin. Though still in one piece, the plates continue to rattle. "We have pancakes," she says quickly.

Stillness returns to the kitchen.

"We're going to have to work on that," Estella tells Kaitlin firmly.

# Chapter 52

## *Caelum*

The dark void of the in-between closes in around Caelum, its emptiness settling like a weight in his stomach. Connor still grips him tightly. Caelum tries to shake him off, but he feels slower, burdened by the heaviness of the in-between. Everything is harder—moving, thinking, even feeling. He forces himself to focus.

"Well, look who we have here," says Valentina.

*Damn,* Caelum thinks. He's outnumbered.

"Go to hell, Valentina—or Cassius, or whoever you are," Caelum snaps, struggling to free himself from Connor's grasp.

"We're already here." Valentina laughs. "It doesn't matter what you call me." She steps closer, moving in front of Caelum. With a swift punch to his gut, she knocks the air from his lungs as Connor holds his arms behind his back. "What matters is *The Book of Origin and Fate* and spreading its word," she says.

Caelum struggles to breathe. It takes him longer than it would anywhere else to recover from the punch. The air is thick here, suffocating, oppressive. He coughs, gasping for breath. "What good would spreading hate and destruction do? So more can join you here? Don't you want to get out?"

"And go where? The other side? Back to life? Been there, done that. Got us nowhere," Valentina says, taking Caelum by his throat. "Dreams get crushed by reality. Hope is eliminated by pain. Love is killed by hate. I like it here—no illusions, no false hope. We get straight to the hellish point," she says, tightening her grip around his throat.

Caelum drives a knee into Valentina, then swings an elbow into Connor. Valentina gasps, doubling over, and Connor stumbles back, barely keeping his balance. Caelum breaks free, taking the opportunity to plant a fist into Connor's face. Valentina recovers quickly, fury flaring in her eyes as she lunges at him, hands poised to choke. Caelum sidesteps just in time, watching her rage build with each failed attempt to reach him. Connor, clutching his face, stomps toward Caelum, determined. With a swift motion, he sweeps Caelum's legs out from under him. The two crash to the ground, rolling and thrashing, fists hammering into each other's sides until neither can breathe.

"You've turned to the in-between in the past. I know you have. After all, you got your hands on a key to this place," Valentina says. "Don't lie to yourself, Caelum. You're a half-soul."

Connor stumbles to his feet, joining Valentina by her side. Caelum, still kneeling, works on gathering his strength. The voices of the depraved in-betweeners echo in his ears. He presses his hands to his head, trying to block them out.

"That was lifetimes ago," Caelum says through gritted teeth, pushing himself to his feet. "I was weak, but I'm not that person anymore. I became strong. I got out of here. I helped others escape—and I can help you, too."

Valentina lets out a sharp laugh, waving her hand dismissively. A vision of Caelum and Estella appears before him. "Look," she says. "You could have saved her from the fire, but you didn't. You gave up on her—and you gave up on yourself."

Caelum's eyes widen as the scene at Rózsa Castle unfolds before him, the fiery chaos playing out like a nightmare. But something's wrong. They don't burn in the flames as they did before. They don't die. Instead, Caelum watches as he hoists the fallen wooden beam off Estella, scooping her up and carrying her out of the fire.

"No," Caelum whispers. "That's an illusion." He grabs at his hair as though he's on the brink of losing his mind. "That's not how it happened. There was nothing I could do!"

Connor steps closer, his face hardening. "Nothing?" he asks. "Are you sure about that?"

*Was it all my fault?* Caelum asks himself. His dark secrets, mistakes, insecurities, and weaknesses start seeping into the cracks Valentina and Connor are creating. All the hurt he's caused presses down on him, making him even heavier. *Could I have saved her?* he wonders, the doubt eating at him. *Did I just give up?* He had given up in the past and got lost in the in-between long before he met Estella. *Maybe I'm lying to myself and pretending to be better than I am. Maybe I* am *a half-soul.* Caelum falls back onto his knees.

Valentina steps closer, her voice dripping with mock sympathy. "See? It's not so bad in here," she says, placing a hand on Caelum's shoulder. "Feels like home, doesn't it?"

"You're messing with my mind," Caelum says, swatting Valentina's hand away.

*This isn't me,* he thinks. He may have once called this place home, but he's better than this now. He buries his face in his hands, focusing on the strength he built to escape the in-between long ago. At the center of his core is that strength, and within it is the spark of love—his true power. He knows love. He's created it. And Estella—she only made his love stronger. They made each other's love stronger.

His energy builds, warming him from within, burning brighter at his core. With newfound power, he pushes past Valentina and Connor. They lunge for him, but Caelum moves faster, fueled by the strength of love. He's closing in on the door to the other side when he stops, turning to face them one last time.

"You can have this," Caelum says, his voice steady. He takes the key to the in-between from his pocket and hurls it at them. Without another word, he steps through the door to the other side, slamming it shut and leaving the darkness behind.

# Chapter 53

Estella

Caelum holds up his hand, and Estella places her palm against his. It's been so long since he appeared in her dreams, ever since he got trapped in the in-between. Seeing him now feels like a cosmic gift. Touching him is heaven—his skin against hers, the connection electric. She wishes this moment could last forever.

Estella stirs awake, only to find Caelum still in the deep sleep he's been in for the past week. Her arms tighten around him. What if he doesn't come back? Now that they're together, she can't bear the thought of losing him. When her time here ends, whenever that will be, she'll return to the other side and then find a way into the in-between. She'll go to hell and back for him if she has to.

Suddenly, Caelum shifts in the bed, and Estella startles. He's been moving around since he entered his trance, but the real Caelum isn't there. He's zombie-like.

But every time he moves, Estella gets her hopes up. Then, his eyes flutter open, and she wonders if he's in there.

"I wish you were here," Estella whispers.

"I am here," Caelum whispers back.

Is she hearing things? Her heart races. Caelum pushes himself upright.

"Is it really you?!" Estella cries.

"Of course it's me."

Estella throws her arms around him. "Don't you dare turn into a ghost again!" she says, squeezing him tighter.

"How long was I gone?" he asks.

"Not as long as last time. About a week."

"That long? It felt like no time at all in the in-between, but time is strange there."

"I'm just thrilled that you're back." Estella smiles, relief flooding through her. "I was dreaming about you before I woke up."

"I know," Caelum replies, a smile playing on his lips. He raises his hand, just like in their dream. "When I got out of the in-between, the first place I found you was in a dream."

Estella places her palm against his once more, their eyes on each other. They sit there, hands pressed together, just like they're in a dream.

# Notes and Acknowledgments

Thank you for reading *Estella and the Dream Traveler*. I'm deeply grateful to my readers and my Instagram and YouTube communities. Connection is the heart of human existence, and I write for you. It's an honor that you take the time to read my work, listen to me, watch my videos, ask questions, and share your insights and experiences.

As a writer, I hope my work resonates with you, providing comfort and a sense of connection. If you enjoyed *Estella and the Dream Traveler* and are curious about my other books, you'll find that there are links to be uncovered between them. I'd love for you to join me on this literary journey.

It would mean so much if you could take a moment to review *Estella and the Dream Traveler* on Amazon and Goodreads. Your reviews make a big difference and help other readers discover my work.

Thank you to the people who helped bring my book to life—Robin Fuller for her meticulous editing, Ann Leslie Tuttle for her invaluable insights in the early development of this book, and Natalia Junqueira for the beautiful cover and interior design.

To my mom and sister, thank you for your love and unwavering support throughout my life. Dad, thank you for lessons that have shaped me.

Finally, to my own little coven—my best friend, Isaiah; my daughters, Nora and Izabella; and our toy poodle, Sunny—thank you for your love and support. I'm eternally grateful for your friendship, companionship, and acceptance of me as I am, complexities and all.

Mercedes Paradiso is the author of *Estella and the Dream Traveler* and *thunder and daisy*, a poetry collection. Though she has a background as an attorney, Mercedes has always been and always will be, most herself when crafting stories and poetry, exploring the complexities of the human condition. She lives with her family and writes in the San Francisco Bay Area.

mercedesparadiso.com
Instagram: @mzparadiso